Praise for Ward Anderson and *I'll Be Here All Week*

"Anderson . . . draws from his real-life experiences for his poignant and humorous debut novel. He crisply captures the highs and lows of being onstage, the loneliness of constant touring, and the compromises one must make to chase a dream career or be with the one you love."
—*Booklist*

"Ward Anderson captures the soul-crushing agony of the road with sledgehammer delicacy. If I had a nickel for the number of times I woke up hungover in Enid, Oklahoma, with a girl named Brandy or Mandy . . . well, I'd have at *least* a nickel. Ward flays open the perceived rock star glamour of stand-up comedy to show us how it really is—lonely, blindingly monotonous, and with a serious lack of adequate toiletries. Thank god the beer is free."
—Aisha Tyler, bestselling author of *Self-Inflicted Wounds*

"Ward Anderson lifts the curtain on the stand-up comedy business, a world he knows well. By turns amusing, sad, powerful, and moving, this deftly written novel might not be the kind of story you'd expect from a veteran comic. Trust me, it's even better. Above all, he speaks the hard truth about life on the road, and it makes for a page-turning read."
—Terry Fallis, award-winning author of *The Best Laid Plans*

"As a stand-up comic, I was especially impressed by how Ward was able to translate to the page the experience and feeling of being onstage, the rush, the drive that keeps you going in the face of very little encouragement, and the obsessive love of the craft. *I'll Be Here All Week* does more than offer a window into the life of a stand-up comic. Any reader would feel like they are actually on that stage, living the life and hoping that they'll get out alive. Underneath it all is a love story that is sweet and funny."
—Ophira Eisenberg, stand-up comic and author of
Screw Everyone: Sleeping My Way to Monogamy

"Stand-up comedy is rarely the subject of heroic tales of struggling artists, but in *I'll Be Here All Week,* Ward Anderson leads us on the hilariously shameful journey of a comedian who is both exhilarated and entirely humiliated by what can only be seen as his artistic passion. It's the humiliation that makes us love Spence, the novel's often hapless protagonist. But it's Spence's final and magnificent triumph that makes us cheer with such pleasure at the end. I loved this book and felt totally bereft when it finally came to an end."
—Michael Dahlie, author of *The Best of Youth*

"Like a good comedy set, with a lot of highs, tons of lows, and subverted expectations at every turn."
—*Among Men*

ALL THAT'S
LEFT

Books by Ward Anderson

I'll Be Here All Week

All That's Left

Published by Kensington Publishing Corp.

ALL THAT'S LEFT

WARD ANDERSON

KENSINGTON BOOKS
www.kensingtonbooks.com

KENSINGTON BOOKS are published by

Kensington Publishing Corp.
119 West 40th Street
New York, NY 10018

All Kensington titles, imprints, and distributed lines are available at special quantity discounts for bulk purchases for sales promotion, premiums, fund-raising, educational, or institutional use.

Special book excerpts or customized printings can also be created to fit specific needs. For details, write or phone the office of the Kensington Special Sales Manager: Attn. Special Sales Department. Kensington Publishing Corp., 119 West 40th Street, New York, NY 10018. Phone: 1-800-221-2647.

Kensington and the K logo Reg. U.S. Pat. & TM Off.

eISBN-13: 978-0-7582-9431-9
eISBN-10: 0-7582-9431-X
First Kensington Electronic Edition: May 2015

ISBN-13: 978-0-7582-9430-2
ISBN-10: 0-7582-9430-1
First Kensington Trade Paperback Printing: May 2015

10 9 8 7 6 5 4 3 2 1

Printed in the United States of America

For my parents

1

The man sitting behind Steven on the plane is eating his potato chips so loudly that it sounds as if he had been starving to death before he opened the bag. Like he is the last survivor of a terrible crash in the mountains and he had to eat the bodies of the other passengers in order to stay alive and this is the first thing he's gotten to eat since being rescued.

Steven didn't bring any earplugs on the plane, and he's spent the past sixteen hours regretting it. He normally keeps a pair constantly packed in his messenger bag, just in case. He was so busy dealing with Robin and the last-minute attempt at packing, finding a flight, and just getting to the airport that he totally forgot he threw away his last pair. Now he's listening to the Neanderthal sitting behind him and wondering if jamming napkins into his ears will do the trick and at least muffle the sound.

CRUNCH!

It's not so much that the man is eating the chips as that he is making a display out of it. He can't just pop one chip into his mouth, close his lips around it, and then bite down. He takes several open-mouthed bites of the chip, making sure to bring his teeth down very slowly to prolong the noise. It sounds as if he is auditioning for a potato chip commercial and wants to show that he can make the biggest crunch as loud and for as long as possible. Steven wonders just how long one small bag of chips could possibly last. This one seems bottomless.

He turns around and takes a long, cold look at the guy, making sure that his eyes display the anger he feels in his ears. A tall, lanky, Asian man around fifty years old, the guy is staring straight ahead, a look of delight on his face.

They're just potato chips, Steven thinks. *How amazing could they possibly be?*

The tall man makes eye contact with Steven, who furrows his brow, sticks his lips into the worst pout he can muster, and generally shoots icicles from his pupils. The Chip Eater looks confused and turns to look over his shoulder to see if Steven could possibly be directing his gaze at anyone else. Realizing there is no one behind him, the man turns back around and faces Steven. With the same dull, confused look on his face, he slowly places another stack of chips onto his tongue.

CRUNCH!

Steven sighs loudly—making certain that Captain Crunch hears him and knows he's annoyed—and turns back around in his seat. He puts his earbuds in, even though his iPod battery died hours ago. He figures that plugging up his ears might help him relax a bit, at least until the bag of chips is gone.

"Are you okay?" the woman sitting next to him asks, having watched Steven fidget off and on for various stages of the flight, which is almost twenty hours long. Like the Chip Aficionado, she is also Asian, which is not at all odd since most people on the flight are, as well, and the plane is headed to Singapore. Young, with a bright smile, she can't be more than twenty-five years old. Steven can't help but think, if he had been in a better mood, he might have thought to engage in conversation with her before the flight was almost over. Instead, he pouted most of the trip.

"Yeah, I'm just a crab, is all," he says, putting his magazine in the seat pocket in front of him. He's been reading the same page for almost an hour now, which tells him that he might as well give up for the time being and just forget about it. "Background noise bothers me."

"It's not just you," the young woman whispers, obviously afraid that Mister Munch behind them can hear her. "He's being loud."

"I'm glad it's not just me," Steven says, but he knows that—most of the time—it is just him. His doctor calls it misophonia. Sound intolerance. Any little thing can give him headaches and just generally irritate him senseless. The sound of people eating is the worst and can actually make him get up and move to another seat if one is available. But it's not just that; it's the sound of candy wrappers or the sound of gum chewing. Even the sounds of fingers tapping on a computer keyboard can make his blood boil. He tried for years to ignore it until Robin made him go see an ear doctor. Until then, he just figured he was an asshole.

Now he's an asshole constantly wearing earplugs. Or listening to his iPod. Or sitting alone, away from anyone who might be making any noise. Steven often wonders how much time he has wasted changing seats in theaters and restaurants just to avoid listening to the sounds people make. He also wonders how many people he knows who can't stand him because of it.

"First time going to Singapore?" the young woman asks and, for the first time, Steven notices that she's very, very pretty. He wonders for a brief second if she's flirting with him. He's always been oblivious to that sort of thing anyway, but it's been even worse the past couple of years. Robin has always made certain that he noticed only her.

"Yes, it is," he says, and looks at his watch. Two hours to go. That's either enough time to have a nice conversation with this young woman and make the flight zip by or enough time to sit awkwardly next to her for what will wind up feeling like an eternity. "You?"

"Oh, no," she says. "My family lives there. My grandparents. I visit every Christmas."

"That's nice." Steven nods.

"You going for business or holiday?"

"Neither," he says, and tries to smile so she won't feel awkward. "Death in the family."

"Oh, I'm sorry," she says, and it seems genuine. In fact, she seems more upset when she hears it than Robin did when Steven told her about it the day before.

"That's okay," he says. "We weren't close or anything like that."

He doesn't know why he just lied to her, but it seemed for a second like he should, so he just let it out. How would she ever know, anyway? When he gets off this plane, he'll never see her again, and she'll feel better thinking that some distant uncle died or something like that. Besides, he doesn't really feel like explaining it to her.

Being Steven's identical twin automatically excludes Scotty from being a distant relative. And, for most of their thirty-four years on the planet, they were actually pretty close. But Steven feels an odd poke in his stomach when he does the math and realizes they haven't seen each other in almost three years. It stings a bit more when he thinks about how—the next time he does see his brother—it will only be Scotty's body. And that will be it.

"Well, good luck with that." The Asian girl nods politely, although she probably isn't any more certain of what *"that"* is supposed to be than Steven is. She turns to look out the window at absolutely nothing. Steven understands and simply looks at the seat in front of him. It's actually a relief, because he didn't want to talk about Scotty in the first place. He feels his headache getting worse and takes off his glasses so he can rub his temples for a few minutes.

Scotty never wore his glasses. Not since he was twenty or so. Before Scotty grew his hair long, it had been the easiest way to tell him and Steven apart. They were roughly the same height, same build. Same everything. When they were kids, even their parents didn't know which one was which half the time. But Scotty snapped out of that the minute he left college. The hair, the tattoos. Steven looked like an older version of the two of them at seventeen, while Scotty went on to look like the two of them at fourteen. He was always Mr. Hyde to Steven's Dr. Jekyll.

And now he was gone.

It was 3 p.m. when the hospital in Singapore called to tell

Steven the bad news. They said that the aneurysm hit Scotty so fast that he was probably dead before he hit the ground. People who had been in the bar with him said he had complained his head hurt. A few minutes later, he was dead. And it was all because of another one of his headaches.

You never wore your glasses, Scotty, Steven thought. Scotty always had bad headaches. Ever since he was twenty. Ever since their parents died. Scotty blamed the headaches on his refusal to wear his glasses. Steven thought it was stress. Or from the accident.

SLURP!

The man behind Steven has switched from potato chips to Coke. Steven actually envies him a little bit. Ten years working as a sommelier, and he has never enjoyed food or drinks as much as this guy is right now. A bag of Ruffles and a can of pop, and this guy is in heaven. It would take a very expensive, very rare steak and amazing, very rare Chianti to get half that response out of Steven.

He looks down at his nails and wishes that his manicure set were in his carry-on instead of his checked luggage. He really wasn't sure if airport security would let him on the plane with it or not. The last thing he wanted was to have his nice nail clippers and scissors thrown away because someone thought he might try and hijack a plane by giving the pilots a nail buff. But now his fingers feel rough, and a little filing would distract him from Mister Noise sitting behind him.

Robin thinks he's a snob. She doesn't think he suffers from misophonia as much as he does from OCD. With all of the grooming and cleaning and rearranging he does, she's frequently called him a "neat freak." Steven thinks of all the times he's heard women complain about the men in their lives being slobs and finds it ironic that the woman he lives with would love a little bit of that.

"Sometimes I want to break things to get your attention," she yelled at him just a week before, standing over him with her arms folded, her curly red hair falling over one eye. "But then I know it would only be a matter of minutes before you cleaned up the mess and replaced whatever was broken. It would be like it never happened at all."

"You're exaggerating," he told her at the time, not realizing that he was arranging a stack of magazines on the coffee table into a perfect square. He doesn't even realize sometimes that he's doing it. But liking things to be in order is hardly the same as having OCD.

She wound up proving him wrong, and it only took two days. Steven came home from work in the evening only to find that she'd gone into the wine chiller, taken the 2005 Henschke Hill of Grace he was keeping, and shattered the bottle in the middle of the living room floor. She didn't even bother to drink any; she just took the bottle and threw it to the ground, leaving it for him to discover, like a vandal who sprays graffiti across a newly painted building. By the time Robin got back late that night from being out with a friend, all trace of the mess was gone, and he was sipping a twenty-dollar bottle of red by himself while watching TV.

Idiot, he thinks to himself, staring at the seat in front of him. He had the chance to talk to her, the chance to work things out. The chance to do something—anything—that would keep her from banging one more nail in the coffin of the past two years. Instead, he just did what he always did, which was nothing at all. The next day he got the call about Scotty.

Not that the death of a family member is ever convenient, but flying across the globe now to bring Scott's body back to Toronto was especially terrible timing. Things with Robin were already pretty awful, and Steven knows that getting up and leaving in the midst of it isn't going to help, especially not with Christmas only weeks away. Robin never met Scotty, but made it perfectly clear that she didn't care for him anyway. She thought Steven was a snob, but she hated Scotty's being the wild child even more. And she hated the fact that he always needed money.

"It's his money," Steven would say to her, every time Scotty called or sent an e-mail. "I can't tell him he can't have what is his."

"Then why does he ask you at all?" she always said, even though she knew he had no choice. That was the deal his parents laid out in the will. There was money, and plenty of it. But neither one of them could touch it without the consent of the other. It was his parents' attempt to keep their little twins constantly the best of friends: to make them partners in all things inheritance.

Scott always needed the money more than Steven ever did. Steven was the one with a great salary, a great apartment. He always got to drink expensive wine and tell other people they should drink it, too. Scotty traveled the world and stayed in hostels and took awful jobs and lived out of his suitcase. The least Steven could do is let him have the money when he came asking. Still, it never made Robin think very highly of Scott. She thought he was a bum.

"I believe people call it 'free spirit,' " Steven told her after another request from Scotty for another wire transfer. That's what people had been calling Scotty for years, even before their parents died. He never had the desire to stay in school like Steven did, even though he was easily just as smart. He liked to travel, to get his hands dirty. He was okay with numbers, but terrible with writing and grammar. He couldn't spell worth a damn. He changed his mind a lot and lost interest in things almost as quickly as he started getting into them.

Then there was the accident.

Scotty dropped out of school almost immediately once their parents were gone. That's when he stopped being a twin altogether and just started being the brother who looked a lot like Steven. Then came the long hair and the tattoos and the piercings. That's when Scotty did the summer on the fishing boat in Alaska, even though he didn't need the money and wasn't going back to school anyway. There was also the scooter rental business, and—of course—all of the traveling.

At least the traveling made him happy, Steven thinks.

It was the only thing that seemed to work. Before that, Scotty would go through weeks of seeming out of sorts or depressed. Then, he'd bounce back and be happy again for a little while.

There would be a new job, or a new woman, or a new idea. But he'd been in Singapore for almost two years. It was the longest he'd ever stayed in one place. Steven figured he must have finally been happy. They'd grown apart and had only spoken on occasion, but things had recently started to look better. That was before last week, when Scotty came looking for money.

BING!

The "fasten seat belt" bell rings so loudly, it snaps Steven out of his thoughts, and he feels himself jump a little in his seat. The pretty Asian girl next to him jumps, but not because of the bell as much as because his reaction startles her. She was starting to doze off while leaning against the window, and he just woke her. Steven figures it doesn't really matter. He can feel the plane decreasing altitude and knows that they'll be landing before too long.

Fifteen grand. That's how much money Scotty came asking for when they spoke last week, not even a week before he died. It was more than he'd ever come asking for, and he never said why he wanted it. And then, a few days later, he was dead. It was all too weird. He was prone to the migraines, but it never seemed to be anything that serious. Yet a few days after he comes looking for a ton of cash, he falls down dead somewhere in Asia.

"He was obviously dirty," Robin had said while Steven packed his suitcase. "He was into drugs or something like that. He owed money to the wrong people."

For once, Steven was inclined to agree with her, although not about the drugs. Scotty hated that sort of thing and was into too much healthy New Age nonsense to be into drugs. Besides, he had money in the bank that Steven let him have whenever he wanted it. Scotty could have easily gotten it—and drugs—if that had been his thing. It wasn't drugs, but there was something shady going on in Scott's life; Steven was pretty sure of that. He just had no clue what it could be.

In the end, Scotty never got the money. Steven dragged his feet on the transfer because the amount was so much he wanted to know what it was all about. He was waiting to hear back from Scotty before he finalized it with the bank. When the phone call from Singapore had come in the afternoon before, he had figured it was Scotty calling to explain. Instead, it was the hospital telling him his brother was dead and how to claim his body.

What the hell were you doing, big brother? Steven thinks. Scotty was born four minutes earlier than Steven, and the two of them had been pointing it out to each other their entire lives. Mostly, Scott didn't want Steven to forget who the eldest twin was.

Steven winces as he fastens his seat belt and reaches for his magazine. He's not very good with landings and tries to read his way through them. Right now, however, he's too busy thinking about his dead brother lying in some morgue in the middle of Singapore and his dead relationship lying in ruins back in Toronto. The magazine will probably go unread until the flight home.

"Merry Christmas, Darling" by the Carpenters pops into his head for no reason, and he suddenly remembers that it's that time of year again. As the plane touches down, he realizes that he forgot to send Scotty a card this year. It's the first time he's ever done that.

2

The heat in Singapore is brutal, and it is matched only by the intense humidity. Steven thought the summers in Toronto were rough, but they have nothing on December in Singapore. He knew it was hot because he did some reading online about the entire country when Scotty wound up there and said he was going to stay for a while. That still didn't prepare Steven for what it was going to feel like when his shirt stuck to his skin the second he stepped out of the airport and flagged down a cab.

He keeps thinking that it's way too hot and humid for it to feel like Christmas, but the decorations are everywhere. He'd heard that Singapore was mostly Buddhist but, looking around, it looks more Christian than Canada. The enormous Christmas tree in the middle of the baggage claim area didn't even have ornaments of Buddha on it. "Let It Snow" was playing on the radio when he passed through customs. Now that the heat is beating down on him, Steven finds himself really missing Toronto.

Dear God, he thinks as he asks the taxi driver to crank up the air-conditioning. *Please, let it goddamned snow.*

The Christmas decorations are not limited to the airport and, while taking the long drive to the Furama hotel, Steven is bombarded by lit-up reindeer and snowflakes and Christmas trees everywhere he looks. The city is in the spirit, even if he's not feeling it. Something about it doesn't seem right. Maybe it's the brutal weather, but it doesn't feel like Christmas, even if it looks like it.

"You American?" the taxi driver says. He is a young Asian man, about thirty years old, with a very crisp, blue, button-up shirt with short sleeves. He makes eye contact with Steven through the rearview mirror, glancing forward at the busy street every few seconds.

"Canadian," Steven says. The traffic is intense, but it's moving quickly. He knew that Singapore City was big, but it towers over him. He's seen skyscrapers before, but these buildings seem twice as big as any of the towers in Toronto.

"Ah, Canada!" The cabbie speaks in short staccatos, his English good but frequently broken. "You like hockey?"

"Sure," Steven says. He figures there's no reason to tell some cab driver the truth.

"Hockey very exciting. Canada very nice."

"Yep."

"Like Canada very much."

"Uh-huh. Can you turn the AC up a bit more, please?"

"What?" The driver laughs. "You want cold? You come here! Canada cold! Most Canadians come here, they don't want the cold!"

"Not this one," Steven says. "It's too hot for me."

"Hot!" The driver laughs harder. "This not hot. Today mild. All week, mild."

Steven cringes at the thought. It feels like the hottest day in July to him. The humidity is easily over ninety percent, and there isn't a breeze in the air. The taxi zips quickly off the highway and right into the middle of the city, where businessmen are wearing three-piece suits as they step out of the enormous office buildings and onto the sidewalk. He wonders how anyone could possibly dress like that in this kind of weather, and looks at his own tweed sports jacket and heavy chinos. It's essentially the same outfit he wears every other day of the week, and it made sense when he left home. Now it might as well be a track suit.

"Furama!" the cab driver cheers gleefully, as if he's never seen a hotel before. The taxi pulls up in front, and Steven suddenly doesn't feel so bad about the clothes he's wearing. He shakes his head as he steps out of the car and is greeted by a doorman who is dressed—head to toe—exactly like Santa Claus. A very thin, very short Singaporean man, he is wearing the big red hat, the very thick red suit, and even the black boots. To top it all off, the guy is even wearing a long, fake, white beard. Steven thinks of laughing, but isn't sure if it's right for him to do so or not. He doesn't know the culture enough to laugh at the people here, and he hears that the police in Singapore cane people for something as simple as chewing gum.

"Hello, sir." Santa Claus walks over and takes Steven's small suitcase. Steven nods as he tries to figure out how to pay the cab driver and do the currency exchange in his head at the same time. In his pocket he has some Canadian cash, some American greenbacks he had in a drawer at home, and a wad of Singaporean cash that looks and feels like Monopoly money.

"Aren't you hot wearing that?" Steven asks Mr. Claus.

"Yes, sir, very much."

"It looks like it."

"Very hot, sir."

"You know that Santa Claus wears that outfit because it's cold where he lives, right?"

"Yes, sir. Very cold."

Santa Claus smiles so big, Steven can see it even underneath the thick, fake beard. He wonders if the guy simply agrees with anything he is told. Steven reaches into his pocket and takes out one of the Singaporean bills he has folded into his money clip and hands it over. The doorman's eyes go bright, and his teeth are clearly visible now.

"Thank you, sir. Very good, sir. Thank you, sir." Santa Claus nods and dips his head forward slightly. It's not a bow, but it is very polite. Steven returns the gesture, wondering just how much money he just handed over and whether or not he'll have anything left for dinner once he figures it out.

The doorman leads him into the lobby and hands Steven the wheeled luggage he pulled out of the car. Steven nods and extends his hand. "What's your name, in case I need anything?"

"Lee, sir." He takes Steven's hand and shakes it as if his life were just saved. His grip is surprisingly strong for such a thin man. "And you are?"

"Steven."

"Oh, good." Lee smiles and nods again, a trickle of sweat beading in his Santa beard. "Thank you, Mister Stevens. Have a nice day."

"No," Steven says. "It's just Steven. Not Mister Stevens. My name is Steven."

"Very good, sir. Have a nice day, Mister Steven."

"No," Steven says, then catches himself. "Never mind. Fine. Thank you, Lee."

With a smile and another vigorous shake of the hand, Lee goes back to his bellhop stand in front of the hotel. Steven wonders just what that Santa suit must smell like at the end of the day. He hopes that all of the doormen don't share the same suit. He also realizes that he actually has no idea what Lee looks like, and will only recognize him as an Asian Santa Claus.

At the front desk, every clerk is dressed in crisp, black shirts and very neatly pressed black pants. The outfit would look very stylish and professional if not for the fact that each employee is wearing a large, fluffy, red Santa hat. It is supposed to look festive, but Steven can't help but laugh at how silly it is. In the past hour, he's been reminded of Christmas more than he would be if he walked through a shopping mall in downtown Toronto.

"Checking in, sir?" The young woman behind the counter smiles at him as he approaches, and Steven wonders if there's any unattractive women in this entire country. Thus far, every female he has seen has been very pretty. He's never had a specific preference for Asian women or anything like that, and his red-headed girlfriend is pretty much the opposite of every woman here, but every female he has encountered so far has been striking. The clerk has a name tag that reads NICOLE.

"Steven Kelly," he says as he pulls his passport out of his jacket pocket and slides it across the counter. The hotel lobby is nice, with dark marble floors and brass rails leading to the bar around the corner. Steven wonders how they got poinsettias all the way on this side of the world and whether or not they can actually grow them here. He's pretty sure the evergreen garland everywhere is fake.

"Yes, Mr. Kelly." Nicole begins tapping on her keyboard and looking at the computer screen in front of her. Then she taps some more. Then she pauses and reads something. Then she taps again. Steven has always wondered just what is on the screens of these computers in hotel lobbies everywhere. Border security does less reading and typing and checking on things whenever he hands over his passport than the average Holiday Inn. After a minute or two of this, Nicole looks up at him again and smiles.

"First time in Singapore City?" she asks.

"First time in Asia, period," he says. He thinks of his passport and the handful of stamps he has acquired over the years. Italy, France, the States. Then pretty much nothing. He chased wine while Scotty chased women. Scotty had tons of stamps in his passport.

"Lovely," she says. Her English is perfect. It doesn't really surprise him, since he read that it's pretty much the main language here. "You will love it here."

"Don't know if I'll be around long enough to fall in love."

"Ah, yes. You are leaving in two days, I see."

"Indeed I am."

"Well, you never know. Just maybe we'll make you stay a while, yes?"

He smiles. "Not if it's always this hot, you won't."

"Afraid so," Nicole says. "Guess we're going to just have to miss you, then."

"Merry Christmas."

Nicole smiles again, and Steven thinks for a second that it's not just hotel employee courtesy. It seems genuine. "You have a message waiting for you, sir," she tells him before he can walk away. "Let me print it out for you."

She steps around the corner, and Steven wonders just what it could be. He grins a little when he realizes that it's probably from Robin, wondering if he has arrived safely and telling him to get in touch as soon as he is in his room. A comforting sense of relief falls over him. He was pretty sure, by the time he left, that she was never going to speak to him again. For the first time in the past twenty-four hours, he feels a twinge of hope. A moment later, Nicole returns and hands him a small printout. The message has been typed out for him, which is impressive. He takes the paper, folds it in two, and places it in the inner pocket of his blazer.

"Will there be anything else, sir?" Nicole asks as she slides a keycard in a small envelope across the counter. She raises a hand that motions toward the elevators directly behind Steven and smiles again. "Do you need a map or directions or a wake-up call?"

"No, thanks." Steven shakes his head and smiles as he wheels his luggage to the elevators and makes his way to the fourteenth floor. He likes to stay on the highest floor possible whenever he stays in a hotel. It makes him feel safer for some reason. Something about the lower floors in a hotel feels slummy to him. Given the choice, he'll always take a top floor.

The room is small, but just what he needs. He figured it wouldn't be huge, as it seems the rest of the world stays in smaller hotels than what he's used to in North America. He remembers the hotels in Italy when he was finishing his degree, with their tiny washrooms and the even smaller beds. He is not even six feet tall, and his feet hung over the bed. The hotels in France weren't much bigger. This room in Singapore City is small, but makes those rooms look like closets by comparison.

He looks out the window and notices that the skyline is busier than the one in downtown Toronto. Singapore City is so much bigger than he thought it would be. The view is a bit overwhelming, but he likes it. He's always been a city guy.

Steven puts his suitcase on the rack next to the desk and unzips it. Immediately, he pulls out the two sports jackets he packed—inside out—and gently unfolds them. Then he turns them right-side-out and carefully gives each of them a once-over.

He's impressed with how few wrinkles either has. He's always been pretty good at packing his suitcase, and the wrinkle-free Oxfords he packed are further proof. The extra pair of brown wingtips at the bottom of the suitcase are a nice alternative to the black ones he's currently wearing, but he wonders why he packed them at all. He likely won't wear them during his brief stay here. But he also knows that, if he'd left them at home, he would have felt like he came unprepared.

Taking off his tweed jacket, he looks at the back of the collar to see if his sweat soaked into it at all. He kicks himself a little bit for not wearing a wool jacket like he knows he should have. But it was so cold when he left Toronto he didn't even think about it. He is about to hang up the jacket when it hits him that he has not read the message Robin left for him. He reaches into his right-side breast pocket and retrieves it. With his jacket draped over his arm, standing in front of the hotel bed, he suddenly feels his stomach churn a little bit.

The message is not from Robin.

Steven sits down on the bed and reads the brief note. Then he reads it again. Neither time does it make any sense.

I have your brother. OK. 1200 Singapore and I will give them to you.
Call me. 65 6738 1334–Dwash.

Steven looks at the message again and, for no reason, looks at the back of the piece of paper. It is, of course, blank, and offers no clues.

You have my brother? he thinks as he reads it again. *And all I have to do is give you twelve hundred bucks in Singaporean cash and I get him back?*

He decides it may very well be the stupidest ransom note he's ever seen. Granted, it's the only ransom note he's ever seen, but the fact that someone would attempt to extort such a little amount of money out of him is ridiculous. What's worse is that the thing being ransomed is apparently his brother, who, last

Steven checked, was dead and waiting to be identified in a morgue somewhere. Is this a ransom note from a morgue thief? Is there such a *thing* as a morgue thief?

Steven thinks that "Dwash" is an idiot. The ransom note is supposed to come before the person is dead, not after. Everyone knows that. As usual Scotty seemed to hang around with some very stupid people.

Mostly, however, he's annoyed because he was really hoping for a note from Robin. He tosses the worthless ransom note aside and picks up the hotel phone.

"Good day, Mister Kelly," a polite voice on the other end says.

"May I have an outside line for an international call, please?"

"My pleasure."

There is a pause, and Steven waits through about ten seconds of on-hold music. Then, the same cheerful voice comes on again.

"Number, please?" the voice says, and Steven realizes he can't tell if it is a man or a woman to whom he is speaking. He gives Robin's cell phone number and waits. There's another ten seconds of music and then a click. Then, there is the faint sound of the phone ringing. He plugs his left ear and waits.

"Hey, this is Robin," her voice mail says to him. "Leave me a message, and I'll get back to you."

Dammit, Steven thinks as he waits for the beep. *It's like 1 a.m. there. Where the hell are you?*

"Hi, it's me," he says. "Just wanted you to know that I'm here, and I arrived with no problems and everything. It was a long flight, but I'm alright. I just thought I would call and let you know." He looks out the window and wonders if he should just hang up and leave it at that. "Anyway, that's it, I guess. Oh! I'm in room 1412 here at the Furama hotel. If you need to reach me. I don't know the number because it's international. But, you know, if you need to reach me, I guess you can probably find it online or whatever, you know. So, yeah." He rolls his eyes at his own stupidity. "So, that's it. Anyway, I just wanted to let you know. I was thinking about you and everything on the plane and, you know, I just felt really bad. That's all. I just wanted to tell you, you know? So. Anyway. I hope you're okay. And I miss you. So, I'll talk to you later, okay? E-mail me or something, and let me know you got this or something. Bye."

Steven hangs up the phone and resists the urge to punch himself in the crotch.

You jackass, he thinks. *If there was a way to sound more pathetic, I don't think you've found it.*

He looks back at the window, runs his hands through his hair, and briefly wonders if he can pay Dwash twelve hundred bucks to push him off a building. When the thought sounds too tempting he gets up and walks to the hotel closet and hangs up his sports jackets. All three of them hang there perfectly, each about an inch apart, and barely look as if they've come all the way to Asia from Canada. For a brief moment, Steven smiles and is a little bit proud of his nice clothes.

"It's like living with a butler," he can hear Robin saying. "I might as well call you Jeeves. You with your pressed shirts and your perfect jackets. I feel like I live with Frasier Crane."

The thought of her saying that makes his head start to hurt a little and, just to prove he can be whomever he wants, he takes the jackets out of the closet and tosses them together onto the bed. He'll leave them there for the next couple of days, just lying on top of one another, folded in half. Just like any other casual guy would do.

He reaches into his suitcase and pulls out his Dopp kit. Unzipping the leather Hugo Boss case, he removes his manicure set and walks over to the window. He lets out a long sigh of relief and—finally—feels like he can relax a bit. It's quiet here, and he likes the view. He starts filing his nails and looks at the Christmas decorations smothering the city down below. This is probably a very nice city, and he probably would have enjoyed it if he'd come here when Scotty was alive. But now it just makes him miss Toronto, and he just sees it as the place that killed his brother.

Looking over his shoulder, he catches his reflection in the mirror. His hair is barely out of place, despite his temples being a little dark from the sweating. His shirt still looks nice on him, even after the long flight. His glasses are clean and straight. Here he stands, a well-groomed man filing his nails while looking out the window.

Christ, he thinks. *I really do look like a butler.*

He puts the file down and sits on the edge of the bed. Again he finds himself wondering if Robin is right—that he's a snob. He's too stuffy, and he possibly has OCD. Maybe Scotty had the right idea all along. Scotty's home was wherever he hung his hat, and he liked to toss that hat wherever it would land. Scotty would have tossed his sports jackets anywhere he pleased. He probably never packed two different colors of the same type of shoe.

But Scotty is dead at the morgue, and I'm sitting in this nice hotel room, Steven thinks and, for just a second, feels guilty. He knows he shouldn't think that way, not with Scotty gone now and not being here to defend himself. But people always acted as if he should envy Scotty when Steven always thought they had it all wrong. He's also not sure why Robin thinks she has it so bad being with him. She might complain about his stuffiness or his cleanliness or any number of things, but she would have hated being with Scotty. He never could have taken care of her the way Steven does.

He looks at himself again in the mirror and thinks he's got pretty nice hair. There isn't any gray yet, and he still has a full head of it. His glasses aren't nerdy; they're actually quite stylish. People at the restaurant have been telling him for years that he's handsome.

A few moments later, he picks up his sports jackets and hangs them back up in the closet. When he does, a slip of paper falls to the ground. He picks it up and realizes it's the message from the hotel desk. There's that name again: Dwash.

Who the hell are you and what kind of name is that? he thinks. He picks up the phone and is about to call the number, but he hangs up instead. It's middle of the afternoon and, although he's tired, he knows exactly what he really has to do before he calls this Dwash person. He picks up the phone and dials the front desk again.

"Yes, Mr. Kelly?" the voice returns.

"I need a taxi, please."

3

If not for the Mandarin writing beside all of the English writing on all of the signs, the morgue in downtown Singapore City would look just like any they show on all the TV shows. Steven is struck by how much it looks just like the one he had to go to fourteen years ago. That was the day he had to identify his parents' bodies. It was just before he went to the hospital to visit Scotty while he was recovering. Scotty was asleep for a couple of days after the accident, and didn't know their parents were gone.

Steven thinks it's weird. He almost had to do this with Scotty all those years ago. There was no airbag in the old Buick, but the seat belt kept Scotty from flying through the shattered window and into the guardrail. Their parents had never liked wearing seat belts.

Back in Toronto, Steven owns a nice BMW. He's had it for five years, and it was barely two years old when he bought it. Although he and Robin live right in midtown and walk a lot, he mostly drives the car to and from work every day, especially during the winter. For over a year after the accident, Scotty couldn't stand to be in a car. When he finally did get back in one, he insisted on sitting in the backseat for the next several months. He absolutely refused to drive. As far as Steven knew, Scotty never did again.

He remembers telling Scotty that their parents were gone and how his brother never cried. He didn't break down or anything like that, but everything in his eyes had looked so dead. It was as if he looked right through Steven while he was talking. Even at the funeral, while Steven gave the eulogy, Scotty never broke down. His face always looked the same. He had that same expression for months.

"Are you ready?" the coroner asks Steven, who has been staring at the same Chinese symbol on the wall for the past few minutes. He's trying to figure out what it means, since there is no English translation anywhere to be found. Here's this one, small poster hanging on the wall behind an examination table, and on it is only one symbol. He wonders if it's actually just one word or a complete sentence.

"Yes," Steven says, and his voice comes out raspy. The phlegm in his throat has built up, and he coughs a little bit to clear it. He's suddenly very cold and is sure he looks very pale. He can feel it, can actually feel his skin getting whiter. For the first time since he got the phone call about Scotty, this all suddenly feels real. He's so nervous, he barely notices the distant humming sound coming from an appliance or a computer somewhere in the background.

The coroner walks into another room that latches like a meat locker. Steven feels sick when it dawns on him that that is exactly what the other room is. A tall, slightly overweight, white-haired man, the coroner has no expression on his face. Behind his very thick glasses, his eyes show no emotion. Steven figures it's probably for the best that the coroner acts that way. When surrounded by dead bodies, it's probably healthy to shut out all the feeling. The old man returns seconds later, pushing a metal cart. On that metal cart, underneath a very clean white sheet, is a body.

Scotty, Steven thinks.

"Are you ready?" the coroner says again. Steven nods his head as he stands over the metal cart. He feels his hands go numb, and that iciness that is in the air runs up his arms. He blinks for a second and feels his eyelashes soak up the moisture of what he won't let become tears.

The sheet comes back, and there is no doubt: Scotty is lying there.

Steven recognizes him immediately. It's that face. It's *his* face. The one almost identical to his own, right down to the bone structure and shape. A sick feeling churns through his entire body, as if he's going to be ill, but there's no vomit inside of him to come pouring out onto the floor. For a brief moment, Steven feels as if he's not standing over Scott, but just slightly removed from it all. It's as if he's watching all this while hovering above the table, looking at his own body lying there. It makes him a little dizzy, seeing his reflection lying cold in front of him.

He blinks and feels one heavy tear roll down the left side of his face. He quickly brushes it away and looks back down at Scotty. For a brief second, he almost expects his brother to look up at him, open his eyes, and smile. That seems like something Scotty would do.

Scotty's hair is even longer than it was the last time Steven saw him. Steven looks him over and can't remember if he had that many tattoos or if some of them are new. Besides that, Scotty looks about the same. A long-haired, tattooed photocopy of Steven, lying on a metal table. Steven feels that churning in his stomach get even heavier.

"Do you recognize him?" the coroner asks.

Steven nods. "Yes. That's my brother. That's Scott."

The coroner moves to pull the sheet back over Scotty, but Steven raises his hand. "Wait."

The coroner stops in his tracks and looks up at Steven, an expression of curiosity on his face. "I'm sorry," he says. "Do you need a moment alone?"

"No," Steven says. "What's that on his face?"

"Bruising. He fell down."

"Because of the aneurysm?"

The coroner nods. "He fell down and hit his face."

"That's what happened?"

"That or he hit his face and then he fell down."

"Which is it?"

"Either way. He had an aneurysm, and he fell down. Either way, he hit his face."

Steven stares at the bruise on Scotty's face. Right along the left side of his forehead, all the way down to his jaw. It's not terribly puffy, but it's noticeable.

"He hit the ground very hard?" Steven asks.

"Yes," the coroner says. "He didn't break his fall. He was dead."

Steven nods and feels another tear find its way out of his eye and onto his cheek. He looks up at the Asian symbol on the wall again, trying to keep the waterworks from coming. He thinks again about how Scotty acted when their parents died. Right now, Steven wants to be just like that. He doesn't want to even blink.

"He looked like you," the coroner says, pushing Scott back into the freezer.

"We're twins," Steven says, staring straight ahead.

"I can tell. I almost didn't have you identify the body. I could tell he was your brother by looking at you when you came in."

"That happens all the time," Steven says, only just now realizing that it never will again. He can't even call Scotty and tell him just how ridiculous this whole thing was today. Normally, that'd have been one of the first things he did.

"Yes, well"—the coroner shrugs—"policy states you had to do it. You understand?"

"Of course. What now?"

"Now?"

"His body?" Steven asks. "What do I do with it?"

"Up to you. We can have it put in a casket, and you can fly him home."

Jesus, really? Steven thinks. He knew he had to do something with Scott's body, but this is the first time he realized it meant actually checking him like luggage and shipping him home. It all seems so creepy, he wonders if he can just leave him here.

"No, no, no." Steven shakes his head. "Nothing like that. What else can we do?"

"We can have him cremated. Give you the ashes."

"You can do that?"

"Yes, of course." The coroner clears his throat. "For a fee."

"That's fine. I'll do that."

"Fine, we will take care of it. Do you want to take his remains back to Canada? There is a lot of paperwork you will have to fill out. Things like that."

Steven shrugs. "I guess so. I don't know what else I'd do with them."

"Some people have them buried," the coroner says. "Some people choose to keep them somewhere at home. In an urn, perhaps."

"Christ, no." Steven looks at the coroner as if he has two heads. "Nothing like that. I—I don't know. I'll probably scatter them somewhere or something like that. Toss them into the ocean or something."

"Many people do that. Although it really isn't legal."

"Even better. That sounds just like something Scotty would do."

Steven almost smirks, still holding back the tears in his eyes. Scotty would do exactly that, in fact. It would be just like him to scatter ashes at the beach or in a park or something crazy, something ridiculous and pretentious and illegal. It's just like something Scotty would have loved.

"Very good, then," the coroner says, and Steven realizes the old man probably doesn't really care. One way or the other, he has to get Scott out of here, and he can't be concerned with where he winds up.

Steven looks down at the empty space where the table was just a minute ago. He realizes that right there, on that table, was his twin brother who he'll never see again. For the first time, he is hit by the fact that it was just a minute ago that he saw Scotty for the last time, and it was to take a long look at him lying lifeless in that cold, awful room. Part of Steven wishes he'd taken that moment with Scotty that the coroner offered him. He stops fighting the tears and lets them fall to the floor. The coroner understands and starts to walk out of the room.

"I'll be just outside," he says as he writes some notes on a file inside a manila envelope. Steven stands there, looking at the wall.

"What is that?" Steven asks, pointing at the Chinese symbol he has been staring at since he first walked in the room. "What does it mean?"

The coroner looks up over his thick glasses and glances over at the poster. "It means *peace*."

4

The Internet connection in the hotel costs him fifteen dollars per day just to use it, but Steven doesn't really care. He feels cut off from the rest of the world, and figures reading the news from back home might make him feel better and a little less homesick. Other people would be out seeing what Singapore City has to offer, at least in terms of food. Instead, he's trying to pretend he's not even there.

Plus, he keeps hoping to hear from Robin.

She hasn't left a message, hasn't texted his phone, and hasn't even dropped him a quick e-mail. He figured by now he would have heard *something*. Apparently she was angrier than he thought. After all, it was just more of the same problems anyway. It wasn't anything new or some enormous fight that sent her storming off into the night, just more of the same.

He doesn't know why it really bothers him. Robin is pretty, and she's smart enough, but they've never had much in common. She'd just as soon guzzle down a cheap cosmopolitan as enjoy any of the superior wine he brings home. Her taste in nice clothes is the only thing they really share. Her love of terrible music certainly has never been endearing. As much as she harps on him about being a neat freak or for being too anal about cleanliness, he could easily be giving back exactly what she doles out. Her tendency to leave a mess in the washroom; the way she leaves her clothes anywhere she feels like it. For all her talk about how fussy Steven is, he knows he could easily call her a slob.

But he would never do that.

The truth is, he knows he's not easy to deal with. He knows that he doesn't compromise enough and that he's very particular in what he likes and what he wants. He knows that he can be crabby in public, especially whenever confronted by the sounds of people eating or any of the number of little things that drive him up a wall. Some people might be snobby and never realize it, but Steven always does. That's why he cleaned up that mess she made with no argument, even after she deliberately broke a five hundred dollar bottle of wine. He knows he's not easy.

He sighs. *Either that or I'm too much of a coward to just break up with her and tell her to get the hell out of my condo.*

He remembers when the two of them met. She was pouring wine at a tasting, and he was there trying to find new additions for the wine list at the restaurant. The same height as he, she had to wear flat shoes to keep from towering over most of the other people there that night. The ballroom at the Intercontinental Hotel had been converted for one night into the site of a huge gathering of sales reps and vineyard employees and sommeliers and restaurant managers. In the midst of all of this was Robin, pouring wine and smiling brightly to everyone.

"This will knock your socks off," she had told him as she poured some cheap Malbec into his glass. She was right, but it knocked his socks off for all the wrong reasons. He spit it into the bucket not so much due to tradition as he did to get it out of his mouth. "Perfect, right?"

"It's very nice," he lied as he dabbed his mouth with a cloth handkerchief he always kept in his front pants pocket.

"You're a bad liar," she said, and shot him a sexy look with her very green eyes.

He laughed and looked over his shoulder to make sure no one else was in earshot. "You agree?"

"Everyone agrees," she said, and leaned in to almost whisper. "I'm not paid to like it. I'm paid to pour it."

"Slumming it" is what she called it: her part-time job work-ing for the Matthews Vineyard. She wanted to do interior de-sign but, until more work came her way, this was what she was going to be doing. She wasn't really much of a wine drinker, she admitted, but she looked good pouring it and flirting with sales reps. She was good at the flirting and, because of that, she sold a ton of wine. Scott would have been tempted by her enough to buy a few cases. Steven wasn't so fooled. That might have been why Robin liked him to begin with. They were sleeping together within a week.

She loved the restaurant, too. Being the sommelier at The Flat was a nice job, but more than a few women had no idea what it meant or how lucky Steven was to be doing it. People in his pro-fession weren't coming out of the woodwork, but neither were the jobs. Being at a place that was casual but pricey was a good thing. Some women he dated just didn't even know what a sommelier was. There was one who had simply called him a "wine waiter." She didn't stick around very long.

One thing Robin never liked was the hours. It wasn't a nine-to-five kind of job and, once those became the hours she was working, Steven's changing schedule began to bother her. On top of that, she tended to love the food at The Flat, but was not at all a fan of the people. She called the general manager "Mister Snooty" or "Felix" behind his back. She hated the waitresses and always complained to Steven that they were obviously trying to sleep with him.

Because she didn't really like anyone else, Robin was always happiest when it was just the two of them at home. Steven had only had his condo in the Minto Midtown high rise for about six months before she moved in, and one of the first things she did was change everything. Just as he changed her taste for wine, she changed his appreciation for decorating. Gone were the classic leather sofas that reminded him of his dad's office. Gone were the framed prints he'd found in art stores. Some guys would have been annoyed at everything Robin did to change the condo, but Steven was happy for it. She really was talented and turned it into the type of home you see in city magazines. People thought Robin's and his place looked like it belonged in the pages of *Toronto Life*.

Steven wondered how many weekends were spent, especially around that first Christmas together, with the two of them never leaving the apartment. They walked naked around the place, making love on every single piece of furniture.

"We have to christen this ottoman!" Robin would cheer as she bounced up and down, her slender body absolutely stunning and surrounded by her handiwork. "Then we break in the bed again!"

They'd order in Chinese food and lie on the floor on the artsy-looking rug she'd found. Wearing nothing but a Snuggie he'd bought for her at Zellers for fifteen dollars, she'd sing along to the Christmas songs he insisted on playing around the house. That first Christmas, she loved those songs. Even the one by The Chipmunks. He'd watch her and get aroused just looking at her sprawled out on the retro recliner she had picked out. He loved her taste. He adored her body and her red hair and her sexy smile. She made him feel less Frasier Crane and more Hugh Jackman.

"You're a classy guy," she'd said at the time. "You deserve to live in a classy pad."

Classy it stayed, but happy it did not. When Robin began doing design full-time, she took any frustrations with that job out on the one Steven did. It didn't matter that he was perfectly happy doing his job, she found ways of hating it.

"Surely you don't have to spend all your time at that place," she'd say at least once a month. "Don't they have some waiters or bartenders that can do most of that?"

They probably did, but Steven loved doing it. So much so that he didn't realize how much time he was spending there and how little he was spending in their classy pad. By the time he caught on to how lonely she was getting, Robin had already moved on to complaining about his neatness. Or his stuffiness. Or his misophonia. She didn't dance naked for him anymore. She just rolled her eyes. A lot.

Steven didn't want to admit to himself that he had probably lost her months ago. It just took his being out of the country for her to finally push away for good.

Checking his e-mail in-box one more time—probably the fifth time in the past half-hour—he finally closes his netbook and leans back in the desk chair. Over his left shoulder, he looks outside and sees that the brutal sun is still very high in the sky, beating down on what is an enormous and busy city. He didn't pack any shorts. Not even a short-sleeved shirt.

Over his right shoulder, he looks at the flat-screen TV and the British newscaster yammering away on the international CNN feed. Next to that flat-screen TV is a small, flat, rectangular cardboard box. It is very simple, very plain-looking, and weighs about five pounds. Inside that box is Scotty.

Steven still feels a bit nauseous and a little embarrassed that he almost threw up right there when they gave him the box. It just seemed so creepy to be carrying his brother's remains in what might as well be something one would pick up at the post office. It's both funny and depressing when he thinks about how he could wrap the box in duct tape and, for very little money, mail his dead brother back home to Toronto. He knows from reading articles on the Internet that it's not all ashes in that box; it's not uncommon for bits of bone and wood to be in there. The thought of this makes him want to vomit, so he never opened the box and has no intention of ever doing so. He'll spread the ashes with his eyes glued shut if he has to.

"Guess it's time to take you home, big brother," he says to the box. The irony was never lost on either of them that, despite being the first born, Scotty usually had to rely on Steven to figure everything out. Scott might not have copied Steven's appearance, but he had always copied Steven's homework.

This thought makes Steven laugh for a second and—without hesitation—that leads into his crying for at least two minutes. It's been like this off and on for the past twenty hours or so, ever since he got back from the morgue. He remembers something about Scotty that makes him smile which then leads instantly to his realizing he'll never smile with his brother again. The waterworks come quickly and then dry up as fast as they came. Sometimes he refuses to believe that Scotty is even gone. The only proof is across the room and looks nothing like him.

Steven gets up from the desk and walks over and touches the cardboard box. He swears it feels warm and hopes he's imagining it. He wonders if human remains can spontaneously combust after they've already been cremated. Then he wonders if he's better off just dumping Scotty's ashes right here in Singapore City. It's the last place he lived, and for over two years. He was even ready to drop fifteen thousand dollars right here. Why shouldn't this godforsaken oven keep him?

Dwash, Steven thinks.

He walks back over to the desk and pushes everything aside, looking for the slip of paper with that guy's number on it. Apparently this Dwash guy thinks he already has Scott. Whatever he's talking about might give Steven some clue as to why Scotty was looking for cash in the first place and what the hell he'd gotten himself into. For all Steven knows, Dwash is some kind of loan shark or mob boss. Does Singapore even have a mafia or loan sharks?

Steven finds the paper and unfolds it. He still has no clue what it means:

I have your brother. OK. 1200 Singapore and I will give them to you.
Call me. 65 6738 1334—Dwash.

Steven walks over to the bed and sits down, picking up the phone on the nightstand at the same time.

"Yes, Mr. Kelly." The owner of the voice on the other end is obviously smiling. "How can I be of service?"

"I need to dial a local number."

"Of course. My pleasure to connect you."

After a couple of short clicks, there is the sound of ringing. After three rings, a man's voice answers.

"Yo," the deep voice says. Steven wonders if this is a common Singaporean greeting.

"Is this Dwash?" he asks.

"Who?"

"Dwash? I'm looking for Dwash."

"Who is this?"

"I got a message in my hotel to call Dwash. Is he there?"

"Aw, hell." The voice chuckles on the other end. "Is this Scott's brother?"

"I'm sorry, but who are you?" Steven says. "And how do you know Scott?"

"It's all good, man. I was a friend of Scott's. Are you in the city? At the hotel?"

"How did you know where I was staying?"

"It took some effort, believe me," the voice says. "But I figured you weren't staying in any fleabag motel."

"You left me a note that you have my brother," Steven says. "What did you mean? Is this Dwash?"

"Is this who?"

"Dwash. The message at the hotel said to call 'Dwash.' "

"Aw, shit, man," the guy says, and laughs. "It's not Dwash. It's D.Wash. Dee. Wash. Like Donald Washington."

Steven shakes his head and thinks about slapping his forehead. "I see," he says. "Well, what did you mean that you have my brother?"

"Have your brother? Where?"

"Christ, man, I don't know. I got a message here that says you have my brother and that I have to pay you twelve hundred in order to get him back. I don't know what the hell you're talking about, but I assure you that you're not going to get anything out of me. I don't care what Scott owed you."

D.Wash makes noises on the other end of the phone that seem to indicate that he is confused and not really sure what to say next. "What? Scott didn't owe me anything."

"Then why the twelve hundred Singaporean dollars to come and get him?"

D.Wash lets out a very long, loud breath. "Keys," he says. "I have Scott's keys."

"His keys?"

"To his apartment. I have his keys, and I want to give them to you."

"Oh. Well, what's with the twelve hundred bucks?"

"Stupid hotel," D.Wash says. He lets out a long sigh and sounds as if he is switching the phone from one ear to the other. His already deep voice seems to get deeper. "They took the message down wrong. Twelve hundred Singapore isn't money. It's a bar. Twelve hundred Singapore Avenue. It's where my bar is. I have the keys to your brother's apartment. Not your brother, and no money. Just his keys. At twelve hundred Singapore Avenue. The Blue Bayou."

Steven looks at the note again:

I have your brother. OK. 1200 Singapore and I will give them to you.

He wants to slap someone. All this time he thought he was being strong-armed for money when it was just a friend of Scotty's trying to give him a hand.

"Jesus Christ," he says.

"Yeah," D.Wash says. "What'd you think? I was trying to shake you down?"

"Thought about it, yeah."

D.Wash laughs. "Nah, man. I wouldn't do that to Scott's brother."

"I did kind of think it made you the worst extortionist in history."

"For real. Listen, you wanna come get these keys? I figured you might wanna get his things out of his place and all."

"I guess so. Did you know my brother pretty well?"

"Well enough to have his keys, right?"

"Fair enough."

"I figure you've got questions, too."

"A few, yeah."

"Well, come on by. I'll tell you what I can. I'll be here all night. It's not too far or anything. Ten minutes in a cab."

"Sure. Gimme a bit, okay?"

"You got it," D.Wash says. "Tell the hotel staff to kiss my ass on your way out."

There is a click on the line, and D.Wash is gone. Steven thinks of taking him up on his advice and starts to dial zero. Instead, he just hangs up the phone and looks around the room once more. The cardboard box sitting next to the TV seems to be laughing at him.

"Screw you," Steven says to it. "And your keys."

5

Walking down to the lobby, Steven feels the heat coming in from the automatic doors that lead outside. Standing in his usual position, still dressed as Kris Kringle, Lee is greeting people as they come and go. He turns around and sees Steven and smiles hugely through his sweaty, fake beard. Like a good doorman, he opens the door by making the exaggerated effort of waving his hand in front of the automatic sensor. As the doors slide open, he practically bounces over to Steven.

"Mister Stevens." He beams. "How are you, sir?"

"Great, Lee," Steven says. "Can I get a taxi, please?"

"Yes, sir, Mister Stevens. Right away." Lee fetches a whistle he has buried in the pocket of his Santa suit and blows into it. From around the corner, a Ford sedan comes slowly creeping over. It looks exactly like a taxi cab from anywhere else in the world. Steven doesn't know why, but he keeps thinking he'll see one that is unique to the area. He doesn't even know if Singapore has its own line of cars.

"There you are, Mister Stevens," Lee says, and opens the door to the backseat. Steven climbs in and, at the same time, slips a couple of bucks to Lee. He imagines that Lee will be disappointed with the amount this time around, but the first tip should still keep Steven off the naughty list for at least the rest of his stay.

"Twelve hundred Singapore Avenue, please," Steven says to

the driver while simultaneously nodding and waving to Lee as he shuts the door. "Winter Wonderland" is playing on the radio, and the air-conditioning is already on full blast. Steven sits back and lets his shirt stick to his back as he gazes out the window.

The city has not slowed down once since he landed. Even now, as the evening is on its way, cars are everywhere and people are all over the sidewalks. Steven has never seen so many motor scooters and Vespas as he does right now. Every other vehicle has only two wheels. The occasional motorcycle goes by, and he spots a couple of crotch rockets. Mostly, however, he notices little mopeds and tiny electric bikes. Occasionally, he spots a random car that he's never heard of before, even though it may be made by Honda or Toyota. He wonders why these cars aren't available in Canada or the US, and then realizes almost no one would buy them. Some of them are barely bigger than the scooters they share the road with.

Steven notices that almost everything is Western. There are signs advertising The Gap and Banana Republic. There are billboards convincing people to buy an iPad. The cab comes to a stop at a red light on a street corner in front of a Kentucky Fried Chicken. Steven wonders for a minute if the people here really love the Western culture or if they simply have no choice. Were they invaded by cheap food and simply chose to accept it? Or do they really love McNuggets? He wonders if there's a Walmart in Singapore and, if there is, did the people here protest it like the people in parts of Canada did when the stores opened there? He sees ads for cellular phone companies and wonders if that's the one thing from here that found its way west. Everything in regard to technology in Singapore City seems years ahead of Canada. But all of the food and the clothes are straight out of Hollywood.

The tall skyscrapers get smaller, and the cab comes to an area where the streets become narrow and a little more crowded. There are fewer office buildings and banks and suddenly more bars and cafés. The restaurants go from being McDonald's and Burger Kings to little independent places with names like The

Flying Pizza and Great Greek and Noodle Hut. It reminds Steven of hanging out in Chinatown or The Annex in Toronto. He wonders if this is where students or artists hang out.

D.Wash is right and, after less than fifteen minutes, the taxi comes to a stop in front of a row of bars at the end of one of the small streets. Steven looks out the window as he is paying the driver and notices a sandwich board with the words BLUE BAYOU written on it. The words COMEDY 2NITE are written in pink chalk, and ONLY $10 underneath that is written in blue. At the top of the sign, a bluebird with cartoon eyes has been half-assed drawn, looking excited about the ten dollars.

Steven looks at the bar, which is narrow but appears to go up three levels. The front patio is open, and people are sitting outside, drinking beers. The dark gray building has bright blue shutters and that same cartoon bird painted right above the front door. It's a very cute, very tacky pub . . . and it looks very out of place in this city. The two Chinese restaurants on either side only make it stand out even more.

Walking through the front door, Steven looks around at the very simple décor and immediately feels like he's at some run-down pub back home. It almost looks like a place one would find on the beach somewhere in Florida, with old people and surfers walking in to have some fried shrimp and a beer. The tables are all wood, and the seats are mostly wooden barstools. Random framed photos of bluebirds adorn the walls, which makes Steven wonder why the place has the name it does. He wonders if there's a Bluebird Bar somewhere in town decorated with photos of a bayou.

"What's happening?!" A very large, bald black man with rimless eyeglasses waves to him from behind the bar. When he does, random people of random ethnicities at the bar turn around and wave, too. There are several Asian people, a couple of white guys, and a black woman. They each smile and yell "what's happening" exactly the same way as the bartender. Steven stops in his tracks and looks awkwardly over his shoulder at the doorway behind him.

"Yeah, you!" the bartender says. Everyone at the bar laughs and turns back to his or her drink and food. The bartender laughs and waves Steven over. "C'mon in!"

Steven walks slowly up to the bar with the confidence of a bad liar at a poker tournament. He pulls out one of the wooden barstools, but doesn't sit down. Instead, he leans on the bar and makes eye contact with the bartender.

"You're Stevie, right?" the bartender says, and extends a very large hand. Steven takes it and notices that two of his hands could fit inside its enormous grip. He's surprised when it turns out the handshake is actually quite soft coming from such a big guy.

"Steven," he says. "You must be D.Wash."

"That I am, my man." D.Wash smiles, and his mouth is somehow bigger than his enormous hands. "That I am. Welcome. Man, you really do look like him."

"I get that a lot," Steven says. He always wonders why people are surprised to find out that identical twins are nearly identical. It's right there in the description. Yet every time someone would meet the other brother, there was always talk of "my, how alike you look." Four years apart and it would be a surprise. Four minutes seems kind of obvious.

"I think you might be a little better looking than your bro," D.Wash says. "All that hair and the ink didn't suit him, if you ask me."

"Thanks," Steven says. "Nice place."

"Hey, thanks, man." D.Wash touches his index finger to his chest, right where his heart would be. "Respect. You want a Tiger?"

"A what?"

"Tiger. It's a beer. You want?"

"No, thanks."

"You find the place okay?"

Steven holds out his hands to his sides as if to say, "Here I am." D.Wash smiles and steps over to the cash register. He pushes a few buttons, and the drawer opens. Then he reaches in and pulls out a set of keys. He walks back over to where Steven is; the smile on his face fades, and he hands the keys across the bar as if he were giving up the lease to his bar. The switch from happy to sad is quick, and it makes Steven a bit uncomfortable.

"I'm really sorry about your brother," D.Wash says. "I'm sorry we had to meet this way."

"I appreciate that." Steven takes Scott's keys and gives them a look. There's nothing much exciting about them or anything out of the ordinary. Three keys and a bottle-opener keychain. Steven recognizes one of the keys as one to his condo back in Toronto. Scotty was allowed to come and go as he pleased, even though he had never been there.

"Everybody liked him," D.Wash says.

Everybody *did* like Scott. What was there not to like? He had money to spend, but never looked like it. He bought most rounds at most bars. He had funny tattoos of women with big breasts. If you didn't like him, he'd buy you a drink anyway, and then eventually you would. How can you not like a guy who lives like a hippie but is secretly a yuppie?

"Thanks," Steven says, and nods. He's not sure really what to say to D.Wash. Instead, he looks at the keys again, as if they suddenly are going to teleport him back to Canada.

"Lemme buy you a drink, huh?" D.Wash says. "Then we can talk a bit about your bro."

"That's alright," Steven says. "I'm not really much of a beer drinker."

"I've heard." D.Wash raises an eyebrow above his rimless glasses and reaches down beneath the bar. When his hands come back up, he's holding a very nice-looking bottle of Penfolds. It's nothing fancy, but it's better than any of the beer in the bar and probably not cheap enough to be the house red. "How about this?"

"Much better," Steven says. "So you know."

"Sure, man. Your brother talked about you all the time. Said it was one of those things he learned from you."

"Wine?"

D.Wash winks. "Drinking."

With a huge grin, D.Wash walks around the bar, nodding to a small Asian girl to take over the drink slinging. She nods and jumps up from her stool and immediately takes his place. D.Wash holds the bottle of wine by the neck, and it looks tiny in his enormous hands. He must weigh nearly three hundred pounds. He looks like a professional wrestler.

"Have a seat." D.Wash points to a small table nearby with two very uncomfortable looking wooden chairs. Steven wonders if the barstool would have been better. He sits down at the chair that faces the street and lets D.Wash sit with his face to the bar.

There are many white people in the bar, and Steven wonders how many of them are locals, tourists, or people on business. D.Wash is obviously American, and Steven wonders if most of his clientele are, as well. He read that there are many British and European expats living in Singapore. He just didn't figure they all hung out together. Now that he sees it, he thinks it makes sense that they'd all frequent the same places.

The sound of the cork snaps Steven out of whatever he was thinking, and he watches D.Wash carefully pouring them each a glass. D.Wash raises his by the stem and holds it in the air. Steven takes his cue and does the same, waiting for the toast.

"I'm sorry we have to meet this way," D.Wash says. "I'm really sorry, man."

"Me too," Steven says, and hopes it's a quick drink.

"To Scott."

"To Scott." Steven touches his glass to D.Wash's. D.Wash proceeds to down what is at least seven ounces of wine in one long gulp. Steven takes a very small sip of his wine and sets the glass back down.

"What?" D.Wash says. "No swishing? No swirling? No twirling the glass or any of that stuff?

Steven shakes his head. "I'm off duty."

"Fair enough."

"Are you American?" Steven asks. He holds his glass by the stem and, without realizing it, slowly shuffles it around on the table in tiny circles. The wine just barely swirls in the bowl, its red legs running down the sides of what is actually a white wineglass.

"Is it that obvious?" D.Wash says, and lets out a long, deep laugh. It sounds volcanic. If the accent didn't give him away, the over-the-top laugh would have definitely pegged him for a Yank.

"It's the accent."

"Ah, yeah. And you, Canadian. Scott had it, too. Always said 'oot and aboot.' "

Steven cringes. He always hates it when people say that Canadians say "aboot." He's never known a single person in his life who said "oot and aboot," and he's positive Scotty would certainly never say it. He hated Canadian stereotypes, and never found them funny, even on TV.

"How long have you been here?" Steven asks.

"Almost seven years."

"Wow. You move here to open this bar?"

"Aw, hell, no. This is just my side biz. Three days a week I teach."

Steven raises his eyebrows. "Really? What do you teach?"

"Screenwriting." D.Wash smiles and nods with a look that obviously says *can you believe that?*

"Here in Singapore?"

"Yup, that's what I did back in the States. Out in LA. I was writing for TV for years. You remember a show called *Mister Malcom's Homeroom?*"

Steven does indeed remember the show. It was an awful program, masquerading as a sitcom for teenagers. Mister Malcom was a black teacher in a stuffy white prep school. He taught the mostly white rich kids how to loosen up, learn to respect each other, and occasionally just learn not to be little assholes. It starred David Davis, who before and since was a very highly paid stand-up comedian. The show was on for years and was simply dreadful.

"That was a great show," Steven lies and takes a sip of his wine.

"It was shit." D.Wash smiles, and his eyes go wide. He pauses for a few seconds and waits for Steven to smile before he continues. "But it paid me crazy and wasn't hard work. Anyway, after that was over, I did some other shit and taught some classes in LA and whatever. Then I got an offer to come out here and teach for NYU."

"New York University?"

"That's the one. There's a satellite campus right here in Singapore City."

Steven doesn't know what to say. "So, you teach Singaporean students . . ."

"How to be sitcom writers, yeah," D.Wash says, and nods as if he can't believe it himself.

"How do you like it?"

"Singapore City? Love it." D.Wash leans in closer. "You get used to the heat."

"Really?"

"Nope," D.Wash says, and laughs again. It's a hearty laugh, fit for a guy his size. Steven laughs, too, and takes another sip of his wine. He sees why Scott liked this guy. Steven's not one for drinking with strangers, but D.Wash makes it seem like that's something he does on a daily basis.

"How did you meet Scott?" Steven asks.

D.Wash taps his index finger on the table. "He was a regular. He liked to watch the comedy."

"I saw that. You have comedians here?"

"Arguably," D.Wash says. "It's mostly amateurs. Some are good. Some are absolute crap. A lot of them are my students. And there are some Brits and a couple of Aussies, too. A little bit of everything. That's why Scott liked it. Every week, he sat upstairs and watched the show."

Steven nods and sips his wine. It sounds exactly like something Scott would have been into. When they were kids, they used to love watching comedians. Scott got ahold of some old George Carlin tapes, and they both had them practically memorized. When they were old enough and at university, they used to go hang at Yuk Yuk's Comedy Club in midtown Toronto and watch the show. Steven smiles when he realizes that the club is long gone, but his condo is only two blocks away from where it used to be. He and Scotty spent more than one night getting drunk there.

"Did he perform?" Steven asks.

"Scott?" D.Wash looks surprised. "Never. Was that his thing at some point?"

"No," Steven says. "Just curious." He asks because, in a way, it is exactly like Scotty. As much as the two of them loved to go and watch stand-up comedy, Scott was way more into it than Steven ever was. While Steven could probably quote any number of routines by George Carlin or Eddie Murphy, it was Scotty who was the connoisseur. He knew obscure guys from the eighties who had never even become TV stars. He could tell you random jokes he had heard twenty years ago and still make them just as funny. Scotty probably spent five nights a month at Yuk Yuk's, even after Steven got tired of going. He knew as much about comedians as Steven knew about wine.

But Scotty never went onstage. Not once. He could tell dirty jokes, and he could make a roomful of people smile and laugh. But Scotty never so much as gave a speech in high school. He was great in a crowd, but horrible under the spotlight.

"He had a lot of friends?" Steven asks.

D.Wash shrugs his shoulders. "I guess. Scott seemed to talk a bit to everybody, you know. He was a social butterfly. Always going from one person to another. But it wasn't like he had a usual group he hung out with, you get me? He would come in alone and leave alone. But he was never alone while he was here."

"I know exactly what you mean."

"He was a good guy. Goddamned shame."

Steven takes another sip of his wine and, as he puts the glass back down, D.Wash refills it before he can refuse. He's actually glad. He has been wanting something to take the edge off since he got here. After the day before at the morgue and now sitting here talking about Scott, it's just what he needs. If D.Wash is going to keep pouring the drinks, Steven's going to keep drinking them.

"What happened?" he asks, and the look on D.Wash's face tells him he was expecting the question to come sooner or later.

"I don't know, really," D.Wash says. "I wish I could tell you more. One minute he was fine and the next . . ."

"Right."

"It all happened really fast."

"That's what the hospital said."

"Yeah, it was."

"Were you there?"

"Yeah," D.Wash says, and pours himself another glass of wine. This time he swirls the glass around a bit instead of just tossing the wine back like a shot of whiskey. "Sort of. I wasn't in the room when it happened."

"Did it happen here?"

"Oh, no." D.Wash shakes his head as if the thought of Scott's dying in his bar is ludicrous. "This was over at Orchard Towers. Middle of the night. I got up to get a drink and when I came back he was on the floor."

"Jesus," Steven says, and feels his throat start to stick.

"Yeah." D.Wash takes a sip of his wine. "Like I said, it happened very fast."

Steven looks at the keys in his hand again. The bottle opener is a stark reminder that Scott was always more of a beer guy than a wine guy. It's funny that D.Wash had a nice bottle of red waiting for Steven. Scotty would definitely have been more comfortable drinking that Tiger whatever beer.

"He live far from here?" Steven asks.

"Five blocks," D.Wash says. "Easy walk. Especially in such lovely weather."

D.Wash winks, and Steven smiles. "I'm not good with the heat," he says.

"No one is, my man."

"The doorman at my hotel was dressed as Santa Claus. Full costume and everything. Even the beard."

"Sounds about right."

"I've seen more Christmas here than I will back home all December."

"They love it here," D.Wash says.

"Why is that?" Steven asks. "Isn't Singapore Buddhist or something like that?"

"Sure," D.Wash says, "but there's a ton of Christianity up in here, too. And Muslims. And Hindu. A little bit of everything. But Singaporeans love festivals. They love celebrations and holidays. It doesn't matter what the occasion is; they love a really festive holiday."

"Hence the love of Christmas."

"You got it," D.Wash says. "And not just here. Over in Jakarta, it's eighty percent Muslim. But you wouldn't know that if you walk down the street this time of year. Everywhere you go, it's Santa Claus this and Merry Christmas and shit."

"That sounds crazy."

D.Wash laughs. "It really throws you off the first time you see it. My first Christmas here, I sat outside on my back porch, sweating into my bathing suit, watching *How the Grinch Stole Christmas* in Mandarin on TV."

"You speak Mandarin?"

"Nope," D.Wash says, and they both laugh.

Steven feels a nice buzz coming on. This was just what he needed. He doesn't want to have to deal with anything else and, for at least the time he's been here, he hasn't thought about Robin. No sooner does she pop into his head then he pushes her right back out again. Maybe it's the company. Or maybe it's the wine. Either way, it's a good feeling. He barely notices that D.Wash slurps his wine and makes a loud gulping noise each time he swallows.

"It sucks that this is what brought you here," D.Wash says after another gulp of his wine. "I bet you'd like it if you stuck around a bit. There's a lot of great shit to see in this city."

"I'm sure."

"Have you seen much of it?"

"Hardly any," Steven says. "I feel a bit out of place."

D.Wash smiles and raises his eyebrows again. "Now you know how it feels to be an Asian man walking around anywhere in North America."

"You may have a point."

"Or what it feels like to be black right here," D.Wash says, and laughs again.

Steven smiles and looks out the window. So many people are constantly walking down the street. The foot traffic never seems to end. Even here, just beyond the patio outside, dozens of people make their way in front of The Blue Bayou. Steven wonders if Scotty stood out when he was here or found a way to blend in with the crowd. For a guy who had a tendency to make such an impression, Scotty was very good at being invisible when he wanted. It's one reason he traveled so well.

"I need to ask you something," Steven says after a few moments of their saying pretty much nothing. "About Scott."

"Go for it," D.Wash says.

"Last week, he came to me asking for money. A lot of it. Any idea what he needed it for?"

D.Wash rubs a hand over his completely shaven head and looks confused. "Damn," he says. "I wouldn't have a clue. Scott never seemed like he needed money. Hell, he barely spent it. I don't know how he could have been hurting."

"I don't know, either," Steven says. "But he asked me a couple of days before . . . this."

"I'm sure it's just coincidence, man," D.Wash says. "I was there, you know? It just happened. Just like I said."

"Right," Steven says. "Still, it was a lot of money."

"Maybe he knew he was sick?" D.Wash says, and shrugs. "Like he knew that this headache shit he was dealing with was bad."

Steven shakes his head. "No, he had the headaches for years."

"Wouldn't wear glasses," D.Wash says, and Steven nods. "Not that it's any of my business, but Scott could have asked me for money. You mind if I ask you how much we're talking, here?"

Steven figures there's no harm in it, although he's never liked talking about money. Not with Scott; not with Robin. Not even with his accountant. But he feels instantly at ease with D.Wash, and goes for broke. "Well over ten grand."

D.Wash almost chokes on his wine. "Damn, you ain't kidding."

"You see my dilemma."

"Yeah." D.Wash rubs his head some more. "I don't know, man. Maybe he was looking to buy a car."

"A car? Here?"

"Yeah, it's a real big deal here, you know?" D.Wash waves a hand at the street outside. "It's not like back home where you just buy one and hit the streets. In Singapore, having a car is a big deal. It costs a shitload of money, too. Take what a car costs back home and double it. Maybe triple. Then, on top of that, you have to get a license, which is not free or even cheap here. Then you've got to get insurance and special permits. It can easily run you twenty grand just to have some piece of shit beater."

"That's nuts, but I assure you he wasn't looking to buy a car."

"No?"

"No chance," Steven says. Scotty hadn't driven in almost fifteen years. Steven doubted he was suddenly going to start in a city where he didn't need to and the traffic was scarier than skydiving. And on the left side of the road, no less. If it was true, and Scotty had been looking to get a car, he certainly hadn't been looking to drive it.

"Well, I couldn't possibly tell you," D.Wash says. "But I know you should probably talk to Dania."

Steven tilts his head back and lets out a long sigh.

"What is it?" D.Wash asks.

"How did I know there was a girl?" Steven says.

Because there was always a girl. Scotty was into entertainment more than wine, and women more than entertainment. And it happened no matter where he went. There was the interpreter when he backpacked across Europe. There was the scuba instructor in Australia. There was some annoying earthy girl way back in Alaska. There was always a girl. Scott didn't go anywhere without getting laid, and he often found a way to fall in love. He did both very easily.

"Well, it always comes back to a woman, doesn't it?" D.Wash says.

"When?"

"Always." D.Wash motions his head at the very petite Asian girl acting as bartender. He gives a wink to Steven.

"Really?" Steven says, realizing that D.Wash is pointing out that he's involved with the girl in question.

"Almost two years. I don't just stay here for the nice weather."

"So I see."

"Scott and I had more in common than beers and funny people, my man."

Steven looks at the petite girl and wonders how D.Wash can possibly be in the same bed with that woman and not break her in half. Instead of saying anything, he simply raises his glass, which D.Wash lightly touches to his.

"So how do I find . . ."

"Dania," D.Wash says. "She works over on the Riverwalk. I'll write down the name of the place for you."

"Thanks," Steven says. "Was she with you and Scotty when it happened?"

"She was always with Scott."

"Then how come you had his keys and not her?"

"She didn't take it very well. I'm sure you understand. When it all went down, we all knew he had a brother back in Canada. Someone had to get your information and give it to the hospital, right?"

Steven had never considered how they had found him. The phone call came and, once he had the news, he didn't bother to think about how they'd gotten his name and number. "So you got my number from his place?"

"Yeah, plus I had to go. I was his PB."

"His what?"

"His PB. 'Porn Buddy.' "

Steven furrows his brow and stares at D.Wash. Steven has no idea what he's talking about.

"Aw, man," D.Wash says, reading the confused look on Steven's face. "You never had a porn buddy?"

"Do I want to know what this is?" Steven says, and tries not to imagine his brother and D.Wash and the petite Asian bartender doing God knows what in this apartment he hasn't even seen yet.

"Aw, man," D.Wash says again. "A porn buddy is a friend who agrees that, if anything terrible should happen to you, he'll go over to your house afterward and get rid of all the porn. So no one else finds it, like a family member or a girlfriend."

Steven almost spits out his wine. It's a brilliant idea, and he never would have been so clever as to think of such a thing. But it sounds just like Scotty.

"Gotcha," Steven says. "And did you do that? Get rid of his porn?"

"Didn't matter; he didn't have any. Didn't even own a computer."

Steven smiles and thinks that Dania, whoever she is, must be one hell of a wildcat for Scotty to not need any outside entertainment. Robin was no slouch in the bedroom, but that didn't change the fact that Steven still subscribed to *Playboy* and had a couple of DVDs in the back of his sock drawer. In fact, he probably kept them still because he knew it annoyed her a little.

"So Dania doesn't live there?" he asks.

"Nah. I don't know where she lives. Just where she works."

"I'll have to go and find her," Steven says. "At least to let her know everything. And thank her. You know."

"Yeah, I do. You taking his body back home?"

"Ashes."

D.Wash winces, as if the thought hurts him. As if he can feel the heat from the crematorium under his feet. "Good luck, my man. You know where to find me if you need anything, right?"

"Thanks." Steven finishes his wine and extends his hand.

"Just one thing," D.Wash says, and looks over his shoulder at his little Asian lover. Then he leans in closer and gives Steven a stern look. "Dania's really cool."

"But?"

"Don't go doing anything foolish. Don't get involved with her."

"Involved?"

"Yeah, you know."

"Involved like how?"

"Like Scott."

Steven sits back and chuckles to himself. It seems like such a strange thing for someone to say. He's on his way to see his dead brother's girlfriend and talk about money problems and scattered remains. It hardly seems romantic.

"Is that what happened?" he asks, wondering if his brother's history repeated itself. "Did Scott fall in love with her?"

D.Wash sighs and smiles in a way that seems more sad than anything else, his large eyes peering from behind his glasses and right through Steven.

"Not just Scott, my man," he says, and raises his glass.

6

The smell in the hallway hits Steven right in the face the second he walks up the narrow flight of stairs to Scotty's studio apartment. It's a combination of spiciness and smoke, as if a bonfire is cooking a wild boar right in the middle of the tiny apartment building. Steven imagines a thick broth with bits of meat and rice and peppers all thrown into one big pot, simmering over an open flame. It smells absolutely delicious. The irony of it all is that he probably just smells a TV dinner being warmed in a microwave. But it's a very exotic TV dinner, to be sure.

Scotty's apartment is on the second floor of this walk-up duplex that has four units in it. His is in a small nook of the building directly above a travel agency. As Steven opens the door, he can immediately see why Scotty liked living here so much. It's not very big, but it's obviously cozy. In one large room, there's enough space for a queen bed, a loveseat, coffee table, little TV, and a small kitchenette. There's not much space, but it's more than enough for a guy like Scotty, who probably spent more time out in the city than he ever spent here. The random books and magazines on the coffee table and nightstand are the only real proof he stuck around long enough to relax and do a little reading.

Steven walks into the studio and gives it a good look. The furniture obviously came with the place, as did the paintings on the wall, which are just cheap prints of ocean views. None of it is particularly Scotty's style, which tells Steven that his brother rented it "as is" and then never changed a thing. Even when he wanted to stick around somewhere for a while, Scotty always lived as if he were about to leave. The entire time he lived in France, he never unpacked his suitcase.

It's freezing in the apartment, which tells Steven that Scott shared his hatred for the boiling climate. The small room doesn't have much going for it, but excellent air-conditioning is at the top of that list. Once inside, there is no trace of Singapore or even Asia in this place. It's quite plain, and has the silly beach photos all over the walls. He doesn't know why, but Steven had pictured Scotty in some beachside hut with open windows and a mosquito net hanging over his bed. Even in the fridge, the cans of Diet Coke and half-eaten pizza slice betray the image of a world traveler that Scotty seemed to portray.

Making his way the entire fifteen feet it must be from the kitchen to the bed, Steven opens the small closet door and takes a look inside. Not surprisingly, there isn't much to see. Several button-down shirts are slung half-assed from wire hangers in various stages of wrinkle. There are several T-shirts hung there, as well. On a small shelf are just as many pairs of jeans and shorts. Inside two garment bags are what appear to be the only suits Scotty ever owned. Steven inspects them and figures they will fit him, but he leaves them where they are. One has a shark-skin collar, and the other comes with a three-button blazer. He's not a fan of either.

Steven looks in the mirror at his own reflection and smiles. He prefers the one-button jacket he's wearing. It's the one with the peaked lapel. The one that even Robin thinks makes him look like a member of The Rat Pack. Scotty never could wear a jacket like Steven could. Steven could wear a white sports jacket and look like a polo player, but Scotty just wound up looking like a waiter.

Steven looks on the shelf inside the closet and pulls out a stack of CDs that are piled in the back. There's some good stuff here, from Michael Jackson to Barenaked Ladies. Then there's stuff that Steven absolutely hates, too. Scotty could listen to the loudest, most annoying drivel. Of course, those are the same words Scotty used to describe the jazz and swing music that Steven constantly had playing around the house. If it was Springsteen, the two of them got along. If it was Sinatra, there would be an argument.

Steven puts the CDs away and takes down a shoebox that has been shoved to the back. It's heavier than it looks, so he walks over to the bed and sits down. Inside is a bunch of worthless knick-knacks that Scotty probably picked up somewhere during his travels. A PEZ dispenser. An Eiffel Tower bumper sticker. Then there are random things Steven recognizes, like old photos and a pair of their father's cuff links. Steven thinks about keeping them, but he knows he'll never wear them. They would find their way into a drawer in his condo and just sit there, like they probably sat in this shoebox for years.

Steven laughs when he flips through some of the old photos. Scotty and old girlfriends, some of whom he bragged would be the women he would marry. There were at least three of those who came and went. Steven always teased Scotty by referring to them as "The Fiancées," even though none of them ever got a ring. Each one only lasted a few months before Scotty got bored with either them or where he was living at the time.

Steven flips through the photos until he comes to one that he remembers the most clearly. It's a picture from when they were eighteen. There's Scotty, standing in the driveway of the house they grew up in. He's wearing his baggy uniform from when he was a delivery guy for Pizza Pizza. Standing next to him are both of their parents, looking proud that their son actually has a job and was supposedly serious about going to university. Steven winces a little and feels that pain again, just like he did in the morgue a few hours earlier. In the photo, everyone is standing in front of the old Buick they were in the night they were killed.

Steven feels that churning in his stomach again and swallows hard.

He remembers getting the phone call and driving to the hospital and finding out his parents were gone. He still can see Scotty with his mouth wired shut because of his jaw being broken. Steven had to help him drink through a straw for weeks. Then there was all the physical therapy and watching Scotty walk with a cane. It was months before he would even get in a car, let alone ride in the front seat. Steven always looked like his chauffeur.

Scotty's having his broken jaw kept him from speaking at the funeral, but he wouldn't have said anything anyway. Steven remembers looking over while he gave the eulogy and being surprised at how blank the look on Scotty's face was. Steven was always a few minutes away from crying, but Scotty just looked blank. He nodded and grunted and tried to communicate as best he could, but it was as if he were still lying in the hospital bed. He didn't even look shocked when he woke up that day and Steven had to tell him their parents didn't survive the crash.

Headaches, Steven thinks to himself. *You never did like wearing your glasses, Scotty.*

Steven flips to the next photo in the stack, which makes him laugh again. It's Scotty, probably a year or two ago. He's wearing a foam arrow through his head and has his eyes crossed and his tongue stuck out. In his hands, he's holding a sign that reads DEFANATELY DRUNK. Steven grins as he shakes his head and puts the photos back in the box.

Steven picks up a notepad and pen lying on the tiny nightstand next to the bed and takes a look. He immediately recognizes Scotty's chicken-scratch handwriting. A long column down the side of the notepad has a bunch of letters and numbers, and Steven can't really figure out what any of it means.

MICK: 1K
STUDIO: 1K
RE: 5,000
EPM: 3K
D: 500

There are several more items in the column, but Steven can't read any of them. He can't even make out what letters or numbers they are supposed to be. He figures some of it is names, some of it phone numbers, but he can't make any of it out. He looks at scribbling again and again, trying to figure out what it means. After a couple of minutes, he figures that it's all about money.

"Studio: 1K" is obviously the apartment Steven is sitting in, and it apparently costs one thousand dollars a month to rent. But he has no idea what "RE: 5,000" is supposed to be about or how much money it refers to. Steven wonders if "RE" stands for "regarding" or a person's name. He also wonders if Scotty owed someone named "Mick" a grand. He tears the piece of paper off the notepad, folds it in half, and puts it in his left breast pocket.

That's some of the money, at least, he thinks. It still doesn't explain fifteen grand or why Scotty owes so many people money. He didn't need to borrow it in the first place. There was still plenty of cash in the bank.

Tossing the notepad aside, Steven opens the little drawer in the nightstand and takes a look inside. He finds a couple more pens, some random change, and a couple of condoms. A few receipts for groceries are crumpled up and tossed in there, although why Scotty kept them remains to be seen. At the back of the drawer is a photograph from a Polaroid Instant Camera, the kind that comes right out of the camera and everyone shakes while it develops. Steven holds it up to the light coming in through the window and gives it a good look.

The photo is a bit yellow and easily twenty years old. Steven can tell this not just because it looks so old, but also because the boy in the photo is wearing clothes that haven't been in style forever. He's a thin, Asian man, probably Singaporean, and couldn't be older than sixteen. He's sitting on a porch swing, waving and smiling broadly to the camera. The photo is a bit worn and has seen better days, and Steven wonders if it even belongs to Scotty at all or was just left in this drawer by a previous tenant. He puts it into the pocket of his sports jacket anyway.

Getting up from the bed, Steven gives the place another once-over. It's really a small apartment. Probably the size of a hotel suite. That's pretty much how Scotty used it, he figures. The place he'd stay until he got tired of Singapore and moved on to the next place he was going to stay.

On top of the TV, there is a framed photo of Scotty with a very attractive Asian woman. Standing in front of the ocean, the two of them seem ridiculously happy and look like something out of a magazine. Scotty with his long hair and tattoos, and the woman with her light brown skin and what appears to be a slender figure. Steven reaches in his pocket and pulls out the note that D.Wash wrote him. He remembers the girlfriend's name.

Is this the mysterious Dania? he thinks.

Steven looks again at the photo and sees exactly why men must fall for her. From this picture she seems quite beautiful. And she certainly had Scotty wrapped around her finger. Steven takes the photo out of the frame and puts it in his pocket with the other one.

Standing in the doorway, he turns around and gives the place one last look. Even though Scotty is gone and stuffed in a cardboard box back at the hotel, Steven feels a weird punch in the gut as he closes and locks the door. It's as if he says good-bye to Scotty a little more each place he goes and with every little thing he does. It makes him impatient to get home and put it all behind him and move on with his own life.

He looks at his phone, but there's still no message from Robin. He's texted her four times, at three bucks per message due to the international rates, and still hasn't heard back. He's begun to realize that she's not mad. She's left him.

Walking down the stairs, Steven knocks on the door right by the entrance to the small building. When the building manager answers, he looks confused for a second and then nods his head.

"You his brother?" the man says. He's a gruff-looking Singaporean man, wearing a blue shirt and blue pants. An ample belly hangs over his belt, and he looks like he was in the middle of dinner by the way he's still chewing his food. Steven notices the man's hands are dirty.

"Yeah," Steven says, and hands over the keys to Scotty's apartment. "The place was furnished, right? It's all your stuff?"

"Yes, the TV he bought. And the clothes."

"You can have them. Or donate them. Whatever."

"You sure?"

"Yes," Steven says. The man nods and smiles politely, as if he understands.

Steven reaches in his pocket and takes out the twenty-year-old photo of the boy. "Any idea who this is?"

The manager takes the photo and thoroughly looks it over, first holding it far away and then holding it close. "No," he says. "Very old."

"Not an old tenant?"

"No, apartment not that old."

Steven takes the photo and puts it back in his jacket pocket. "Did my brother have a lot of visitors? People hanging out with him?"

"Not home very much. Spent most of the time with girl-friend."

Steven holds up the photo of the woman who he thinks is Dania. The manager nods his head and smiles. Apparently everyone thinks she's good on the eyes.

"Thanks for everything," Steven says, and starts to walk away. He turns around in the doorway. "How much was his rent here?"

"Twelve hundred."

"Did he owe you any money?"

"No," the manager says, and Steven admires his honesty. "He was always on time. Good tenant. Good man."

"Thank you very much," Steven says, and opens the front door to the building.

"Excuse me," the manager calls after him, and Steven peeks his head back in the door. "The apartment. I clean it out. What if I find money?"

Steven smiles, again. He knows that, if there were any cash in that place, Scotty wouldn't have come asking for the fifteen thousand. Besides, there was nowhere it could have been hidden in that tiny place. "You won't," he says.

"But if I do?"

Steven smiles. "Merry Christmas."

7

Steven is surprised to find a Hooters restaurant in Singapore but, sure enough, there it is. Right along the brilliantly named Singapore River, in an area just as cleverly referred to as the Riverwalk, a string of restaurants, bars, and tourists traps awaits unsuspecting travelers such as himself who may be seeking a little reminder of their home turf. There is an American joint called The Burger Shack, which is blasting The Beach Boys' Christmas album on its front deck overlooking the water. Then there's G. Golly Molly's, with photos of Little Richard and Elvis plastered all over the place. Next to the requisite Starbucks sits a hot dog stand and, just a few doors down is Hooters, complete with an orange neon owl hanging outside. If he wanted to feel like he were anywhere but the Far East, Steven has come to the right place.

Up the river a little bit, he sees a person standing on a tall makeshift tower that rises easily twenty stories above the ground. Just a tiny figure in the distance, the person wears a helmet and a harness and, clipped to the harness, a bungee cord. He can hear the sound of a grown woman screaming as she steps off the tower and falls toward earth. Suddenly, the bungee cord snaps into action, and the woman bounces back up into the air, still screaming as if she narrowly avoided certain death. Steven smiles because, essentially, she really just did. That, and he can't believe that people still bungee jump. Of all the touristy things he would do in Singapore, he can't imagine flying all the way across the world to go bungee jumping.

The irony of the fact that he's thinking this while standing in front of a Hooters is not lost on him.

Scotty loved Hooters, so it surprises Steven to find that this Dania woman doesn't work there. He knows his brother dated his share of Hooters waitresses in Toronto. And by "dated" Steven really means "slept with." He and Scotty used to go there all the time when they first went to the University of Toronto. Scotty kept at it long after Steven thought the novelty had worn off. Eventually, Scotty must have tired of it, as well, because it is not at Hooters that Dania works, but at a place called The Shark Fin, directly next door.

On the outside, The Shark Fin looks like any of the other dozens of bars and seafood restaurants along the river. It's got bright lights on the outside and a sandwich board out front advertising drink and menu specials. Here you can get mahimahi for only fourteen dollars Singapore, which is only ten bucks in Canadian. There's also a special on margaritas. Since Steven makes a living pairing booze with food, he shudders a bit when he thinks of this combination. It sounds awful. Still, the restaurant is nicely lit on the inside and obviously a little more upscale than it appears outside. He wonders if they actually serve shark fin on the menu. He'd heard you couldn't get it anymore.

Walking in the front door, Steven takes off his aviator sunglasses and switches them with his usual, horn-rimmed eyeglasses with matching prescription. He can get by—if only barely—without either of them, but he feels naked when he's not wearing one or the other. Yet another thing he and Scotty never had in common.

He feels the air-conditioning hit his face and pauses for a minute to enjoy it. It's the same pause he takes each time he walks into any building in the entire city. He is pleased to see he won't have to do much searching for Dania, since the woman in the photo is standing about five feet in front of him. Leaning on the hostess's stand, writing notes in a reservation book, she is taller than he thought she would be. In the photo with Scotty, she must not be wearing shoes because, in the heels she has on right now, she's easily three inches taller than he. Her short black skirt does not do a good job of covering what is a very strong-looking pair of legs.

She really is beautiful.

Steven doesn't approach her immediately, but stands in the doorway for a minute, giving her a once-over. She's attractive in a unique way, and he can't quite figure out what it is about her that he finds so interesting to look at. She's slender and has clear, dark skin, and obviously takes care of herself. But it's not as simple as her being fit and pretty. She has a commanding presence and seems in control of everything around her, even though she's just a hostess in a restaurant. The best way to put it is how his father would have: She comes off as one tough broad.

"You must be Dania," Steven says as he finally walks in. He makes certain not to speak too loudly so as not to startle her. She still has her head in the reservation book when she raises her eyebrows and then, after a couple of seconds, looks up and makes eye contact. She looks at Steven for a second and then squints her eyes.

"No," she says, and shakes her head. There is a slight accent when she speaks, but it's not Singaporean or any type of Asian dialect. It sounds almost British. "I'm sorry. She's not working today. Can I help you?"

"Oh? You're not she?"

"No, sir. But I get that all the time."

Steven stands there for a minute with his eyebrows digging downward. For a second, he wonders if he and Scotty aren't the only twins to hang out in this restaurant in the past week. He drums his fingers on the hostess stand just once and then reaches in his sports jacket pocket. He takes out the silver pen that Scotty gave him as a present when they turned thirty. "I'm sorry, my mistake. Do you know when she'll be here?"

"I'm sorry, sir," the hostess says. "I can't give out that kind of information."

"Of course, I understand." Steven smiles. "Do you think I could leave her a message?"

"Of course." She tears a sheet of paper out of the back of the reservation book and hands it to Steven.

"You don't mind?"

"Not at all."

"Terrific." Steven scribbles a note on the piece of paper, folds it in half, and writes FOR DANIA ONLY on the backside. Then he hands the paper back to her and smiles. "I really do appreciate it."

"No problem," she says. "I'll make sure she gets it."

"That's great. Thanks so much for your help."

"May I tell her who asked?" She raises her eyebrow, still holding the note out as if it may catch fire at any moment.

"Oh, she'll know," Steven says, and raises a finger to his forehead as a polite salute. He smiles one last time and, putting on his sunglasses while then putting his regular glasses in their case, steps back out into the early evening waiting outside. Looking over his left shoulder, he sees another person in the distance, hurtling to earth and then bouncing back up, laughing and screaming at the same time. He looks for the nearest available restaurant where he can sit outside and be very conspicuous and easily seen. Unfortunately, that place is Hooters, and it's hardly the place that Steven wants to visit anywhere else, let alone in Singapore City.

What are the odds of getting a glass of wine that isn't complete swill? he thinks with a wince. He sighs to himself, accepts his fate, and walks up to where the tackiness lives.

Stepping up to the outdoor patio, Steven makes eye contact with a waitress wearing a tight white tank top and skimpy orange shorts. Not only does the Hooters restaurant look just like they do back home, but the employee uniform is still exactly the same as it has always been. Steven figures that's exactly why it's successful. He knows it's exactly why Scotty was a loyal customer. A very attractive, surprisingly busty young woman offers back a deliberately sexy smile and waves to him.

"Sit anywhere you like." She extends a hand to the patio,

which has all but two tables available. Steven takes a small one right at the very back of the patio, up against the water. With his back to the river, he has a great view of the Riverwalk and the people walking from one end to the other. He wonders how many of them are travelers and how many are locals. Although this is obviously a big tourist trap, he's certain that many locals develop a love for some of it. It can't just be traveling businessmen who have dinner here or at G. Golly Molly's.

"Hey, there." The same sexy Hooters waitress who greeted him when he entered walks up and puts a cocktail napkin on the table in front of him. "I'm Jasmine. You from out of town?"

"What gave it away?" Steven says. Jasmine laughs as if he actually said something funny.

"Where you from?" she asks.

"Toronto."

"Canada!"

"That's the one."

"That's great," she says, and smiles. "I love Canada."

"Ever been?" Steven asks.

"Not yet. One day."

"I'll keep an eye out for you."

"Sounds good." She laughs again. "Can I get you a beer or something?"

"What red wine do you have?" he asks, pretending to look at the two-page paper menu he picks up off the table.

"I don't know. We only have one. No one ever asks for it."

"First time for everything, I guess."

"No food?"

"Nope. Just the award-winning wine you have."

"Okay, be right back."

Steven watches her walk away and wonders again if there are any ugly women in Singapore. From the hotel to Hooters, he's run into nothing but gorgeous women everywhere he goes. Sure, he expects to find hot women at Hooters but, at this rate, he's expecting to see a homeless woman who could be a swimsuit model. He wonders if it's really possible that Scotty had only one girlfriend in this city.

A full three minutes later, Jasmine returns with a tiny wine-glass with some red substance in it that some people would call wine. Steven thanks her and raises the glass in a toast. To her credit, Jasmine giggles and winks and essentially makes Steven blush before she walks over to a table of three other men and starts talking to them. Steven cringes as the wine burns his lips, tongue, and then throat. He finds himself instantly missing D.Wash and The Blue Bayou.

When the hostess from The Shark Fin comes storming over, Steven looks down at his watch. It's been just over ten minutes since he left and came over to Hooters. She makes a beeline to his table, where she stops and stands, three feet in front of him, with her arms folded across her chest.

"What took you so long?" Steven asks.

"What the hell is this?" the hostess says, and holds out the sheet of paper that he left for Dania.

"That's a note for Dania," he says, and sips his wine.

"Yeah, I can see that." She tosses the paper onto the table. Steven smiles as he unfolds it and reads what he wrote inside:

I will be waiting outside when you are tired of lying to me, Dania.

"But you weren't supposed to read this." He looks innocently up at her. "This note was only for Dania."

"How did you know it was me?"

"Because you came outside looking for me after reading a note that was addressed specifically to Dania."

"I'm serious." She practically stamps her foot. Steven almost finds it cute. If he weren't annoyed at being lied to, he'd proba-bly smile.

"Are you a twin? Do you have a twin sibling?" he asks.

"No."

"Well, I am, and I can always tell when someone knows my brother. Because, when they see me for the first time, they're al-ways a little stunned. Like they're seeing double. Which they are. It's the same look you just gave me. Looking at something that seems familiar, yet isn't." Steven chuckles to himself. He's gotten used to people looking at him like they've already met even when he is first introduced to them.

"So you knew I was lying just by the way I looked at you?"

"Not really."

"Yeah? Then how?"

Steven reaches into his jacket pocket, takes out the photo of Scotty and Dania, and then tosses it on the table. "I already knew what you looked like."

Dania looks at the photo on the table, then up at Steven. Her eyes look cold. "Clever," she says.

"Not really."

"I forgot about that picture."

"Apparently. Have a seat?" Steven extends a hand toward the chair on the other side of the table.

Dania stands there for a minute, thinking it over. The look on her face isn't one of annoyance as much as it is caution. She looks over her shoulder back at The Shark Fin, then at the Hooters waitress in the other direction. She gives Steven a long, hard stare and then finally sits. Steven takes another sip of his wine and takes a second to admire her long, black hair. It goes all the way down to the middle of her back. He thinks it must be a real chore to get it that shiny.

"Why did you lie to me?" he asks.

"I'm sorry," she says, and appears to mean it.

"I'll get over it if you can tell me why. In that photo you seem pretty happy with my brother."

She looks up at him, and her eyes are suddenly sad. "I was."

"Then why?"

"I don't know." She shrugs and looks down at her hands. They appear strong, despite the perfectly manicured nails. "Things aren't so good here right now. At work, I mean. Plus I thought if you were mad at me and caused a scene . . . I can't afford to lose that job."

Steven looks at her for a few seconds before he speaks. "Did you kill my brother?"

The shock on Dania's face is the only answer he needs, but

she gives him one anyway. "God, no! I would never . . . I *loved* Scotty."

Steven smirks for a brief second. Nobody called his brother "Scotty" but him—none of their friends or family members, not even "The Fiancées."

"Then why do you think I'd be mad at you?" he asks.

"I don't know," Dania says, and looks down at her fingers again, fidgeting with her nails. "I mean, we never met before or spoke, and then Scotty just—"

She doesn't finish the sentence, nor does she seem like she's even thinking about it. She just stares at her fingernails and then over her shoulder toward the other restaurants along the river. Steven doesn't say anything, but he makes certain no one on the patio is watching them. In the background he hears "Rockin' Around The Christmas Tree."

"I mean . . . Jesus!" she says, and clears her throat. "You look like him. I just didn't know what to say. I just saw him a few days ago and then . . ." She looks back up at Steven and stares right through him. "You look. Just. Like. Him."

"You never saw a photo of me? Nothing?" Steven asks.

"Nothing. When you walked up, I just didn't know what to do. It's been really hard, you know. Since . . ."

"I know," Steven says, quieter than he meant for it to come out. He waits a second for her to make eye contact with him again. From her pocket, she pulls a tiny square of Kleenex and dabs her eyes with it. A minute later, she looks as if nothing out of the ordinary happened at all. Steven is glad, because watching her tear up almost makes him feel like crying, too.

She is striking. Sitting here, he really gets a good, long look at her. The sleek legs; the stunning cleavage peeking through the white button-up shirt that hugs her body; the beautiful hair. Even when she speaks, her slightly British accent is very seductive. Steven figures it took Scotty all of five minutes to fall for her.

"What can you tell me about Scotty?" he finally asks.

"What do you mean?"

"About that night? I don't want you to get upset. I just want to know what happened."

"I don't know. We were having a good time. Everything was great. And then it just suddenly hit him. It all—"

"—It all happened so fast. I heard."

"You spoke to D.Wash?" she asks, and Steven nods. Dania smiles and nods her head back at him. "He's a sweetheart. He's a good man."

"I caught that."

Dania cracks her knuckles, but Steven doesn't hear it. He looks over his shoulder for a second at the water. The sound of another bungee jumper is in one ear and the sounds of rocking Christmas tunes are in the other. When it gets like this, it's actually perfect. Background music never seems to bother him, and loud groups just become white noise after a while. It's the little things that drive him crazy. The tiny noises. He often welcomes the music and the cheering. Enough noise will drown out the sounds of people chewing. Or slurping their beers. Or—God forbid—belching. Hating the sound of belching has nothing to do with misophonia. Steven just thinks it's crass.

"So, no one saw it coming?" he asks. "He just fell down dead?" Dania's face drops, and Steven holds up his hand as an apology. "Sorry. I didn't mean to be so blunt like that."

"S'okay," she says. "But, yeah. It was just like that." She looks down at her hands again. "It was awful."

Steven takes a small sip of his wine. He thinks of ordering another, but he doesn't think Hooters is where he wants to order it. He wonders if there's a nice wine bar on the Riverwalk. "Do you know anyone named Mick? Someone Scotty might have known?"

"Not that I know of. Why do you ask?"

He tells her about the piece of paper with the names and various numbers. The look on her face tells him that she has no idea what he's talking about. "I don't remember his knowing anyone by that name," she says. "And he didn't owe anyone money."

"Was he trying to buy a car?"

"He was afraid of cars."

She really did know him well, Steven thinks.

"Do you have any idea why he came to me looking for money?" he asks.

"He did?"

"Yeah, last week."

"I really can't say. He didn't need it."

"No, he didn't."

He reaches in his pocket and takes out the photo of the teenage boy. He slides it across the table and, without any reaction, she takes a look at it. "Do you know who this is?" he asks.

"No, I don't. Who is it?"

"I don't know. I found it in Scotty's apartment."

"Maybe it came with a picture frame," she says, and smiles. Steven returns the smile and chuckles lightly.

"Yeah, maybe."

"It's an old photo," she says. "Scotty hasn't lived here that long. It's probably nothing."

"Maybe not, but Scotty kept very little. When he did, it was because it was something important to him."

"If an old photo is so important to him, then why is this the only one?"

Steven shrugs. She has a good point. Here he is walking around with a photograph that, for all he knows, Scotty found somewhere and uses as a bookmark.

"How long are you staying?" she asks.

"Just today. Then I go back to Toronto."

"And Scotty?"

"Him, too," Steven says, and catches himself. "His ashes." Dania nods her head, and Steven is surprised that this doesn't seem to faze her whatsoever. He expected a little shock or even a few tears.

"Do you want them?" he asks her. After all, she was the girl-friend in his life.

"God, no." She looks at him as if he just punched him in the face. "No, I don't want that at all."

Steven holds up his hands in surrender. "Just thought I'd ask."

"Thank you, but no. I will miss your brother. Dearly. But I don't want his ashes. He was enough trouble already."

"Trouble? How do you mean?"

Dania lets out a long sigh and runs a hand through her hair. "Trouble in that he was a crazy, Canadian white boy who went and got me all crazy, too. He had a look that made me want to do everything for him. But he was all over the place. He was very special, but he was a handful. Do you understand?"

Steven does understand. It was pretty much how most women described his brother.

"D.Wash says he loved you," he says.

"I guess you could say the feeling was mutual."

Steven can't help but think about Robin. Dania and Scotty couldn't have been together as long as he and Robin had been together. But he's pretty sure Robin never felt about him the way Dania feels now. He imagines that, even if he died in a fiery plane crash while flying home from Singapore, no one would ever see the look on Robin's face that he sees from Dania right this moment. He also thinks letting go of Robin would be easier for him than leaving Dania could have been for Scotty. The look on Scotty's face in that photo was proof of that.

Maybe the money was for an engagement ring, Steven thinks. He can only hope Scotty would have been that smart.

He reaches into his pocket and takes out some money and tosses it on the table. "Don't you have to get back to work?" he asks.

"I'm off," she says. "I was about to leave when you walked in. I have to get to my other job."

"Two jobs, eh?"

"I only do the restaurant thing during the day. I also sing in a band."

"Really?" He raises his eyebrows. Now she's obviously Scotty's dream girl. It all gets clearer every minute he talks to her. "What kind of music?"

"A little of everything," she says, which Steven recognizes as the standard answer musicians give to that question. "We have a regular gig over at Orchard Towers. In The Cocktail Room."

"Sounds very nice. Did Scotty watch you perform a lot?"

"All the time. That's where it happened, you know? Where he . . ."

"—I know."

There is a long moment, and neither one of them says anything. Dania watches a bungee jumper off to the side, and Steven stares at the orange lightbulbs all around the Hooters. For the first time since his plane landed, he feels a cool breeze blow through his hair. He only just now realizes that he hasn't felt terribly hot the entire time he's been sitting on this patio. He also realizes that the waitress never came back to check on him.

"The service here is lousy," he says, and smiles at Dania. "I bet it's better at The Shark Fin."

"Most definitely."

"You should get a job here. I bet the money is better."

She rolls her eyes and, for a second, almost looks annoyed. As if it is a sore subject. "They would never hire me here."

"Of course they would!"

"No, I have a bad reputation."

"That's not what I heard. D.Wash says people tend to fall pretty hard for you."

"He's crazy. Like I told you, I only attract trouble."

Steven leans forward and takes the note he wrote to her and folds it into a little square. "Thanks for taking care of my brother. I have no doubt you meant the world to him."

"I'm sorry he's gone," she says quietly. "He was really something special."

Steven smiles and stands up. "That he was."

Dania stands up too, and Steven is suddenly reminded of the fact that she's a few inches taller than he is because of her stylish heels. He looks up at her and suddenly feels weak. As if she could put him over her knee and spank him like a child. She points at the note in his hand.

"Your handwriting is better than his," she says.

"It always was."

"Computers did it. Made everyone bad writers. Typing and e-mail and keyboards. No one writes letters anymore."

Steven has to agree. He can't remember the last time he wrote anything that wasn't a Christmas card. The last birthday card he got from Scotty was an online greeting.

"Take care of yourself," he says, and extends a hand to her. Dania looks at it and then gives Steven a long stare. Her eyes seem very sad again, and he suddenly feels awkward. Then she pulls him close and puts her arms around him. It's a very forceful hug, but it feels just right. He doesn't quite know if it's sweet or sexual, with her firm body pressed so closely against his. But he knows it's exactly what he needs. She squeezes him tightly, and he returns the gesture. Four seconds later, she lets him go.

"You're so much like him," she says. It's obvious she's still looking at Steven and seeing Scotty standing there. "You look and sound like he does. Like he did."

"Always have."

"But you're different, aren't you? Just like he said about you. The glasses and the hair. The nice clothes. All of . . . this. Makes me wonder which one of you was the real thing."

"I think we both were. But we really did have more in common than people realize. More than just how we look."

Dania smiles and waves to him as she starts to walk away. Steven can tell that, the second she's alone, she's going to have herself a very big, very long cry. He knows that she's doing a good job of holding it back right this minute, but it's inevitable. He understands. She just sat and talked to the identical twin of her lover. An identical twin she never met until that lover was dead. It's bound to be a bit overwhelming.

"You're probably more like him than even you realize," she says.

"Think so, do you?"

"Yeah." She smirks. "You look like trouble, too."

8

Look at you, you sad son of a bitch. Steven hears the cardboard box of ashes speaking to him the way Scotty might if he were sitting here right this moment. Here Steven is, a Canadian in Singapore, all the way on the other side of the world, and he's sitting in his hotel room watching TV. There are probably a million exciting things to do in this city, but he's apparently content to sit here and wait for room service. Scotty would definitely be appalled.

Out the window, the lights on the tall skyscrapers are a clue that there is a nightlife going on out there that even a twin in mourning could enjoy. In fact, a twin in mourning *should* enjoy it, rather than wallow in his despair in front of a TV speaking almost every language other than English. Even the worst local food would probably be more exciting than the steak and potatoes that will soon arrive on a rolling cart up the service elevator.

"If you've seen one crowded, polluted, stinking town . . ." Steven says aloud. He chuckles that he managed to remember the line. It's lyrics from the song "One Night In Bangkok," from the Broadway musical *Chess.*

But this ain't Bangkok, and you're not a chess player in an eighties musical, Scotty's ashes scoff at him from across the room. *You're just a fop drinking wine in your underwear.*

Steven looks over at himself in the mirror. He does look quite silly. Still wearing his patterned accent socks and pressed Oxford shirt, he discarded everything else but his boxer briefs. The two bottles of Cabernet he bought in the hotel bar are keeping his pants company on the ironing board across the room. He opened one bottle a half hour ago and was planning on saving the other for tomorrow. The more he sits here and stares at either the TV or the window, the more he begins to think that both bottles will be empty by midnight.

He sings the line about a night in Bangkok and the world being your oyster to himself. He doesn't like oysters. He's never been to Bangkok. He's in Singapore and doesn't really care. Might as well be Vietnam for all he knows or cares. He couldn't find any of them on a map if he tried.

"So, this was where you chose to stay?" he asks the cardboard box. "After all that time in France and Italy and Australia? After months in Alaska, even, you chose to stay here in God's sauna."

Hell, yes, I stayed here, Scotty says back to him. *Did you see the woman I was screwing?*

Indeed Steven did. In fact, Steven has little trouble remembering Dania since he left Hooters only a few hours ago. For once, he is pretty impressed with his brother's taste in women. Maybe it was the exoticism she put out there or that allure that a lot of Asian women have on Western men. But Dania was definitely more interesting (and more interesting to look at) than other women who came in and out of Scotty's life. There were plenty of attractive ones, to be sure. Some were probably even stunning. But Dania had something about her that was enticing. Steven's not knowing what that something was probably made her seem even sexier. He imagines that's what Scotty thought, too.

Steven looks at the clock on the nightstand. Just after 9 p.m., which means it's just around 8 a.m. back in Toronto. The glass of wine has given him just enough liquid courage and lack of good judgment to pick up the phone and try dialing Robin one last time. There has been enough time since he last tried. A call right about now wouldn't seem so desperate, right? She is his girlfriend after all. She should want to know that he's okay, right? His brother did just die and everything, right?

Don't try to pull me into this mess, Scotty tells him. *I never even met the woman. She didn't even like me.*

The phone rings three times, and Steven is about to hang up when the voice mail doesn't pick up. Instead, there is silence on the line. Then, a second later, he hears the sound of someone inhaling and exhaling very slowly. Then, after another second:

"Hello?" Robin's voice already sounds annoyed. It's as if she knew that Steven was calling, didn't want to pick up the phone, but knew she probably had to at this point anyway. She's still mad at him, has already decided to leave him, and isn't ready to even deal with speaking to him about it yet.

He can tell all of this simply by the way she says "hello."

"It's me," he says, and prays she doesn't ask whom.

"Hey," she says. For a brief second, she sounds like she did when they first met. Just that one word is enough to do it. "Hey" sounds like the greeting of someone who wants to talk to the person on the other end of the phone. "Hey" is friendlier than "Hello."

"Hey," he says back, trying to see if it sounds as carefree when he says it. It doesn't.

"You still in Singapore?" she asks.

"Yeah, everything okay back home?"

"I'm fine. Just heading to work. What time is it there?"

"Just after nine," he says. He wonders how long he can steer the conversation this way and keep the small talk going. He's surprised to find how comforting he finds the sound of her voice.

"Did you take care of everything? With your brother?" She says "brother" with a coldness he picks up on. It's as if she's caught him cheating with another woman and there never was a twin all these thirty-four years.

"Yes," he says, and looks over at Scotty's ashes. "I had him cremated. I was going to bring him back to Toronto with me."

"Oh." She sounds surprised. "Did they give you an urn or something?"

"No, just a box."

"Really?"

"Yeah."

"That sounds creepy."

"It is, a little, I guess."

"I don't think you can just bring a box of ashes on the plane with you." She is definitely twirling her hair around her right index finger while she talks. She always does that when she's on the phone. "There's got to be some health issues or something like that, right?"

"You're probably right." He thinks of how odd it is to even have a box of remains, let alone to be packing it in his suitcase and checking it onto a plane. "I don't know. I'll figure something out."

"I don't know why you don't just leave them there," she suggests, as if she's told him to leave behind a pair of old gym shoes.

"Because he's my brother, and I flew to Singapore to get him."

"No," she says, and almost sounds sweet. "That's not your brother anymore, Steven. It's just his ashes. It's his remains. You don't have to bring them home." She pauses for a minute, and he can hear her still getting ready. Putting on makeup or lipstick or something like that. They're talking about his dead brother, and she's just going about her daily routine. "He probably wouldn't have wanted you to do that, anyway."

"I don't know," he says, even though he's pretty sure she's probably right. He looks at the cardboard box and, for a minute, thinks it might be funny just to check out of the hotel and leave it here. Scotty probably would have liked that—his last hurrah on this mortal coil being a practical joke on some unsuspecting hotel maid.

"Look," she says, and Steven wonders if this is when she drops the axe. "I've got to go. I've got to run out and meet a client."

"Sure, I understand."

"I'll talk to you when you get home, okay?"

"Yeah, sure," he says. Before he can hang up, he stops himself. He knows that it's now or never and that he doesn't want to wait until Friday. "Hey, I'm sorry about the other day. You know, before I left."

"I know." She sounds annoyed. "I don't wanna talk about it, okay?"

"Sure, but I just wanted you to know I didn't like the way we ended it. I know what you were trying to tell me. With the bottle and everything. I should have talked with you about it."

"It doesn't matter."

"No, it does matter. I want to be better about these things. It's a good idea. I don't like it when things go that way. I don't want you thinking I don't listen or I don't care."

"It is what it is."

He pauses. He's always hated that expression. Mostly because it doesn't actually mean anything. But also because he knows it's usually what people say when they have accepted a decision they have made. He wonders what decision has been made this time. "What does that mean?" he asks.

"Nothing. We'll talk when you get home."

"No, you never say that unless you've just done something. So, what does that mean?"

She lets out a long, loud sigh. He takes his ear away from the phone for a minute and lets her finish cursing under her breath.

"Look, I just think it's time to move on, okay? Both of us. It's just—it's just time, okay?"

"Move on?" he says as if he's never heard the words, let alone seen them coming for days. "You mean, what? Move out? Are you moving out?"

She sighs again. "I think that's best, yes."

Well, I'm not moving out, he thinks. *It's my goddamned condo. You don't even pay rent.*

"We can figure something out when I get home," he says. "This is probably harder with me being all the way over here. Maybe we can take some time apart and figure things out once the holidays are behind us."

He can hear her scoff through the phone and knows she overdid it on purpose. "The holidays," she says.

"What?"

"You and your goddamned Christmas. What do we need to

wait for, Steven? It's over. You know it, and I know it. It's been obvious to everyone for months, for Christ's sake."

"It hasn't been that bad."

She laughs. "Of course it has. I think even your brother could tell better than you could."

That one hits between the eyes and stings for a second. He says nothing and just sits there and looks at the cardboard box. She's probably right, but he still thinks it was an awful thing to say.

"I'm sorry," she says after a few seconds of silence. "I didn't mean to say that. But this is what I'm talking about. I get mean with you, and I hate that. I don't want any of that with us anymore."

"Neither do I."

"It just doesn't work anymore, Steven. You like what you like, and none of that is something I like. You love your structure and your schedules and all of that. I can't live like that."

"I know. I'm sorry."

"Jesus Christ," she says. "I don't want you to be sorry. You don't have to be sorry. That's what I'm talking about. You're just you. There's nothing wrong with that. It's just not who I am. And I can't live with your trying to be something else just because you think it's what I want. For God's sake, have some balls for once in your life. Stick up for yourself."

"That's not fair. I stick up for myself all the time."

"Being passive aggressive isn't sticking up for yourself," she says. "I'd prefer it if you straight out told me to go fuck myself once in a while, instead of just ignoring me and pretending everything was just hunky dory when you know it isn't."

"I don't talk like that."

"Exactly! That's my point. I need to be with someone who does. Don't you get that? There's nothing wrong with you, Steven. But I can't be with you, no matter how goddamned perfect you are. Get it?"

Steven pours himself another glass of wine. He's glad he thought to buy two bottles instead of just the one. "I get it. I'm sorr . . . I understand."

"It's better this way. It's just time for me to move on."

"Sounds like you already have."

"It's been brewing for a while."

"Doesn't matter. Where are you going to stay?"

She pauses for a second, and he can hear her putting on her shoes while trying to balance the phone on her shoulder. He imagines that she's dressed in one of her sexy black suits. It always makes her red hair really stand out. She tends to dress this way with new clients. "I've already done that. I got my own place."

"What?" Steven sits up in his chair so fast he almost spills the entire glass of wine all over his nice white shirt. "You've already moved out?"

"Yes. I moved everything yesterday."

"Jesus, I've only been gone a couple of days. You found a place already and moved there?"

"I told you that it's been brewing."

"No shit. I'm glad my brother's death turned out to be so convenient for you."

"Screw you. That's not why this happened, and you know it."

"I guess it is what it is," he says. The silence on the other end of the phone tells him that the line hit home and she's about three seconds away from cursing at him, hanging up on him, or both.

"I have to go," she says, and sounds surprisingly calm. "I'm sorry."

Steven looks at himself in the mirror and doesn't think he looks so silly anymore. He thinks he looks a bit sad and pathetic. Not since he was fourteen has a woman broken up with him over the phone. It feels just as awful now as it did twenty years ago. The biggest difference now is that he doesn't have his parents or brother to run and cry to when he puts down the phone, which only makes him want to cry a little bit more.

Scotty always moved on from one woman to the next, never really seeming to let it bother him whenever a relationship fell apart. Several half-assed engagements came and went, and Scotty never seemed to mourn their losses for more than a couple of days. Steven was the one who sulked for weeks, always wishing he could be like his brother and just go find another warm bed when the current one got cold.

"All this time I thought we were fighting," Steven says, not realizing how quiet his voice sounds. "Turns out we were finished."

"I said I'm sorry, and I meant it." She actually sounds sincere.

"How much did you leave me with? When you moved, I mean. The furniture and all that?"

"Enough."

Steven pictures a half-empty condo with an oddly bare bookshelf next to his oversized reading chair . . . and not a lot else. She didn't like most of the paintings, so at least the walls will have plenty left on them. And the bed was there long before she came along. At least he'll have enough to live with for a while.

"You aren't really surprised at any of this," she says. It's not a question.

"I guess not."

He suddenly wonders what he'll miss the most: the sex or the furniture. He really enjoyed both—especially when they came as a package—but since he's gone without one for a while, he figures he'll miss the other the most. Just thinking like that makes him aware that it's best she's moving out, even if it does kind of put a damper on Christmas.

"Good-bye, Steven," she says at last. She means it just like it sounds and, a second later, there's a click on the line and nothing more.

Steven hangs up the phone and looks around the hotel room. The idea that he has no one to go home to makes the room seem even smaller than it did before, and suddenly the extra day in Singapore seems like it will last an eternity. One would think that getting dumped would make him not want to go back to Toronto for weeks, but, instead, it just makes Steven want to be home twice as fast. He'd rather be drowning his sorrows at The Keg on Yonge Street than in some Furama hotel in Asia.

There was a time, about eight years ago, when he and Scotty

both happened to be in the same country at Christmastime. Scotty managed to meet and "fall in love" with some yoga instructor from Calgary, and Steven was dating Diane, the nurse. Both Steven and Scotty wanted very much to impress the women in their lives, so they rented an isolated cabin way up in northern Ontario.

"You do the driving, and I'll do the rest," Scotty had said when Steven came to him with the plan that November. And the rest he certainly did. Scotty found the little two-bedroom cabin and made all the arrangements. Then, he bought two cases of reds and whites and packed them in the trunk of Steven's old Jeep Cherokee. Scotty topped it off with enough sexy jazz for three full days of nothing but drunken sex by the fire and Christmas gluttony. The four of them had the best Christmas ever, snowed inside that cabin all weekend.

Even long after Diane and the yoga girl had moved on, Scotty and Steven still talked about that weekend. It had only been three days, but it had been three days of pure holiday bliss. Scotty didn't complain about his headaches or about having to get in the car. Steven only took sweaters and jeans with him and didn't care about shoving his clothes into an old duffel bag. The wine was cheap. The whole weekend had cost well less than the fifteen grand Scotty came asking for last week. It was just a cheap cabin with some cheap wine. Christmas and snow and women.

Steven wished he were in that cabin right now.

There's a knock on the door, and Steven realizes he's been staring out the window for a full ten minutes. The smell of steak fills the room as he opens the door and the room service waiter wheels the small metal cart over the threshold.

"Hello, sir," the waiter says. He's wearing the standard hotel uniform: all black clothing and a ridiculous Santa hat. Steven shakes his head and smiles, the wine finally doing what it's supposed to do. "How are you, sir?"

"I'm fine, thanks." Steven motions to the opposite end of the small room. "Just leave it over there, okay?"

"Very good, sir," the waiter says, and does exactly that. "Will there be anything else?"

"No, thanks," Steven says, and hands the man five dollars. "I appreciate it."

"Thank you, sir."

"Wait a second."

"Yes, sir?" The waiter turns around, the same big smile still on his face. "What can I get you?"

"I'll give you fifty dollars for that Santa hat."

Ten minutes later, Steven digs into his medium-but-supposed-to-be-medium-rare steak. He looks at himself in the mirror as he pours his third (or fourth?) glass of wine. He thinks that the hat perfectly complements his attire. The only thing missing is the pants.

And some music.

He reaches over to his laptop and pulls up his music collection. He keeps dozens of Christmas songs in a special file for just such an occasion. At home, he'll attach speakers to his laptop and decorate the tree or something while listening to that playlist. He figures that this is just as good an occasion as any. If he can't be in that little cabin in the middle of the snow, he can at least try and make this hotel room feel a bit like it.

The first song coming out of the laptop speakers is "River" by Joni Mitchell. As she sings about Christmas fast approaching, Steven takes a big long sip of his wine and leans back in his chair. He clicks off the lamp next to the hotel desk so that the only remaining light in the room is the city lights coming through the window and the dull blue glow from his laptop screen. It's not exactly a fireplace, but it will do.

Steven stops chewing long enough to listen to the next verse. Then, he washes down his steak with another big gulp of his wine. He pours himself another glass and looks over at the other bottle sitting near the cardboard box of Scotty's ashes.

At that moment he realizes that Robin was right. He never fought for her. He never fought for them. Even when she said good-bye and hung up the phone, he just let her go. He barely even protested.

"To hell with her," he says out loud and for no reason other than the wine he's already had and the new bottle he knows he's going to open. Standing up, he lets his napkin fall to the floor as he shovels another piece of steak into his mouth. He walks over to the other bottle and brings it back to where he was sitting. He raises it in the air and points it at the box.

"Between your dying on me and the girlfriend's leaving me, I'd say this is turning out to be one shitty Christmas, big bro."

Sorry to screw up your holidays, Bing Crosby, Scotty's ashes jab back. *I promise you that the view is much worse from inside my current studio apartment.*

"Touché."

Maybe if you were chasing women instead of chasing relationships, you'd enjoy both a whole lot more.

"Now you're just rubbing it in." Steven takes a long gulp of his wine.

What now? Scotty's ashes ask.

"Merry Christmas, Scotty, my boy," Steven says. "Let's get drunk."

9

You really are a sad son of a bitch, you know that? Scotty's ashes say from across the room.

"You're starting to repeat yourself," Steven says to them as he tries to slowly gulp down the last sip of the second bottle of wine. He pretends that, if he drinks the last bit slowly enough, the booze in the glass will somehow last longer and that he'll savor it more than if he just downed it and swallowed as fast as he can.

Try as he might, he hasn't been able to drink himself into another time or place. He looks around and, despite the strains of Dean Martin singing "Baby, It's Cold Outside," he doesn't believe it for a second. Not only is it not cold outside, but inside is still a hotel in the middle of Singapore City, and the wine is all gone. There is no mistaking the fact that Steven's already on his way to being drunk, but, at the moment, something inside of him tells him that the only surefire pathway to Christmas cheer is if he drinks more, passes out, and dreams of it.

"This looks like a job for room service," Steven says, and picks up the menu off the nightstand. He figures that just ordering a third bottle of wine in no way means he has to actually drink the entire thing. He could have a couple of glasses. Or maybe just half the bottle. There's no definite commitment just because the booze is open and next to his empty glass. Besides, it's practically a vacation. No one would begrudge him a little party on vacation.

But you're not on vacation and you're not at a party, Scotty scolds him from his box. *You're drunk in your hotel room in one of the most exotic and exciting cities in the world while talking to the remains of your dead brother.*

"Screw you," Steven says. "At least I'm here keeping you company."

Gee, thanks. Now I'll somehow be less dead.

"One more crack like that, and I'll be scattering your ashes in the toilet. You'll spend eternity in the pipes," Steven slurs, and laughs. He realizes how absurd it is that he's talking to a cardboard box, but he's had enough wine that he doesn't really care. He never got to have a last conversation with Scotty so, at the very least, he can let himself have one now. No one has to know.

You've got the rest of the year to feel sorry for yourself, Scotty says. *And at least the entire month of January. Right now, you should be out seeing what the nightlife in Singapore City has to offer.*

"I should be seeing what the sandman has to offer as my head hits that pillow."

And wake up with a terrible hangover in this place? Forget it. You can sober up as you take in the scenery. The heat alone will do it.

"And just what, pray tell, am I supposed to do if I leave this room? I haven't the first clue where to go."

Did you not speak to my beautiful girlfriend earlier today? She practically gave you an engraved invitation right there.

"She did? Wouldn't that be awkward?"

You look just like the guy she was sleeping with, idiot. Scotty is practically pleading now. *How awkward could it possibly be?*

Steven knows better than to answer this question, mostly because he knows he's not really talking to Scotty. It wouldn't be the first time he talked himself into a really bad idea because he let himself drink too much. He's got more than one scar to prove that, when enough alcohol is in him, the uptight snob gives way to the reckless fool.

You should do something while you're here, Scotty's ashes

say. *Why wait until you wind up in a box like this one? Live a little.*

"To hell with that." Steven stands up. Immediately, the two bottles of Cabernet he just drank hit him in the face, and he has to pause for a minute to keep his balance. He's a little drunk, but not so much that he can't stand or walk. He can carry on conversation. He knows he can manage without blacking out. After all, he's a professional drinker. He can function better than most people would. Sure, he's used to spitting out the wine half the time, but he swallows his fair share, too.

He looks at himself in the mirror. The Santa hat has made the top of his head sweat a bit, but he doesn't think he looks as drunk as he is. He could probably walk in a straight enough line to fool the average person. Spitting on the sidewalk in Singapore is illegal, but he's not sure if public intoxication is. He figures that, as long as his drool doesn't hit the curb, he can probably hope to not be caned.

He looks at the cardboard box. He's told himself he would never look inside. It's too disgusting. Besides, it's not really his brother in there. It's just a bunch of gravel that someone shoved in there for Steven to have something to take home. It's not Scotty.

"You stay here," Steven says to the box. "I'm going to go on an expedition."

I was the free spirit, Scotty says. *Everyone said so. Now you're going exploring without me.*

"I'm a free spirit, too."

Bullshit.

"Am so."

You don't really believe that, Scotty says. *You've always hated that expression. Even Dania can tell that about you, and she just met you.*

"Guess I'll have to show you," Steven says, and looks around the room. Tossed in the trash can are two long, slim paper sacks that one of the bottles of wine came in. Steven fetches them out of the trash and gives them each a once-over. There are no holes in either; doubled up, they can be pretty thick and durable. He looks over at the box of ashes.

"You want to go for a ride?" he asks.

Steven feels better now that he's thrown up a couple of times. He's not sure if it's the wine that finally caused him to vomit, but he's pretty sure that handful of ashes that ran down his hand didn't help. The random bits of bone or whatever the hell that was had a way of disgusting him even more than he thought they would. What's worse is that he didn't expect the smell. Not that it smelled nasty or like a dead body or anything like that. It's just that he didn't expect to smell anything. Whoever called cremated remains "ashes" is a complete liar, too. Steven can attest that a handful of gritty rocks and muck is not at all ashy.

He pats his left breast and feels the folded-up paper sack in the inner pocket of his blazer. It causes a noticeable bulge and is not exactly comfortable, but he figures he'll get used to it. It's completely the opposite of what anyone would have expected him to do and—for that alone—he likes it. He's pretty certain that he never would have dared do something as ridiculous as this had he not downed as much wine as he did, but that doesn't really matter. If other people can get tattoos when they get drunk, then he can carry around his dead brother's ashes in his pocket.

Getting into the taxi, Steven pulls out the little piece of notepaper he has with all of Scotty's chicken-scratch nonsense written on it. On the other side, he has written down some things Dania said to him.

"Can you take me to The Cocktail Room?" he asks the cab driver. The driver turns around and looks at him as if he's just asked for a ride to Winnipeg. It might be because Steven is still wearing the Santa hat.

"Where?" the driver says.

Steven looks at the sheet of paper and the other things he has written. "Orchard Towers. Do you know where that is?"

The driver laughs and starts the meter. "Of course," he says. "Four Floors of Whores."

"Four what?"

"You will see," the driver says with a grin.

Steven puts his head back and closes his eyes for just a second. He wants to see if throwing up helped to clear his head a bit and maybe even sober him up enough so he doesn't look like a fool when he gets out of the cab. He also hopes he doesn't get dizzy and throw up again. If spitting is illegal in Singapore, then vomiting in the street is surely frowned upon.

He laughs to himself at his own stupidity. Rolling up a newspaper and using it as a funnel. Pouring Scotty's remains down that funnel and into the doubled-up paper bags. He'd probably regret it if not for the fact that he thinks it's actually something Scotty would have liked. Scotty found stupid behavior funny. He seemed to think foolishness was brave. Steven figures that, if his brother would have been fine with it, then he has no reason to think otherwise.

Enjoy the ride, big brother, he thinks.

Steven looks out the car window and stares at the Christmas lights everywhere. The taxi takes a turn down one particular street, and the display becomes ridiculous. There are twice as many lights and twice as many Santa Claus figures. It almost looks like a parade. From a huge lighted display, so big it covers an entire street corner, soap suds are being shot into the air to resemble snow. If he were sober, he would hate this. Right now, however, he thinks it's perfect and he smiles.

Steven wonders if Scotty was actually happier than he is. It's something Steven has wondered at least twice a year or so for the past decade. Sure, Steven traveled a good bit. He got to see Rome and Florence and Paris. He got to drink the best wine and eat in the best restaurants. He had a job that people envied and thought sounded interesting and different.

Everyone except for Scotty.

Scotty never seemed to envy Steven. He was too busy doing not much of anything, just traveling and sleeping with different women in different cities. He tended bar and waited tables. He did dock work and scrubbed the decks of ships. When he got bored, he moved on. Steven thought all of this sounded terrible. He liked his nice car and his hardwood floors and his high-rise view of midtown Toronto.

So why did people think Scotty was happier?

The taxi pulls up to an intersection, and Steven already wonders if this was a bad idea. The streets went from being deserted to suddenly being packed with pedestrians. People are walking everywhere, from one corner to the next, and even right in the middle of the street. Taxis and other cars have to drive around them. Drunken old men with British accents walk with their arms around tall Asian women dressed to the nines. And they're all coming out of the same building.

It's more than one building, actually. Steven can see this as the taxi pulls up to the corner and stops. It's several office buildings all on top of one another, with people coming out of several entrances on all four sides. Even from inside the taxi, he can feel the bass from a dance club thumping through his feet. There's a party going on somewhere, and it's very nearby.

"Here we are," the taxi driver says. "Four Floors of Whores."

"What?" Steven asks again.

"Orchard Towers," the driver says. "Go look. You see."

"O . . . kay." Steven reluctantly hands money over to the driver and gets out of the cab. He pats his left breast, just to feel secure.

"Nothing free there," the cab driver says as Steven closes the door. A woman runs up, and, just as quickly as it arrived, the taxi disappears with her inside. Steven finds himself standing on the corner, surrounded by dozens of people probably more drunk than he is. That thought should comfort him, but instead makes him feel a bit queasy.

Turning around, Steven stares up at the tall buildings in front of him. They look like ordinary office buildings. It's certainly not the kind of place where he thought he would find Dania playing with her band. But the thumping bass and laughing drunks and scantily clad women obviously point to this being the center of it all. Steven adjusts his blazer, checks to make sure his zipper is up, and heads up the short flight of steps into the building.

Once inside, there is no mistaking that this is the place. It might look like office buildings on the outside, but it's all night-clubs on the inside. And there are many of them. On the ground floor alone there seem to be at least five different bars and clubs with people stumbling in and out the front doors. Steven walks into the middle of the open area, which resembles a shopping mall, and looks upward. Sure enough, there are four floors.

And, sure enough, there are whores.

Steven thinks that the moniker is a little insensitive. Yes, there are women—many of them—and they're everywhere. And they are all dressed in very revealing clothing. But probably no different than women at any other club anywhere else. It looks a lot like downtown Toronto from where he's standing.

Walking into the first bar on his left, Steven is immediately confronted by an Asian woman wearing a tight black bodysuit. He can make out every single hidden detail on her body with just one, quick glance.

"Heya, handsome," she says, and hooks her arm around his and presses her body as close as possible. "You come have a drink with me?"

"I've had enough, thanks," he says, wondering if he's slurring because he is indeed drunk or because he's tongue-tied around the half-naked women.

"You sure?" the woman says, and smiles while batting her eyes. It's almost comical and yet still quite sexy.

"I'm pretty sure," Steven says.

"Okay, then." The woman smiles again and walks away. Only seconds later, another woman appears on his left-hand side and pulls the same routine.

"Hey, cutie," she says. This one is also Asian and also beauti-ful. But she's wearing a short white miniskirt and fishnet stock-ings. "Where you from?"

"Canada," Steven says, and smiles. The entire place is huge. He'll never find Dania in here, even if this is where she's working.

"Canada?" the young woman says. "You like to dance, Canada? You dance with me?"

"No dancing," Steven says. "Sorry."

"Please?"

"Sorry."

"Drink, then?"

"No drinks."

The woman shrugs and smiles. Steven wonders if she's going to get angry, but she does not. She keeps the smile even as she turns and walks away, looking back over her shoulder at him.

The next twelve feet Steven walks, the same scenario plays out a couple more times. He begins to wonder if it's something about him that's attracting all the women. At first he wonders if it's because they're not used to seeing a white guy in this place . . . until he looks around at the other patrons in the club. Every other one is a white guy. There are men speaking with thick British accents and others who sound American. There are a lot of fat, old, bald men and—right by their sides—tons of Asian women. In fact, that's the entire bar: white men and Asian women. It isn't hard to tell that the women aren't all necessarily from Singapore, either.

Steven steps back out into the hallway, fighting off the advances of yet another young woman as he does. When he gets to the middle of the large complex, he looks up again at the three upper levels of bars and clubs. On the third floor, just two escalators up, is a bar with a neon martini glass hanging over the doorway. Stepping around random drunk people, Steven makes his way up the two moving staircases, toward that neon sign.

The Cocktail Room.

Here goes nothing, he thinks as he steps through the double doors. Instantly, he feels a thousand times more comfortable than he did downstairs at the noisy dance club. This place is calm, and the music is nice. He hears a slow ballad being sung in the background and likes it better than the noisy bass down below that he can still feel thumping through his shoes. There are candles on the tables and couples sitting, watching the stage in the corner. Through the darkness of the room, he looks to the lights of the stage. Standing there, softly singing that ballad, is Dania.

She looks amazing. Dressed in a short black skirt with tight boots, she leans forward as she cradles the microphone in both her hands. Her lips are bright red and sexy, and she's wearing a black button-up blouse that reveals just the right amount of cleavage to make Steven stare a few seconds longer than he probably should. As usual, her straight black hair falls perfectly down her back, to just above the top of her belt.

It takes Steven a minute to let his eyes adjust but, once they do, he finds his way to a little table in the corner of the room. Not too far away, but not so close that Dania can see him. The last thing he wants to look like is a stalker. He sits down and orders a drink from the nearest waitress. Then, he turns his attention back to the stage. Everyone in the room is looking at that stage and with the same intensity that Steven has right now. He is glad he's not alone; everyone is smitten with Dania.

Calm down, dude. That's my girlfriend you're gawking at. Scotty's ashes sound muffled from within Steven's blazer pocket. Steven ignores them and just keeps staring.

The music stops, the small audience applauds, and Dania thanks them with a sultry, deep voice.

"Thank you very much," she almost whispers into the microphone. Her eyes scan the room to see her admirers. It's then that, despite his efforts to hide, Steven sees her notice him. She makes direct eye contact with him, smiles, and looks away. For a second, he's certain he just saw her blush. She smiles again, looks his way, and winks. Now it's his turn to blush.

Maybe it's the wine or the fact that Scotty's remains are stuffed into his pocket, but Steven is suddenly struck with the realization that he's sitting in the room where his brother died. It's almost as if he feels guilty for being happy in a place where something so tragic happened only days before. A weird mixture of calmness and guilt flows over Steven, and he's not sure how happy he is anymore. He feels oddly nostalgic and homesick while feeling excited and sheepish at the same time. He's pretty sure it's the wine. He normally feels only one emotion at a time, and that's usually annoyance.

The music starts up again. It's some old song by Madonna. Dania instantly changes gears and puts on her best upbeat rock persona. Again, every eye in the place is glued to her as she gyrates and leans into the microphone stand. She closes her eyes for much of the song but, when they open, she's looking across the bar at someone else. Steven's eyes follow hers until they come to the target of her gaze.

A short, stocky Singaporean man sits at the bar off to the side of the small club. Wearing a sharkskin suit and mirrored wraparound sunglasses, he almost looks like a sleazy mafia guy. That is, of course, if Singapore even has a sleazy mafia. Although Steven can't see the man's eyes, he knows that he's staring Dania down, looking right through her. His expression is cold and serious. Steven looks back at Dania, who is now looking back at him. When he glances back to the bar, the sleazy guy is gone.

There are three more songs before Dania thanks the audience and waits as the smattering of applause dies down. The band plays one last number without her as she exits the stage and disappears into a back room off to the side. Steven figures that's the end of the show and wonders if he'll ever see Dania again at all, much less again tonight.

It's only just then that it dawns on him he doesn't feel drunk anymore. Sometime between the taxicab and Dania's singing some song by Cyndi Lauper, he has managed to sober up. He's not sure if it was the music or the vomiting or the club sodas that did it, but his head has returned to just a slight buzz. It's a good thing, too, because it's only a couple of minutes later that Dania taps on his shoulder. Steven is certain that talking to her while three sheets to the wind would have ruined his night.

Don't screw this up, idiot, Scotty scolds from his isolated pocket. *You're representing both of us now.*

"Hello, stranger," Dania says with that sexy smile that she just had onstage, now right here in person. "You look awfully familiar."

"I get that a lot around here," Steven says.

Dania laughs. "Yeah, I guess you would. What brought you out?"

"You told me you sing. I wanted proof."

"Ah, yes, I did. So, did you get it?"

"Get what?"

"The proof, silly."

"Oh!" He feels like an idiot. "Yes. Yes, I did. You sound great."

She seems to blush again. He remembers the way Robin used to twirl her hair and figures that Dania's is too long to do that with. "Aw, you're sweet. Thanks. I'm glad you came."

"This is quite the place."

She rolls her eyes. "Ugh. How much have you seen?"

"Just a couple of places on the first floor and here."

"I'm sorry to hear that."

"Why?" He shrugs. "Everyone was quite nice. Everyone. Everywhere."

"Yeah, I would imagine. You got any money left?"

"Of course," he asks. "Why?"

"They don't call this place 'Four Floors of Whores' for no reason," she says. Suddenly, Steven realizes that it's actually what everyone calls Orchard Towers, and not just the taxi driver.

"They're prostitutes," he says, his suspicions confirmed.

"Yep," Dania says.

"All of them?"

"Pretty much."

"I kinda figured."

"It's pretty obvious, yes."

"No wonder everyone was so friendly," he says.

Dania puts her head back and laughs. Hard. She looks directly into Steven's eyes and smiles. "You're drunk."

"Maybe just a little. How could you tell?"

"You don't hide it well."

"Neither did Scotty," he says, remembering how they both tend to slur when they drink.

Dania puts a finger over Steven's mouth. He starts to speak, but she leaves the finger there. When he tries to speak again, she shushes him quietly.

"Shhhh," she says. "Don't talk like that anymore. It's bad luck."

"What is?" he asks from behind her index finger.

"You know," she says. "Talking about the past. No more of that."

"But, I—"

"Don't do it. We did enough of that today."

Steven smiles and says nothing. In fact, it feels good not to even think about talking about Scotty anymore.

"He's still with you," Dania says. "Just leave it at that and be happy."

"Literally," Steven says, and opens his jacket. "We decided to get drunk together."

Dania sees the paper bag protruding from the inside pocket and stares for a second, confused. Then her eyes get wide as she realizes just what's in the bag. "Oh, my God," she says. "Is that what I think it is?"

Steven nods. He waits for Dania to slap him, or scream, or run away. Instead, she puts her hand over her mouth and laughs. Hard. Again.

"Oh, my God," she says again, laughing so hard she snorts. "Oh, that's great. He would love that."

"Yeah," Steven says. "I think he would."

Dania's laughter is cut short when, out of nowhere, the sleazy man in the sharkskin suit appears right beside them. Still wearing his mirrored sunglasses, he looks none too pleased. He makes a face at Dania as if she just ran over his dog.

"Can I help you?" Steven asks. The man tosses him a mean look and says something in a language that Steven doesn't understand. Dania looks hurt at first, but her facial expression turns angry quickly. She says something back to the man in that same language. Then the man turns his icy gaze at Steven and continues yelling.

"I have no idea what you're talking about." Steven shakes his head, shrugs, and looks to Dania to translate. Instead, Dania grabs the little man by his chin and turns his face back to hers. She points her other finger in his face and continues yelling at him. He yells back at her and then, with an angry sneer back at Steven, turns and walks away. Steven feels his bottom jaw hit the floor, amazed that no one got punched in the face just then.

"What the hell was that all about?" Steven asks, watching the sleazy guy storm off.

"Forget it," Dania says. She looks as if she's about to spit on the floor. "He's nobody."

"Didn't seem like nobody," Steven says.

"Trust me," she says, "he is. C'mon, let's get out of here."

She takes Steven by the arm and walks him out a side door and into another hallway. The place is full of more drunks and prostitutes. Steven laughs and thinks of *The Wizard of Oz*. Lions and tigers and bears, and drunks and prostitutes.

Oh, my, Scotty says from inside Steven's jacket pocket. Steven realizes he's still a bit drunk.

Dania takes him into another bar, just around the corner from where they were. Steven looks up and sees the name of the place is The Crazy Horse just before the double doors open and he finds himself in yet another place with more entertainment and more people drinking. This time, techno music plays, and a few very sexy, scantily clad women are dancing on a tiny stage in the corner. It looks like any strip club in any city in any country, except the women are all clothed. They're not wearing much, but what they are wearing covers the naughty parts.

"Wow," Steven says. "This place has everything."

"Actually, it's pretty much all the same thing," Dania says, and sits him down on a barstool. She nods to the bartender, who seems to recognize her. The bartender instantly pours a couple glasses of vodka and sets them down in front of the two of them.

"Nothing free here," Steven says, and smiles, remembering the cab driver's last words to him.

"What?" Dania asks, taking a long sip of her drink.

"Are all the women in this place really hookers?"

"All except for the singers and the waitresses," she says. "And sometimes the waitresses are, too."

Steven thinks for a split second about the fifteen grand his brother came asking for last week as he tips back his vodka. "But not the singers, right?"

"Not the singers," Dania says, and gives a sly grin. "But I'll bet the money is better."

Steven looks at the three women dancing on the stage. They're all so sexy. Each has an amazing body and sleek, tan legs.

"Are they hookers, too?" he asks, motioning to the tallest, sexiest of the three.

"Well"—Dania cocks her head to the side—"not exactly. Maybe. I guess. For the right money. But it's more complicated with them."

"What do you mean?"

"I mean it takes a lot to look like that," Dania says. "You don't just tear those clothes off and go at it. Most men couldn't handle them if they got them home, anyway."

"Yeah," Steven says. "They really are something."

"That's one way to put it."

"Wha . . . ?"

Dania smiles and rubs Steven's back like he's a child. It's not sexual or affectionate so much as it's comforting. He turns to look at her and just enjoys the moment. She looks at him like she adores him.

"You're really sweet," she says. "A bit naïve. But sweet."

"What does that mean?" Steven asks. He doesn't know whether or not to take offense.

"It means I like you," she says. "The world needs more sweet men, trust me."

Steven decides he likes that. He turns back to watch the show and takes a sip of his vodka. He thinks it must be watered down, because he tastes hardly any booze whatsoever. He looks at his watch and sees that it's after two in the morning. He doesn't even feel very tired. Maybe he somehow avoided the jet lag. In fact, he feels pretty awake right about now. That's when he notices

Dania has put her hand on his knee. He wonders if she's just affectionate that way.

"That man at the club," he says, and looks at Dania. "Was that Mick?"

"Sweetie, there is no Mick," she says, and squeezes his knee. "I already told you that."

"Is he the boy in the photograph?"

"There's no boy in the photograph, either."

"But he knew my brother. That guy."

"Gave you that look, did he?"

"Yeah," Steven says.

"That's Nez. He's my manager."

"You have a manager?"

"That's how it works here," she explains. "Everyone does."

"He didn't act like a manager."

"That's because he's an asshole."

"Well, he didn't like my brother very much, did he?"

"No," Dania says, and watches the dancers onstage very closely. One of them turns and looks at her as she spins around the brass pole in the middle of the tiny stage. When she and Dania make eye contact, Steven wonders if they know each other.

"I could tell from the way he looked at me," Steven says, as if he needs to explain it to her, even though he knows he doesn't. "A lot of people don't like me at all because they don't like my brother."

"I like you," Dania says, and squeezes his knee again. He reaches down and puts his hand on top of hers. He knows he shouldn't, but, for that one brief moment, it's a bad decision he's willing to make.

They're all wrong about us, Scotty mumbles from inside his paper bag. *You're the one who can't be trusted. You're the rebel.*

Steven smiles and—looking Dania up and down—realizes why Scotty had so much fun being a free spirit.

10

Steven stumbles getting out of the taxi, and Scotty's bag of ashes almost falls out of his jacket pocket and onto the sidewalk. Laughing, he tucks the bag back into place and turns around to help Dania get out of the cab. She winks at the cab driver and laughs as loudly as Steven just did. She's obviously just as drunk as he is.

He runs his hand through his hair, which is hanging in his face from a combination of sweat and humidity. He catches a glimpse of himself in the reflection of the hotel's glass front doors. Besides the nice jacket, the rest of him looks a bit worn out. His shirt is untucked, his pants baggy and hanging off his hips, and his hair—despite his best efforts—is hanging over his right eye.

How did you manage to get drunk twice in one night? Scotty asks from inside his hidden pocket.

"Shut up," Steven says.

"Who are you talking to?" Dania asks, stumbling in her high heels.

"Nobody," Steven says, and puts an arm around the small of her back. She's so thin, he'd probably be hugging himself if he tried to put his arms around her.

The two of them walk through the automatic doors and into the hotel lobby. Dania is singing "Baby, It's Cold Outside," and Steven tries to remember the male part of the song. He's doing a bad job remembering the lyrics, which makes Dania laugh while trying to sing her part. Hotel employees look more annoyed than amused as the two of them stumble across the floor.

"This evening has been . . ."

"I'm drunk as hell right now. . . ."

"So very nice . . ."

"I think that cab driver had lice."

Dania laughs and, in the middle of the lobby, takes off her heels and stumbles toward the elevator. Steven sees the desk clerk staring at him and, for a quick second, thinks about buying his Santa hat off of him. Then he realizes he's already wearing one he bought earlier in the night. He's smart enough—even in this condition—to just keep walking to the elevator and make a quick exit.

Back at his room, Dania leans on the wall as Steven tries to find his hotel key. He's always been bad about remembering which pocket he put the card in. When he finds it, he first puts it in backward. Then does it wrong again the second and third time. Finally, they both fall into the hotel room, Dania still singing the same Christmas song she's been singing for an hour.

"Say, lend me a comb," she sings as Steven takes off his jacket and kicks off his shoes. His wingtips took a nice scuffing tonight. Scotty would be proud. Thinking about his brother like this reminds Steven that the ashes are still in his pocket, so he takes out the paper bag and puts it into the cardboard box the remains came in. Then, just to be absolutely carefree and crazy, Steven tosses his sports jacket onto the floor.

"I'm a wild man, I tell you!" he yells much too loudly for someone who is in a small hotel room. Dania stops singing and looks shocked. Then she smiles and looks at the jacket on the floor. Singing quietly to herself, she walks over, picks up the jacket, and hangs it neatly on the back of the desk chair. Then she walks over to the window and looks out at the view of Singapore City.

"Looks so pretty from up here," she says. "Like we're in New York or Chicago, almost."

"Think so?" Steven asks. He's seen both of those cities and thinks this one looks nothing like them.

"It's not real," she says. "This is the Singapore you see in photos. Or on the Internet. It's not the Singapore that I know. Not even the *city* that I know." She turns around to look at Steven, standing just a few feet behind her. "I wish you could see it."

"That's not in the cards, I'm afraid," he says, and taps his watch. "My morning flight makes the rules."

"No good. You didn't even get to eat real Singaporean food."

"I didn't eat any Singaporean food."

"What the hell is wrong with you, white boy?"

"Hey, I'm a sommelier. I have a very delicate palate."

Dania scoffs. "I think you have a delicate vagina, is what I think."

Steven pulls the front of his chinos and looks down at his underwear. He makes a shocked look and then looks back up at Dania. "It's small, but it's definitely a penis, I assure you."

"Okay, but next time you stay longer. And let me show you some real local food."

"Yeah, next time. You got it."

"Hey, never say never."

"Whatever you say."

Dania looks one last time out the window and lets out a quiet humming sound. It's as if she's still singing and letting out air at the same time, almost a whistle. Her face gets serious for a minute, and then she turns to Steven.

"Okay," she says, "you're here and you're safe. Set a wake-up call, and then I'll know my job is done and that I got you back here alive and well."

Steven salutes and does as he's told, calling the front desk and making certain that he has plenty of time to get to the airport. He's thrilled to find he doesn't need nearly as much time as he does back home in Canada. He showed up in Toronto three hours before his flight. He thinks Toronto's airport doesn't handle international flights well.

Hanging up the phone, Steven sits on the edge of his bed and looks around. He closes his eyes for a brief second and is pleased to see that the room doesn't spin when he does.

"That's a good sign," he says.

"What?"

"I'm not shitfaced."

"You're not what?"

"Shitfaced. It means really, really drunk."

"That's funny."

"Yeah, I got it from . . ." Steven opens his eyes and looks over at the box with ashes in it. "A friend of mine." He realizes that it's not a word he really ever uses.

It's just then that Steven realizes that he was just really starting to become friends with Scotty again. After years of barely speaking—except for holidays and birthdays—things had seemed to be looking up for the first time in a long while. Six months ago, Scotty talked about coming back to Canada for a month or two, just to get home and be back in Toronto. Steven didn't realize at the time how much he had wanted that to happen.

I wouldn't have liked that bitch you were dating, Scotty's ashes say from inside their box. *And you know it.*

The fact that Robin just dumped him doesn't bother Steven so much as knowing that the very thing Scotty would have hated is gone and now Scotty won't be coming to visit anyway. Steven realizes that he technically has two things to be mourning tonight, but only one matters to him. The other, he feels, doesn't deserve it.

You're thinking of the wrong woman, Scotty says.

"Should you not be encouraging me to put the moves on your girl?" Steven says under his breath to Scotty.

"What?" Dania asks.

"Nothing."

Bro, I'm dead. Scotty says. *What the hell do I care what you do now?*

It's at that point Steven realizes that he's drunk and that the only person doing the talking is him. He's saying exactly what he wishes Scotty would say . . . but probably never would. Scotty was just as territorial as anyone.

"Are you happy?" Dania asks, and snaps Steven out of talking to himself. "Going home to Canada?"

"Yes and no. I'm glad to go home, but there's not much left to go home to."

He tells her about Robin. About his condo that will be mostly cleaned out when he gets there. And about how having no family left leaves him with little to celebrate this year.

"You love Christmas," Dania says. "Scotty told me. That's why he couldn't invite you here this year. He said you can't stand being anywhere that's not cold at Christmas."

Steven smiles. "That's true." He looks up at her, still standing at the window. "I think we have a problem, you and me."

"I think you're right," she says, then catches herself. She clears her throat. "What do you mean?"

"You seem to know everything about me, and I know nothing about you."

"Ah. I'm one big secret."

"So it seems." He stands up again and looks out the window. It's funny that Dania doesn't like the view. It's the one part of this city he has liked since the moment he arrived. It may not look like the view outside his condo, or the skyline in New York or Chicago, but it's close enough. Other people like to feel as if they are on vacation; he prefers to feel like he's home.

"You, too," Dania says after a minute, making eye contact with Steven through his reflection in the window. "One big secret."

"Hardly."

"Very much so. There's someone hiding behind those glasses. Underneath the nice clothes."

You look like me, only better dressed, Scotty's remains whine from across the room. Steven shakes his head and ignores it.

He steps closer to her and smells her hair. He's only a foot behind her now and knows she must feel his breath on her neck. But she doesn't move. She doesn't seem at all uncomfortable. He's had too much to drink, and should back off. But she doesn't move or seem to want him to, either. So he just stands there and lets the faint smell of flowers fill his nose.

"You agreed we have a problem. What did you mean?"

"That I know so much about you," she whispers now.

"No." His voice gets quieter, too. "That's what I said. You were thinking something else."

"It was nothing," she says, still looking at his reflection, her back to him.

"Tell me," he says, and steps slightly closer. Her breath gets a little heavier, and she inhales deeply before she speaks again.

"It's just that . . ."

"Yes?"

"You hide your true feelings."

"Am I hiding them now?"

"No," she says, and turns to look at him. Her face is only inches from his. She's almost as tall as he is, even without her shoes. "You pretend to be one thing, but you're another."

"Am I?" He's actually whispering now. He wonders if he should back away. Neither one of them moves. This is probably a bad idea, but neither one of them moves. "Like my broth—"

Dania puts her mouth on his and presses her lips against his tightly. At the same time, her hand comes up and gently rests on his left cheek. Her lips are soft and her touch is so gentle, Steven feels all the blood in his face drain away. Her hands are almost as big as his, and yet her touch is so soft. Before he can move, before he opens his mouth, she pulls back and looks him in the eyes.

"No more," she says. "I don't want to talk about him again."

"What *do* you want?"

She kisses him again, more passionately this time. Both her hands make their way around his face, his chin, through his hair. He knows this is wrong, but he lets her do it anyway. He doesn't know which one of them is making the mistake, but he's willing to let it happen. He wants it to happen. He kisses her and runs his hands along her neck, her waist, up her arms.

She stops kissing him and pushes him back a few feet. He can still feel the alcohol in his head. He still can't stand very straight, and he wonders if he'll regret this when he's sober.

Scotty's ashes aren't talking to him anymore.

"I want to make you feel good," she says, and kisses his neck. "I want to make you happy."

Steven closes his eyes and feels her mouth on him. No one has ever said that. For the first time, he wonders if anyone has ever really made him happy. Dania's mouth on his neck makes him smile, and he runs his hand through her very long, silky hair.

"Sit," she whispers in his ear, and pushes him back on the bed. He looks up at her, standing in front of him, and wonders if she's as drunk as he is. Will she regret this tomorrow? Are Scotty's ashes right? Is this only because Steven looks almost exactly like the last man she did this with . . . and only days or weeks ago?

Who cares? he thinks to himself. *Isn't this what you want?*

"Shhh." Dania stops him when he tries to speak. It's as if she knows what he's thinking and doesn't want him to worry. She really wants him to be happy. She reaches up and slowly unbuttons her blouse, revealing a very thin, tan body. Steven immediately thinks her breasts aren't real, but are still amazing. As she lowers her skirt, he can't help but stare. Her entire body is gorgeous, from head to toe. Every inch of her is tan, toned, and striking.

Completely topless, but still wearing a pair of black thong underwear, she walks over to where he's sitting and kneels in front of him. He reaches down and puts his hands through her hair, pulling her face close to his. She runs her mouth down his chin, his neck, and his chest. Working her way down, she unbuttons his shirt with each kiss of his body.

Steven reaches down and holds her shoulders. He tries to pick her up and bring her onto the bed with him, but she will not let him. Instead, she looks up into his eyes, unbuttoning his pants at the same time.

"You stay there," she says. "Just let me take care of you."

Steven closes his eyes and feels Dania's hand push him backward onto the bed, until he's lying down with his feet still on the floor. In the background, he can hear the toilet in the next room. It's making noise as if someone needs to jiggle the handle to keep the tank from constantly trying to fill. He can hear the air conditioner in the background and a slight rattle it's making. The refrigerator in the room is humming louder than it should be.

"Wait," he says, opening his eyes and feeling instantly sober.

"What?" Dania lifts her head and looks him in the eye, her hair falling over one side of her face.

"Just . . . wait."

"What is it, sweetie?"

"I . . . I don't know."

Dania sits up farther, resting on her elbows, still straddling Steven's body. He feels her skin, so warm against his, and it gets him excited while making him uneasy at the same time. He wants to grab her and make love to her, but that very thought makes him feel so . . . sad.

"What do you want, sweetie?" she says, her voice sounding sultry and soothing.

"Is this because I look like him?"

"Shhh." She gently runs a hand across his stomach. "I told you not to talk like that."

"But is it because we look the same?"

Does it matter? Scotty is patiently watching from the darkness.

"You don't think that, do you?" Dania asks, covering her breasts with one of her arms, as if she's suddenly embarrassed at being exposed.

"I don't know," Steven says, rolling over on one side to look at her. She's more beautiful than any woman he's been with. Part of him thinks he's a fool for stopping what she started. Scotty would agree.

"What *do* you know, then?"

He pauses for a minute and lets his head stop spinning and lets the sounds of the refrigerator and the air conditioner and the toilet stop annoying him. Then he reaches across the bed and touches her shoulder, feeling several strands of her hair that are falling across her body.

"I know that the only thing I've liked since I came here is being with you," he says.

She looks deeply in his eyes for a moment without saying anything. Then she reaches up with the hand she was covering herself with and touches his hand that is resting on her shoulder.

"I think we both wanted this because we both needed this," she says. It makes perfect sense. Steven doesn't say anything. He just smiles gently and touches her face.

"Stay?" he asks.

"Of course."

He pulls her close, not thinking of the clothes he's wearing or whatever she isn't. Without practice and without a bit of hesitation, the two of them fit their bodies against one another, Steven spooning against Dania, wrapping his arms around her as she cradles him close to her. He smells her hair and pulls her tightly to him as he quickly—and happily—feels himself drifting off to sleep.

11

Steven thinks the elevator is running much slower than usual. It normally takes a lot less time to get all the way up the building. He watches the numbers light up as he continues his ascent. He could swear that the building used to be only eighty-six floors, but he seems to just keep moving upward. By the time he reaches the ninetieth floor, he wonders how much longer until he finally reaches the top.

He's startled by the loud bell that rings out as the doors open. The hallway outside is dimly lit and appears to be empty. Even though he's pretty sure this isn't where he's supposed to be, Steven steps out of the elevator and around the corner. The hallway is long and straight, with only a few doors here and there on either side. He keeps slowly walking, occasionally looking back at the elevator behind him.

"You're not supposed to be here," a voice says over his left-hand shoulder, and he turns to face it. A security guard is standing there, holding a bag of potato chips in his hand. He's shoving handfuls of them into his mouth as he stands there, but Steven doesn't seem to notice any noise.

"I don't know where I'm going," he says.

"You're not there yet."

"I know, but this is where I wound up."

The security guard takes off his hat, and his hair falls down to his shoulders. Steven thinks the man looks ridiculous, but he doesn't say anything. He looks down at his own clothes and realizes he has no business criticizing anyone else. His pants are torn and dirty, and he's wearing an old T-shirt with stains all over it.

"Make sure you're on time." The security guard puts on a pair of glasses and walks away.

"I'm already late."

Steven takes a deep breath and rolls over, feeling a sharp pain in the back of his head. The pillow is wet, and he has a terrible taste in his mouth. He knows that if he doesn't drink a lot of water right now, he'll wake up with a much worse headache and probably a terrible hangover. As it stands, he thinks he might still be slightly drunk.

Another anxiety dream, Scotty's ashes tsk-tsk from across the room. *Some things never change.*

Steven ignores the wisecrack and walks into the bathroom. He stands at the sink and gulps several glasses of water until he's certain he's had enough to stave off any serious dehydration. If need be, he'll have some beer on the flight to chase away any hangover that might linger. Or he'll load up on sleeping pills and hopefully be nearly comatose all the way back to Canada.

Walking back to the bed, his eyes adjust to the darkness, and he sees a figure move in the corner. Dania is standing by the window, wearing one of his Oxford shirts and looking out at the city skyline outside. She doesn't turn to face him; she stands completely still, her arms wrapped around herself. Steven wonders if the protocol in this situation is to walk up behind her and hold her or to just lie back down on the bed and wait for her return. He chooses instead to do neither, and stands behind her with his own arms folded across his chest.

"It's a beautiful view," he says. "Too bad it feels like the inside of a toaster out there."

"Hardly," Dania scoffs. "A toaster oven is a dry heat."

Steven chuckles and steps closer. Dania looks back at him with a slight smile. He wonders if this is the part where he puts his arms around her and kisses her shoulder softly or any of that. Instead, he walks over to the window and stands beside her, leaning on the windowsill and feeling the blow from the air conditioner. He faces her and tries to ignore the wine headache swirling around in his skull. He also tries to not be so obvious when checking out the silhouette of her body underneath his shirt that she's wearing.

"Couldn't sleep?" he asks.

"Too much to drink."

"Me too."

"I think we pushed it a little hard."

"More than usual, I'd say."

"Could've been worse."

"All things considered, yeah."

"You look different without your glasses." Her voice is deep and sultry, as if she is singing onstage again, just like earlier in the night.

"Like him?"

Leave me out of this, Scotty calls from the darkness.

"No," Dania says, "not like him. Different."

"Different how?"

She pauses and scrunches up her face, as if she knows what to say but not how to say it. "You look serious all the time. With or without the glasses on your face. But without them you look sad."

"You mean old?"

"No. I mean sad. You don't sleep well."

"Not tonight, no."

"Not usually."

He smirks and looks back out the window. He says nothing because she's absolutely right. If it's not a weird dream, it's a lot of tossing around in the bed. If it's not that, it's random bouts of insomnia. He feels as if there's always something left undone, even when he's restless with nothing to do. One reason he loves an incredible view is because it gives him something to look at when he's having trouble sleeping.

"You sleep well?" he asks.

"Not really."

He furrows his brow and takes a deep breath. He doesn't know if it's late at night or very early in the morning at this point, but the city looks extremely busy regardless. He wonders if Singapore City is the type of place that is constantly going, twenty-four hours a day. For all its energy and culture, Toronto shuts down promptly at 2 a.m.

"The accent," he says. "I can't place it."

She grins. "A little here and there. This is here. London is there. I was born here, but my parents moved us over there when I was eight years old. I moved back about ten years ago."

"London, England?"

"No, London, Afghanistan." She looks at him as if he has two heads. "Of course London, England."

"We have a London in Canada too, you know."

"Really?"

"Yep."

"Learn something new every day."

Steven smiles. That's something Scotty used to always say. It was usually after Steven had just taught him something. Come to think of it, Scotty seemed to say it all the time. He had a stable of regular catchphrases he doled out whenever the situation called for it.

"You came back here to pursue the singing career?" Steven asks. It certainly seems like the UK would be a better place for an aspiring pop star, but what does he know?

"I wanted a change that felt familiar," she says, and turns away from him and looks out the window. A full minute passes before she says anything, the sound of the air-conditioning filling the silence between words. It startles him when she speaks again.

"Do you really think I wanted to be here because you look like him?" She's quiet and keeps her gaze aimed at the brightly lit skyscrapers in the distance. The air-conditioning is loud, and that awkward rattle has returned.

"No," Steven says. "I don't know. Maybe. Is that terrible of me?"

She says nothing, but shrugs her shoulders. Scotty is surprisingly quiet in the background.

"It's happened before," Steven says. "It happened all the

time, really. All the way back to high school. I had girlfriends who wanted to be with him because he looked like me without being me."

"You shared them?"

"They left me *for* him."

"Really? Didn't you resent him for that?" she says as if she pities him, and he wishes he hadn't told her.

"Sometimes, but it was never anything serious. He just played with them and moved on. It's what he did."

The corner of one side of her mouth goes up, and Steven realizes what he just said. He catches himself and tries to rewind a step. "I'm sorry. I didn't mean it like that."

"It's okay; I get it." She smiles. "Did you ever pretend to be each other?"

All the time, Scotty chimes in.

"Sometimes. We switched classes here and there. I took his English finals for him a couple of times. He took more than one calculus exam for me."

She smiles big and touches him on his hand, which is resting on the windowsill. He grips her hand lightly, and she returns the squeeze harder.

"What about with girls?" she asks. "Did you ever pretend to be him?"

Tell her about Kathy Varillo. Scotty snickers mischievously.

"Once." Steven snorts remembering it. He was only sixteen.

"What happened?"

"I lost my virginity."

Dania's eyes go wide, and she smiles so big it seems as if her mouth will swallow the rest of her face. She laughs hard and loud and smacks him playfully on the shoulder. Her hair falls in her face as she laughs, and she casually tosses it back over her shoulder with just a flip of her head. She bites the tip of her tongue lightly between her teeth and looks back out the window while still chuckling softly. For a moment, the air conditioner dominates the conversation again.

"If it's not because I look like him, then why was it?" Steven feels her hand grip his tighter when he says this, but he still can't help but wonder. Only earlier in the day she was his brother's lover and he was a stranger with the same face. The one thing they have in common is the one thing they're both mourning.

"You like Tony Bennett more than you like Frank Sinatra," she says, and it's true. "You won't eat a steak if it's overcooked. And you didn't like *The Catcher in the Rye*."

Steven doesn't say anything. He just squeezes her hand again and looks back out the window. When he glances slightly right, he can see her reflection in the window and sees that she's looking him up and down, her eyes searching his entire body.

"Scott loved *The Catcher in the Rye*."

"Big surprise," Steven scoffs.

Screw you, Scotty chimes in.

Dania continues, "You taught him how to tie a necktie. And your favorite TV show as a kid was *Miami Vice*."

"Scotty tell you all that?"

She nods. "He told me everything about you. That's why I wanted to be here tonight. I wanted to be with you because I felt like I already knew you."

"I feel the same way." Steven senses her leaning in to be closer to him.

"You do?"

"He told me everything about you, too."

"Liar." Dania smiles just before she presses her lips against his. Steven smells the perfume in her hair, and it instantly arouses him just like before. It's also the first time a woman seems to have moved from Scotty to him instead of the other way around. He wonders if that would have been the case had he shown up months earlier just for a visit while Scotty was still alive. He shakes this thought out of his head as quickly as it enters and lets her kiss linger for a moment before he pulls back to look into her eyes. He doesn't know anything about this woman. As special as she might have been to Scotty, he never said a word about her to Steven. Just like all the other women that came before her. Steven wonders if he's making a big, bad mistake.

Why stop now? Scotty laughs. *Who are you going to offend at this point? Me?*

"Were you happy?" Steven asks Dania, feeling as if his gaze could burn through her.

"Usually," she says. "But he didn't like Tony Bennett."

Steven smiles as she takes him by both hands and leads him back to the bed. With one, smooth movement, she pulls him onto the bed as she lowers herself backwards, softly landing on the bed so they lie facing each other. She runs her hand through his hair and presses her mouth against his again.

"Sleep well," she says, softly running her fingers over his eyelids to close them. For the first time in a long time, Steven thinks he will, even if it's only for a couple of hours. In the background, he hears absolutely nothing.

Dania wakes up slowly and rubs her temples a bit. Her head must be pounding after tossing back the drinks she did. She didn't gulp down several glasses of water like Steven did in the wee hours of the morning. Opening her eyes, she takes a minute to get adjusted to the light and then another few seconds to get her bearings. Steven imagines that she doesn't wake up in strange hotel rooms every morning. At the very least, he hopes not.

She sits up in the bed and looks down. She's still wearing Steven's button-up shirt that he gave her to sleep in. He always keeps the air-conditioning very high in the room. She was shivering, even with his body next to hers, so he gave her the shirt. She smells the sleeve and smiles.

"Morning. Or afternoon. Whatever," Steven says quietly from the other side of the room, cradling a cup of coffee in his hands. Dania turns to see him sitting at the desk, his tousled hair hanging over his face. He knows he looks exhausted, despite the huge smile from ear to ear. He extends the coffee mug in her direction. "Want some?"

Dania smiles. "Maybe later," she says, and stretches again. Looking over at the nightstand, she glances at the alarm clock for a second and then back at Steven. Then the smile on her face instantly drops, her eyes go wide, and she snaps her gaze back to the clock.

"Your plane!" she yells, standing up. "You missed your flight!"

"It's okay," Steven says without a single hint of annoyance or frustration. In fact, he's still smiling. "I rescheduled it."

"You did what?" Dania asks.

"I changed my flight. I figured I could stay a few days longer."

"Really?" she says, and catches her breath. "Why did you do that?"

"Seemed like a good idea at the time," he says.

"You're crazy."

"Yeah, probably."

"I thought you had enough of this place."

"I'm already here. I should at least see more of what Singapore has to offer."

"Oh, really?" Dania smiles and walks over to him. She leans in to kiss him, and he gently pulls her close until she is sitting on his lap. He takes a deep breath and smells her hair. "What about getting home? Your job? Your beloved winter?"

"It'll wait," Steven says. "I've got some time off coming to me."

"What brought this on?" She smiles and kisses him.

"I don't have anything to go home to just yet," he says. "And I just found a reason to stick around."

12

"Where the hell am I and what did you do with the rest of the city?" Steven asks as he steps off the sidewalk and crosses the street. The tall skyscrapers are gone and have been replaced with small shops and cafés. But, unlike the area around The Blue Bayou, this entire area is more colorful. It is also completely void of all the Western chains and theme restaurants. There are no English pubs or anything of the sort here. This area looks like the Far East Steven expected when his plane first landed.

Dania laughs. "This is Singapore City. This is the *real* city."

"The real city had those towers and fancy streets and cars, my dear."

"Wrong again. That's the banks and all the financial stuff. This is where the real people live. This is where the real shops are. The real food."

"Ah, yes," Steven says. "I smell the food."

In fact, the entire area has a very strong, very overwhelming smell. On this little corner, right on Kandahar Street, a blend of curry and pepper and all kinds of aromas hits him right in the face. With each corner they turn and each open door they pass in front of, Steven is aware that there is a lot of eating going on in this area. And all of it will probably wreck his stomach.

"Don't be such a baby," Dania says when he tells her this. Her slightly British accent is so damned sexy that he wonders why they left the hotel at all. He'd prefer an afternoon of intense lovemaking followed by just listening to her say his name all day long. Of course, sightseeing is the second best thing.

Steven smiles and squeezes Dania's hip with the hand that is resting there. He's never liked sightseeing. He prefers to go from Point A to Point B and be done with it. But the company he is with makes wandering around something he could get used to. Whether he's taking in the local scenery or just looking at Dania when she smiles, Steven finds himself content.

Rows of small shops sell pashminas and other wrappings. There is lots of silk clothing and random other accessories. There are handbags, too, and—of course—plenty of food. If it's not a specialty shop, then it's some sort of restaurant. Or what appears to be what people in the West would call a diner. It all looks very busy and smells very enticing. It reminds Steven of China-town without the Chinese.

"It's really something," he says, and—for once—he's talking about the city and not Dania's figure. This area is fascinating to look at, with little shops and delis and people selling everything from espresso to area rugs. As he steps around another corner, his jaw drops at the enormous gold building just off to the side, a few blocks down. "What is that?"

"That's a mosque," Dania says. "You do have mosques in Canada, yes?"

"Of course. Just not like that. That's huge. And it's . . . well . . . it's huge. And gold and colorful and fancy."

"This entire area has a large Muslim population. There's a reason people call it Arab Street."

"So I see. Is that what you are?"

Dania laughs. "Hardly. They won't have me."

"Them and Hooters, it seems."

"Yes, that's it. One always follows the other."

She squeezes up to Steven and, although she is right up against him, he doesn't feel so hot anymore. "I was raised Protestant, if you can believe that."

"Makes sense. The accent gives it away."

"That's the stupidest thing I've ever heard."

"Made sense when I thought it."

Dania stops for a second to look at some fabric a woman is selling in a tiny shop on the corner. Steven stands outside and continues to look around the area. They're barely outside downtown, where the huge mirrored skyscrapers tower over the streets. The skyline looms just in the distance as a constant reminder that this is a huge city with huge businesses right next door. This area, as set away from all of that as possible, is still right next to the metropolitan craze.

Off to the side of the skyline, Steven sees a large, Gothic skyscraper that seems set apart from everything else. Dark and brooding, shooting up into the sky, it looks nothing like any other building in the area. It's like no other building in Singapore City, really.

"Hey." Steven takes Dania by the hand as she steps out into the street with him. "What on earth is that building all about?"

"Oh." She smiles. "That's the Batman building."

"The what?"

She rolls her eyes and chuckles. "The Batman building. I forget what it's called. But that's what it looks like, right? Something out of a Batman movie?"

Steven looks at it again and, sure enough, she's right. The Gothic architecture and dark brick and dark gold exterior cast a shadow over the entire area it overlooks. It surely looks like something he could see the Caped Crusader standing aloft on. It even has gargoyles.

"It's owned by some Taiwanese billionaire," Dania says. "He was a big fan of Batman. So, he wanted a building that looked like what he thought a Batman building would look like. And there it is."

"Get the hell out of here. You're making that up."

"No, it's true. That's the story."

"So what is it used for?"

"Just an office building. I think there's a restaurant, too."

"I'll be damned. Is there a Spider Man building, too?"

"Yes, it's on the other side of the city. It's blue and red and shaped like a web. I should show it to you."

"Really?" Steven is astonished and honestly finds himself excited to see that. Until, of course, he realizes that Dania is putting him on. The look of embarrassment on his face is enough to make her laugh and kiss him, so he doesn't mind being played.

"There's all kinds of different buildings here," she says. "Nothing is the same. Just a little ways down from the Batman building, there's a flat skyscraper." She points her finger toward a long sliver that pops up in the distance. "You see, there?"

"Yes." Steven shields his eyes from the sunlight.

"That building was designed so, when you look at it from a certain angle, it looks two dimensional. Like one long sliver. Or a sheet of paper."

"Damn, that's weird."

"That's what this city is like. There's no rhyme or reason. People throw up whatever buildings they want. It means that it's more than just the people that are diverse."

"And yet I can't chew gum here," he says. Dania gives him a slug in the side.

Turning another corner, Steven can't help but admire how different all of the buildings look. Back in Toronto, they would all have essentially the same shape but different storefronts. Here, he is amazed by the changing outline of every block.

"Hungry?" Dania asks, reading his mind or perhaps hearing his stomach rumble. She points across the street to a dark red building with two tall spikes jutting out of the top in opposite directions. One spike faces east, the other west, like arrows about to be shot into the distance.

"That's interesting," he says. "Is that a restaurant?"

"It's Minang."

"Mine-wha?"

"Minang. Minangkabau. Let's eat there. You'll love it."

"Alright," he says, and lets her lead him across the street. He is still amazed by the grip this woman has. Such a thin woman, yet her hands are almost as strong as his. She pulls him by the arm, and he has no choice but to follow.

Inside the restaurant, the two of them are greeted by a young woman dressed in a long red gown. She wears a headdress that looks just like the roof of the building, with two long spikes sticking diagonally upward and sideways. She is very polite as she takes them to their table.

"Do you trust me?" Dania asks. It's a question that Steven would answer "no" to when most people ask it. But, for some reason, he feels okay this time around. "To order food for us, I mean?"

"Of course," he lies. He's certain his stomach is going to hate every part of what he's about to do to it. And the spices in the air tell him he's going to be no good at his job for at least a few days when he returns.

When the waitress arrives, also wearing the tall headdress, Dania gives a very detailed order to her while Steven smiles and pretends to understand.

"You're going to love this," she says to him, and squeezes his hand. He smiles and decides that when in Rome . . .

She kisses him sweetly and, for another moment, Steven tries to forget the fact that he has cuddled up to his dead brother's lover. Every so often, the reality of it comes smacking him in the face, and he wonders if he's doing the right thing. He has a nagging feeling that he is not. Still, all of this feels too good for him to simply do nothing. He knows how he feels when he's with Dania, so he tries to ignore that creeping sense of doom in the back of his mind. He reminds himself—much as it hurts to do so—that Scotty is gone. The only two people who should care at all are sitting together right now in this restaurant.

"What's with the hat?" he asks, motioning at the red spikes everyone in the restaurant is wearing. It's quite the elaborate uniform, and Steven is pretty sure he's not the only person in there who is thankful that the place is heavily air-conditioned.

"On her head?" Dania nods toward the hostess at the front door, still easily visible from the table. "I told you, it's Minang-kabau."

"And that means . . . ?"

Dania takes a sip of her water and rubs Steven's hands in hers. "The Minang people are from Indonesia. The island of Sumatra. That's what this place is. Indonesian food."

"Okay, I'm with you so far."

"Well," she continues, "hundreds of years ago, their land was invaded by the Javanese—"

"—A ruthless band of coffeemakers."

"Shhh." She puts a hand over his mouth. "The Javanese prince wanted their land, where the locals farmed. For the Sumatrans, it was customary in those days to settle disputes with a bullfight. Water buffalo. But they did not fight with a man against a bull. It was two bulls fighting against one another."

She takes another sip of her water while Steven tries to figure out the geography in his head and follow along. She brushes her long hair over her shoulders and out of her way.

"So, to keep their land and their homes, the Sumatrans challenged the prince to a bullfight. The prince was known to have the biggest, meanest bull that had ever been challenged. He accepted the challenge without thinking twice. He knew that his bull was unbeatable."

"Damn those princes and their unbeatable bulls."

"The prince and his people returned a few days later with their prized bull. An enormous, angry water buffalo. They set him free in the arena, ready to kill the first challenging bull to enter. The Sumatrans released their bull into the ring. Everyone was shocked to find that they challenged him with a frail calf with little nubs instead of horns. This little bull that sheepishly walked into the ring."

A plate of rice arrives, and Dania looks surprised. It's as if she has just been caught telling a secret. The waitress smiles and disappears again, back into the kitchen. Dania leans in closer to Steven.

"Well," she says, "the prince and the Javanese people all laughed. This puny calf was no match for his great buffalo. Even their bull seemed unimpressed. Follow me?"

"Edge of my seat."

"What no one knew was that the Sumatrans had starved the little calf for two days. And those little nubs it had for horns? They had sharpened them until they were like little daggers on the top of its head. So when they released the little calf into the ring, it was so hungry for milk that it mistook the big bull for its mother. It ran up to the big buffalo and ducked under its belly, looking for an udder it could suck on. Those razor-sharp horns tore out the big bull's stomach and killed it."

"How very clever."

"Clever, yes." Dania takes a sip of her water. "The Sumatran people ran into the arena cheering and applauding. They yelled, 'Minang kabau! Minang kabau!' "

"Which means?"

"The bull wins," she says, and smiles as if she is very proud of herself. As if she wrote the story herself and just told it for the first time.

"Hence the pointy hats."

"Horns."

Steven leans in to kiss her and, as he does, more food arrives. There is a mix of noodles and rice and meat and all things spicy. If he were looking for calm, boring, bland food, he came to the wrong place. He wonders if he has Pepto Bismol in his suitcase back at the hotel.

"Oh, God," Dania says, and leans over the plates. "This is going to be good. You just wait."

It's then that she leans across the table and takes a handful of rice. She doesn't use a spoon or a knife or even the chopsticks on the table. She actually reaches with her hands and scoops the food from the serving dish to her plate. Steven watches in wide-eyed horror as she repeats this process with each serving tray and each item of food she has ordered them.

"Bon appétit," she says with her sexy smile that Steven suddenly doesn't find so sexy. A thick sauce puddles on her plate, and she takes a handful of rice, rubs it through the sauce, and then scoops it all into her mouth.

"What the hell?" Steven says, staring with his mouth open.

"What?" Dania asks through mouthfuls.

"Are you seriously going to eat that with your hands?"

"Yeah, that's how we do it here."

"That's a"—he tries to remember the name—"Minang thing or something?"

"No, it's a Singaporean thing."

"Really?"

"Well, not over where you're staying. But this is how the locals eat."

"With their hands?"

"Yes, try it."

"I don't think so," Steven says, and picks up a pair of chopsticks.

"Oh, come on. Live a little."

"Oh, I'm living," Steven says, and remembers again whom he is with and how he met her. He wonders if Scotty ate with his hands. Then he dismisses that thought because he doesn't want to think about Scotty right now. Besides, he's certain that's exactly how Scotty ate. It seems like something he would have liked very much.

"Eat with your chopsticks then, little bull," Dania says, and winks. "I will eat like a big buffalo."

Steven holds the chopsticks up to his head as if they are horns. He makes a snorting sound that makes Dania laugh and almost choke on her food. She sips her water. It's so loud, it reminds him of the man sitting behind him on the plane a couple of days ago. He wonders if everyone in Singapore is so noisy when they eat. If not for the smile on her face, he knows his misophonia would drive him to get up and run out of the restaurant.

He's not sure if, back in Toronto, he'd be madly in love with Dania or appalled by her. Anyone else smacking her lips and scarfing her food the way she does would bring out the worst in him. Something about Dania's doing it makes it a little easier for Steven to tolerate it. He thinks he must really be smitten to sit here and take it. He tries to remember if he felt the same way in the beginning with Robin. He also wonders if years of listening to Dania eating like this would wind up making him resent her, as well.

"Tell me more," he says.

"More what?"

"More anything."

"What do you want to know?" She smiles and shovels more rice into her face with her bare hands.

"Tell me everything. Tell me all about you."

"Oh, honey." She smiles and winks at him. "I so wish there was more to tell. The bull story is the best I've got."

As he digs his chopsticks into his food, Steven is hit in the face with the spiciness of it all. He's had spicy food before, but this is something new to him. It's not the clean intensity of the wasabi he lightly pats on his sushi back home. It's also not as simple as the peppery Thai food that Robin always loved to order in. This is hot and peppery and burns the tip of his tongue right down to his lower intestine. It's overwhelming and delicious. He stirs more rice into the meal in order to cut the heat a little bit. He knows he'll need more than a couple of refills of water. Dania sees all of this play out on his face and winks.

He looks at the way she smiles at him and can't help but wonder what she sees in him. It's not that he doesn't think he's a good man or that a woman shouldn't like his company. In fact, he knows that many would consider him quite the catch. But if this woman was so in love with Scotty—and Scotty was so different than Steven—what is it she's so attracted to if not just the familiar face? Could it really be as simple as Tony Bennett?

He puts that thought out of his head for as long as he can and just enjoys himself. Still, as much of himself and his life story as he shares with Dania, he realizes how little he knows about her. The bits and pieces he puts together only tell him so much. He can tell that, as affectionate as she is, she is keeping him at a distance. If it's to keep him away, it doesn't work. Instead, it probably makes him want her that much more.

Dania slurps up a handful of food, and Steven lets his eyes linger over her figure for a moment as an easy distraction. He tries to hear the music in the background instead and listens for a rattling air conditioner that might save his panicked ears. Then he looks back over at her and she's grinning, knowing exactly what she's doing to him and having fun with it. He laughs despite himself and reaches for more water. And then more water.

Steven realizes that, if she were to ask him right then and there, he'd probably give Dania the fifteen thousand dollars. He imagines that's what Scotty had in mind all along. If a woman like Dania isn't worth that kind of money, then what on earth could Scotty possibly have needed it for? He didn't want a car, didn't need it for rent. Steven figures she's worth that much just for him to have this time with her.

It's a price he would gladly pay.

He knows he should look for the better in people. But he can't help it. He keeps wondering how long it will be before she turns to him and asks him to pay it.

13

Steven has a bit of a skip in his step as he practically bounces through the front door of his hotel. Despite the sweat rolling down his back, he thinks nothing of the heat and, for the first time since he arrived, he finds the Christmas decorations in the hotel lobby to be cute instead of tacky.

"Mr. Steven!" A familiar voice greets him as he steps through the automatic doors. Still dressed as Santa Claus, Steven's favorite doorman is obviously smiling hugely from underneath his fake white beard.

"Good afternoon, Lee," Steven replies without taking off his aviators. "Getting out of the heat?"

"Yes, sir." Lee smiles. "Very good, sir. Anything you need?"

Without breaking his stride, Steven continues through the lobby, calling to Lee over his shoulder, "Everything is great, Lee. Just great."

And everything *is* great. Regardless of the fact that he's in the middle of what is actually a very tricky situation, Steven feels just fine. Despite having just lost his brother, having been dumped, and having gotten involved with his brother's lover whom he has to leave for good in a couple of days, all is well. In fact, for the first time since long before Scotty died, Steven thinks his smile is genuine.

"Have a Holly, Jolly Christmas" is playing over the speakers in the hotel, and Steven finds himself humming along. That

Christmas spirit seems to have finally hit him. It's odd that, when he hears the music this time, he's not homesick at all.

He always feels a little depressed when the season comes and goes. The week leading up to Christmas is always great, with everything from the music to the feel in the air to make him happy. By the time January rolls around, he often finds himself in a bit of a funk that's hard to get out of until February.

It's not that he simply loves Christmas that much. Just like everyone else, he can get tired of all the festive hoopla. It just seems to be the one time of year when he doesn't have other things to worry about. His restaurant is booming in December, and the work is easy. All the stresses that come with relationships go away and, for years, it was the only chance he ever got to see or really speak to Scotty. And, for just six brief weeks per year, it's a time when background noise doesn't make him crazy. Something about the classic sounds of the season in the air drowns out all of the mayhem he normally hears every day. And something about people's good nature during that time of the year makes him a little smoother around the edges, as well.

Stepping out of the elevator and walking to his room, Steven wonders if he can curb his schoolboy crush long enough to take a nap. Running around with Dania all morning and afternoon was exhausting, not to mention the fact that she kept him awake and drunk most of the previous night. It's finally starting to catch up with him, and he figures he's due for at least a couple of hours of rest while she is off rehearsing with her band and setting up for her gig later that night.

As he puts his key card in the slot, he gets a weird feeling at the back of his neck. The "Do Not Disturb" sign is no longer hanging on the doorknob. He was sure it was there when he left with Dania earlier that morning. When he opens the door, his room is immaculate and clean. As great as that is, he was perfectly content to leave everything unmade.

He looks around just to make sure everything is in order. His blazers are hung perfectly, and his shoes are in the right spot. He tips an imaginary hat at Scotty's ashes, still in their paper bags, resting inside the box his remains came in.

Screw you, man, Scotty's ashes say.

"Right back atcha," Steven says back to the ashes.

He sits at the desk and switches on his laptop. After spending a few brief moments reading about nothing going on back home, he sends off a few e-mails and then checks to make certain he's not missing anything at work. As luck would have it, the walls still stand, the wine has all been ordered, and the place has not exploded or burned to the ground in his absence—all good things, indeed.

Just for the hell of it, he Googles "Orchard Towers." There he immediately finds photos and—even on this Web site—the description "Four Floors of Whores." He sees much more excitement on this Web site than he did at the actual place, which makes him wonder if he was there on a slow night. According to Wikipedia, Orchard Towers is home to not only prostitutes, but international prostitutes from all over the world. Russian hookers, Chinese hookers, and—yes—even just run-of-the-mill local Singaporean hookers.

He does some more reading to find that there are many bands just like Dania's that play in the Towers. There is also a ton of local food, all kinds of bars, more hookers and some drug dealers, as well as transvestites, beggars, and thieves. All in all, it makes for what no one would consider a great family tourist location.

Glad you had a good time seducing my girlfriend. Scotty's ashes are pouting on the other side of the room.

"Remember Gina St. John?" Steven asks, the memory of an old college girlfriend still fresh in his mind. Scotty seduced her after she lost interest in Steven.

Touché. Scotty shuts up after that. Steven smiles and goes back to searching the Web.

He thinks of Dania and her singing. She's really quite good and, although there were many people watching her sing, she is miles better than the place where she works. He wonders if The Cocktail Room is as good as it gets in Singapore City, or if there are better, classier places where she could be working. Then he figures that maybe, like many other musicians, she's just happy to have any work at all.

He closes his laptop and goes over to the bed to lie down. As he takes off his shoes, he looks over on the nightstand at the stack of belongings housekeeping had neatly set aside. There are Scotty's notes and random photos, pictures of their parents that Steven took, and Steven's random receipts from the past few days. He stops for a second and looks through them. It's then that the warning bells go off in his head.

The photo of the boy is missing.

Steven flips through the stack of papers and photos one more time, although he knows he didn't miss anything. He never makes mistakes like that and keeps everything in perfect order. No, the photo simply is not there. He looks under the bed and finds nothing. In fact, the bed goes straight to the floor, so there's no way to hide anything there anyway. He looks in the nightstand drawer, then the desk, and then—just because he hasn't looked there yet—the bathroom. Nothing. The photo isn't tucked into anything like his suitcase. It's not on top of the TV or next to the cardboard box containing Scotty's bag of ashes. It's simply gone.

What the hell? he thinks. His first instinct is that he lost it. He had it in his pocket, and he lost it at some point between last night and today. After all, he took everything out of his right-side jacket pocket at some point while he was drunk and put it all on the nightstand. For all he knows, the photo was lost all the way across town.

The next thing he thinks is that housekeeping somehow lost it, threw it away, or vacuumed it up. But then he realizes how silly it sounds to think an old Polaroid got vacuumed, so he immediately drops that thought. Why would housekeeping lose only one photo and have everything else perfectly in place?

Then he thinks that Dania took it.

But he can't think of when she might have gotten hold of it, since she spent most of her time with him in that room and barely left his sight. Besides, he would have just given it to her at

Hooters when he first met her. All she had to do was say it was hers and ask. Not only did she never do that, she acted like she didn't know or care about it at all.

He's pretty certain that he simply misplaced it but, now that it's in his head, he can't seem to let it go. It's not like the photo was getting him anywhere, anyway. No one seemed to know a thing about it. It was just some old photo that had probably been lying around Scotty's place since long before he even moved in.

Still, Steven feels it gnawing at him, so he puts his shoes back on and walks back down to the lobby. Walking up to the first young woman with the Santa hat he finds, he immediately recognizes Nicole from when he checked in.

"Hi there," he says. "Do you remember me?"

"Yes, sir." Nicole smiles back. "Mr.—"

"Kelly."

"Yes, of course, Mr. Kelly. How can I help you?"

"Well, today housekeeping made up my room—"

"—Did they do a satisfactory job, sir?"

"Oh, yes," Steven says. "Great job. But, anyway, I had some personal belongings in my room, and something is missing now."

"Oh, dear." Nicole is genuinely surprised and a bit upset. "What kind of things? Something valuable?"

Steven says, "Nothing like that, no. It was just some paperwork. A photo, actually."

"A photo?"

"Yes," he says. "Like a little photograph. You know, a Polaroid?"

"I'm sorry, sir." Nicole shakes her head slowly. "I don't know what you mean."

"Just an old photograph. Taken from a camera." Steven has never tried to explain what a Polaroid is before and suddenly realizes he can't. "Anyway, all my things are there and were left in a neat little stack for me, but this one photo is gone."

"I'm sorry to hear that."

"Yeah, well"—he scratches the back of his neck—"I was just wondering if maybe someone had found it?"

"A photograph? Here?" She looks confused.

"Not here, no," Steven says. "Like housekeeping. Did they accidentally pick it up or anything like that?"

"Sir." Nicole leans in politely. "Are you trying to ask me if our cleaning staff took your belongings?"

"Oh, no," Steven says as if he's just been caught calling her mother a whore. "No, I wouldn't say that at all. I just wanted to know if it might have been an accident, or if they might have picked it up by mistake."

"Well, Mr. Kelly," Nicole says, "I can assure you that housekeeping doesn't have it and didn't pick it up by mistake. It just does not seem likely."

"Sure, I get that," Steven says. "Is it possible that someone else got into my room?"

"Absolutely not," she says matter-of-factly.

"How can you be so sure?"

"People do not do that here, Mr. Kelly." Nicole smiles. "The laws are much too strict. To break into your room would be very, very foolish. Just a ridiculous thing to do."

"Sure," Steven says, "I understand. But people commit foolish crimes all the time in Canada, where I'm from."

"Perhaps," Nicole says, and looks at him with very serious eyes. "But they do not do it here in Singapore."

"Alright, then," Steven says. "I guess I just misplaced it. Thanks, Nicole."

"Maybe your friend has what you're looking for," Nicole calls to him as Steven starts to walk away.

"My friend?" Steven asks.

"The woman you were with last night."

"Oh," he says, and feels his face get red. "You saw us here. Together. Last night."

"Yes, sir." Nicole smiles and picks up the ringing hotel phone. "Maybe she can help you."

14

The whores are on all four floors in great number tonight as Steven makes his way into Orchard Towers and straight up to The Cocktail Room. As he steps in the dark room, he can already hear Dania singing a song by either Celine Dion or Barbra Streisand. He can't remember which one. As his eyes adjust to the darkness, he sees that the place is pretty packed. He still wonders if this place is the best venue her manager could find. Chances are it pays the best, what with the steady flow of tourists and locals and johns parading through.

Sitting at the same table as before, Steven sips on his only sort-of-terrible wine and watches Dania go into another song. As the tempo changes and she really starts to rock, Dania takes on a bit of a different persona than the sultry sex kitten she becomes during the ballads. There's something rough and crude about her that strikes Steven as a bit odd. It's almost as if she seems familiar, but as if she's also a completely different person. It all feels like déjà vu for a minute. He imagines a lot of people felt this way when they met him after they had already met Scotty.

Dania sways her hips and dances and thrusts her pelvis to the song. It's intimidating and reminds Steven just how forceful she can be in bed. How she can be submissive at one moment and then completely in control the next. God help the man who ever winds up on the receiving end of her anger.

Midway through the rock song—something that sounds like it might be by Melissa Etheridge or Bonnie Raitt—Dania looks across the room and makes eye contact with him. She throws him a sexy smile and a very obvious wink. More than one man in the audience turns to see who is on the receiving end of that wink. Steven almost blushes from the knowledge that at least a few of those men are jealous that it's him.

That's right, you sad sacks, he thinks to himself. *I'm the guy. I'm the one she's looking at.*

The music changes again, and Steven feels an odd chill run down his neck. Dania whispers something to the band, and they bring the music down to a slow, jazzy style. The club immediately goes from rock to jazz as Dania leans in on the microphone and, sexy as ever, begins to croon. Then, it hits Steven what she is doing: She's singing directly to him.

In that one moment, there is no one else in the bar. There is no one else Dania is performing for or trying to entertain. It's almost as if the band isn't even there. If she weren't standing all the way across the room, Steven would reach over and gently caress her face while she sang.

It's Vince Guaraldi she's singing, and the song is "Christmas Time Is Here." A gorgeous—and gorgeously slow—Christmas song. It's one of his favorites and a constant staple for him this time of year. He doesn't remember when, but he must have told her at some point how much he loves the tune. She's looking right at him as she sings the opening lines. Looking back at her as she croons the song, Steven wonders if D.Wash was right.

He wonders if he's falling for this woman.

Steven only just now realizes that no one has ever sung to him before. He wishes that he could go to the stage, pull her down, and carry her home. He wants to put her on a plane and take her back to Toronto with him.

Then he sips his wine and thinks he's insane. He's falling in love with his dead brother's girlfriend. A woman he's only known a few days. It's exactly the sort of thing he never does. The kind of thing he detests when he reads about couples who barely know each other and get married. It's the kind of thing people do when they don't have real structure or responsibility in their lives.

It's just the sort of thing Scotty would have done.

Dania sings her way into the final chorus of the song and Steven shakes off his doubts and second guessing. He stops thinking and lets himself enjoy the moment, the music washing over him and erasing his usual worries. Just as he is ready to lose himself completely in the song, drop to his knees, and propose to Dania right in front of the entire club, everything comes to a screeching halt.

Nez has approached the stage.

The short, annoying man must have just walked into the club, unbeknownst to Steven, Dania, and every member of the band. Everyone seems to be enjoying the song, but that apparently makes Nez angry. By the time Steven even notices that he's there, Nez is right at the stage, losing his mind.

He yells something to Dania, who tries to pretend he's not there and keeps singing. Audience members are yelling for him to sit down, shut up, and just generally get out of the way. This doesn't even faze Nez, who keeps yelling gibberish at Dania and the band. Then, he walks up to the side of the stage and points his finger angrily at the guitarist. When Nez doesn't get the answer he wants, Nez reaches up and, pushing the guitarist back, pulls at his microphone stand.

"What the hell?" the guitarist clearly mouths, which causes Dania to take a step back. Steven sees this and wonders if he should do anything. Then he remembers every warning he's ever gotten since coming to Singapore about how he should mind his own business. He simply sits there and watches it all unfold. For a second, he's sure he sees Dania look over at him.

The guitarist reaches over with one hand and pulls the microphone stand back from Nez. For a second, there's a tug of war between the two men until Nez lets go and the guitarist yanks the microphone free. The music stops, the band seems freaked out, and Dania quits singing. There is silence for a moment as Nez stands in front of the stage and leers at Dania.

"Get the hell out of the way, asshole," someone yells from the audience. Nez doesn't even break his icy stare that is piercing right through Dania's forehead.

"One," Dania looks right at Nez as she speaks. She starts snapping her fingers and keeps counting, "Two, three, four."

The music goes upbeat again, and the band switches into another rock song. Nez glares at Dania and steps away, walking back over to the bar near the back of the room. Apparently he got what he wanted. Everyone in the audience seems to shrug it off as they get into whatever upbeat tune Dania is rocking out to. She smiles as if nothing happened at all.

It all seems so bizarre. Steven isn't even sure what just happened. Nez heard a Christmas ballad and lost his mind, which instantly makes him the biggest Ebenezer Scrooge Steven has ever seen. For a guy who is the manager of a band, Nez has a way of acting like he runs a sweatshop. All he's missing is a whip to crack.

Steven takes a sip of his wine and holds his glass in the air. He hopes Dania sees the toast he's giving her. After a minute she looks over at him and blows him a kiss. He winks back at her and smiles.

When he turns his head to the left, Nez is standing right there and, a few feet behind him, a stocky bodyguard in a black suit with a black shirt is standing with his arms folded. Steven feels a lump in his throat, but stands up as straight as he can. Nez is oddly intimidating for a man several inches shorter than he. His jaw is stuck out, and he appears to be grinding his teeth as the light shines off of his slicked-back hair and sharkskin suit. Steven thinks the guy looks like a total slimeball.

"Can I help you?" Steven asks.

"She's mine," Nez says through his teeth. His eyes almost look as if they can shoot lasers.

"I think you mean she's your client," Steven says, realizing that he's close enough to Nez to feel Nez's breath hitting his neck. He looks over his right shoulder to see Dania, still midsong, watching the two of them. She doesn't look happy.

"I get her work," Nez says. "I record her music; I do the booking. She's mine."

"Fine by me. I'm not looking to get into the music business."

"You don't understand, do you?"

"I don't care, if you really must know."

"You're in the wrong place."

"And I'm just a tourist."

"Go to Crazy Horse, tourist. That's your place."

"I like the music here."

"You're not even the first. You know that?"

"Yeah," Steven smirks. "But I knew the other guy pretty well."

Nez scoffs and shakes his head. "He wasn't the first, either."

Steven doesn't let the insult bother him, despite the fact that he clenches the fingers of his left hand into a fist. He wants to choke Nez with his necktie, but—for a change—Steven isn't wearing one. Instead, he simply smiles and raises his wineglass.

"Cheers," he says, and turns back to watch Dania onstage, wrapping up her song.

Nez cracks the knuckle of his index finger using the thumb on the same hand. He looks at the bodyguard behind him, then back at Dania on the stage. Then, with that same, angry stare, he looks back at Steven. Leaning close, he speaks so softly into Steven's ear, it's almost a whisper.

"You be smart," he says. "Or get what your brother got."

With a dismissive shove to Steven's shoulder, Nez walks away. Steven stands there for a minute before he realizes that his mouth is wide open and that his knees are wobbling a little bit. His hands are shaking. He knows it's not out of fear. He just can't remember the last time he was instantly this angry. Nez walks back over to the bar, turns around, and gives him a smug little smile. Steven thinks this is the first time he's ever wanted to kill a man.

The music stops and, through the applause, Steven hears Dania leave the stage. The crowd loves her, and she smiles and waves and takes a bow. Steven doesn't notice any of this, as he's still staring at Nez, who is standing just behind the bodyguard.

"Hey, you." Dania kisses him on the cheek. Steven doesn't even look at her.

"What the hell was that all about?" Steven asks, finally looking at her when she puts her hand on his chin and pulls his head toward her.

"That?" Dania asks. "That's Nez. I told you, he's an asshole."

"I see that. What was he doing?"

"He has this stupid idea that we shouldn't be doing slow songs. He thinks that too many ballads turns people away. And he hates the Christmas tunes when we do them."

"He's an idiot. An asshole and an idiot."

"No kidding. That bullshit with pulling at Tommy's gear. Yanking at the mic like that. The mic cost eight hundred bucks."

Steven feels those hairs on the back of his neck stand up again. "What did you say?"

"The microphone," Dania says. "It's really expensive."

Microphone.

Mic.

Mick.

Steven almost laughs. His mouth is open again, and he realizes he's staring at Dania for a full thirty seconds before he hears her voice.

"Hey," she says. "What's going on? Steven? What is it?"

"Christ," Steven says. "Scotty. Was he trying to be your manager?"

"Scotty? Of course not. He didn't know anything about music."

"Yeah, but he was trying to buy equipment. Microphones. Things like that."

"Why do you think that?"

"That's what 'Mick' means," Steven says, trying to find the slip of paper in his pocket. Then he realizes it's back at the hotel. Then he thinks of asking Dania about the missing photograph. "Scotty had a list of things he needed money for. 'Mick' wasn't a person. It was a thing. He couldn't spell worth a damn, is all."

"I think you're reaching."

"I think I'm right."

There is a loud noise from across the room. Dania and Steven both jump as they see Nez slapping his hand on the bar to get her attention. Steven wishes he had the power to blink and make Nez's head explode into a million pieces. He imagines it would make a lot of people in the bar very happy.

"Asshole," Dania says. "Just ignore him."

"Wait," Steven says as Dania starts to walk away. She seems surprised when he reaches out and grabs her by the elbow. "I need to know something."

"What is it?"

"Nez said something to me. About Scotty."

"To hell with him," Dania says, and starts to walk away. Steven pulls her back.

"No, I'm serious," he says. "He said I should back off or get what Scotty got. What does that mean?"

"It means nothing. He's just being a little prick."

"Don't tell me that," Steven says. "I can tell there's something going on. You need to tell me, Dania."

"It's nothing."

"Is it? Scotty had an aneurysm. He had headaches. What's this asshole talking about?"

Dania looks over her shoulder at Nez, back to the stage, and then finally back at Steven. Her bright eyes suddenly look heavy and sad. Steven doesn't like the strange feeling that has hit his stomach. Across the bar, Nez is still tossing out his smug glare.

"Look," Dania says, "I'll tell you everything later, okay?"

"Not later," he says, and brushes off her hand when she tries to caress his face. "Now."

Dania takes a long, deep breath. Letting it out, she leans in closer to Steven and holds his hands in hers. "Scotty did have an aneurysm, sweetie," she says. "But it killed him during a fight with Nez."

"What?" Steven says loudly enough for more than one person in the bar to stop what he is doing and look over.

"It all happened really fast. They were arguing. Nez hit Scott in the head. Then Scott stumbled backward and just . . ."

"He just what?"

"He just died," she confesses. "He got hit once and grabbed his head and just died."

Dania is still speaking, but Steven can't hear her. He feels as if he's at one end of a tunnel while listening to her yelling at him from the other end. Everything he sees is red. He feels his blood already boiling and his hands shaking even worse than they were before.

The bruise on Scotty's face.

Nez.

Scotty always had headaches.

Nez hit him.

"That man killed my brother," Steven says to no one.

"It wasn't like that." Dania tries to touch his face again.

"Yeah"—Steven pushes her hand away—"it was exactly like that."

In an instant, Steven has pushed Dania aside and is storming across the room to where Nez is standing behind his bodyguard. The look on the goon's face when he hits the floor, gasping for air and clutching his neck, is almost worth the pain that surges up Steven's arm. One swift blow to the throat will take down most men of any size; Steven learned that fact a long time ago. Years of working in bars and dealing with drunks who can't handle their liquor has made Steven much quicker than people would guess. It also has made him better with his fists than anyone would have ever thought. The bodyguard is on his knees in an instant. Steven finishes him off with a right hook to the jaw that lays him on his back.

The look on Nez's face is nothing less than terrified.

Steven pulls Nez off his barstool and shoves him into the corner. People are watching, but no one seems to care enough to get involved. If anything, they are entertained. Steven hears the band starting to play again and the heavy beat of the bass drum filling the air. He doesn't realize that it's not the bass drum at all, but the blood in his head as his heart pounds against his ribcage.

"You sonofabitch," Steven screams at Nez, whose eyes are so

wide, he looks as if he might start crying. "You ruined everything! You killed my brother!"

Steven wraps his fingers around Nez's neck and squeezes. He watches the color in Nez's face go from white to red to blue very quickly. Before Steven knows what he's doing, he has reached into his jacket pocket. The inner left-hand pocket of his very nice, very pressed, unwrinkled sports jacket. From that pocket he pulls the bag of Scotty's ashes. A second later, he's tearing open the bag. Then he's releasing his grip on Nez's throat.

A second after that, he pours the remains into Nez's mouth.

Nez gets Scotty's remains all over his face, in his mouth, and down his throat. Steven holds Nez tightly against the wall as he sees his brother's dust and bone spill everywhere. Nez chokes and spits. He falls to his knees and hurls up the filth that is all over his face and in his mouth. Scotty's ashes are everywhere. Steven tosses the empty bag to the floor and listens to the pounding in his head as it gets even harder and faster.

Nez is on all fours now, gagging and close to puking. He knows exactly what it is that he just swallowed. He wipes Scotty out of his eyes and tries to spit out the remains that are still in his mouth. He looks ridiculous, crawling around on all fours, covered in Steven's dead twin.

Steven simply stands over Nez, looking down at him with disgust. He notices that some of the ashes are on his own pants legs and shoes. He doesn't care. He waits for the pounding to stop. He looks over his shoulder and sees that the bodyguard is slowly getting to his feet.

There is a hand on his shoulder, and Steven wheels around to punch whomever is grabbing him.

"Wait!" Dania's voice is strong and loud. It snaps Steven out of whatever trance he's in, and his head instantly is filled again with the sounds of the bar. Someone is laughing in the back. Nez is coughing on the floor. Steven takes Dania in his arms and holds her tightly against him. He feels her heart beating almost as fast as his.

"We have to get the hell out of here," Dania screams at him, but she still sounds far away.

"What?" Steven asks, as if he didn't hear her the first time.

"You do not want to go to jail here!" Dania screams at him, takes him by the hand, and practically shoves him out the side door. Steven finds himself in a dark hallway with a metal staircase that leads them all the way down to the street. Before he even realizes what's happening, Steven feels the familiar heat and humidity of the nighttime air. He feels the pavement under his feet. An instant later and he feels the cool leather of the backseat of a taxi.

Another instant after that he feels Dania's strong hands holding his.

"It's okay," she says, and holds him close to her. He catches his breath and waits for the thumping in his chest to slow down. He feels her hands touch his face and he buries it in her chest. He waits for his hands to stop shaking. When they do, he waits for tears that never come. Instead, he presses his face harder against Dania's body and feels her grip get even tighter.

It feels as if an entire day passes as everything slowly calms down. Steven hears the sound of the car tires humming across the pavement. A car horn blows in the background, and the radio is playing what sounds like an Asian pop song. When he raises his head again he sees that Dania has obviously been crying, but she is fine now. She looks at him and shakes her head.

"Are you okay?" she asks.

"Yeah. You?"

"I am now. That was crazy."

After another thirty seconds of silence, Dania suddenly smiles, and they both find themselves laughing. It starts with a couple of chuckles until they both just let go. The taxi driver looks confused in the reflection in the rearview mirror, wondering if his passengers are drunk or insane or both. There's no reason for it—and he doesn't know why—but Steven can't stop smiling.

"I'm sorry," Dania says after a while of them just staring at each other. "That I didn't tell you sooner, I mean. About Nez and Scott."

"Don't be."

"Still . . ."

He puts his hand over her mouth and shushes her. "It's okay."

"Do you mean that?"

"I have to."

They say nothing for at least five minutes, both staring out the same window, watching the Christmas lights outside. Steven feels Dania's thumb gently caressing the back of his hand. He can smell her perfume and her hair, and is a bit alarmed to feel himself getting aroused. He barely notices the taxi driver is whistling, which usually drives him crazy.

"That was amazing." Dania breaks the silence and kisses him.

"I still can't believe I did that."

"Now do me a favor?"

"What's that?"

"Take me back to your hotel."

"Deal."

With that, they are silent again for several minutes. Steven buries his head in Dania's neck and kisses her skin. He smells her perfume that he has come to recognize. He smells her beautiful, long hair. He caresses every inch of her shoulders. His heart is starting to pound again, but he likes it.

"Do you feel bad?" Dania asks quietly as the cab pulls up to the hotel. "About what happened to the . . . ashes?"

"No." Steven looks up at her and smiles. "I think it was perfect."

"You do?"

"Yeah, I think Scotty would have loved it."

15

Dania is humming a song under her breath, and Steven loves the way her body feels pressed against his. His pale white skin contrasts with her tan, toned figure. He smells her hair and her perfume together, filling his nose with a combination of exotic herbs and flowers. He loves the way her skin always feels warm.

It's been several days of this, as well as many spicy meals and excellent nightlife. There has been shopping and parks and walks along the river. Dania has sung to him, and he's lain in bed listening. She has slurped soup, and he has tried not to plug his ears. It's been so nice, in fact, that Steven has almost forgotten why he came to Singapore in the first place. When the thought does enter his head, he reminds himself that Scotty would want him to be happy. That, and he knows he's doing exactly what his brother would be doing under the same circumstances.

It's going to rain. Outside, the sky is getting dark and, even though it's early in the day, the shadows are falling into the room in a way that makes it seem much later than it really is. The clouds are ugly and waiting to pour down upon the busy city. In the distance, the thunder he hears tells Steven that the best place to be is lying in this hotel bed with the pretty woman next to him.

He hears the thunder louder than she does.

He's never commented on her breasts, which—obviously implants—still feel very soft and perfect. Worth every penny, they fill out her form just right. He is stretched out on his back, Dania lying out across him, her left leg crossing over his torso. She runs her strong hands across his chest as she sings quietly in his left ear. This is as intimate as it has gotten, but he could stay here like this for about a decade and not think a thing about it.

He knows that she's only a few years younger than he is, but the difference might as well be at least ten years or more. Her tan skin is very smooth, and there's not a wrinkle to be seen on her face. Even with her having lain here for what seems like days, her hair falls perfectly, as if it had been just washed and dried.

Dania is quietly singing "Christmas Time Is Here," as if giving him an encore. Or finishing the song she didn't get to complete in the bar a few nights ago. Steven watches the darkness fall across the room and lets her warm breath beat against his neck.

"I wish I could bring you home," he says. "Back to Canada. I wish you could see it this time of year."

"Your favorite time of year."

"I bet you would love it."

"I'm not very good with cold weather," she says, and squeezes him tightly as she yawns. "Too many winters in London."

"I don't mind it. You'd think I would. Three-plus decades in Canada and you'd think I'd be more into the weather here. All this heat."

"Maybe you just need to give it more time."

Good luck, he thinks. *My vacation time only goes so far.*

"Maybe one day," he says, "I can come back and spend more time."

"Maybe."

Steven feels her soft kiss on his shoulder, and he smiles. He can't remember the last time he lay in bed like this with Robin, just staring at the walls and listening to the sounds of nothing. Feeling each other's warm bodies and nothing more. With Robin, it seemed as if they'd reached a point where all they were doing was waiting for another chance to have sex. There was never time anymore to just relax and be next to each other.

"I have a coffee shop I always go to," he says after a few minutes of listening to Dania's breathing. "Right near my condo."

"I prefer tea."

"You can get that there, too. It's just a Second Cup."

"A what?"

"Like Starbucks, only Canadian."

"Ah."

"It's just a few blocks down from where I live. On Eglinton Avenue." He rolls over onto his left side and faces her. His eyes looking right into hers. "There's a fake fireplace in the back. An electric one."

"You people and your fireplaces. Right in the middle of the freezing cold. Looking to get as hot as possible."

"You got it. But that's where I sit, in the back of this coffee shop. Every chance I get. Sometimes several times a week."

"And do what?"

"And? And do nothing. I just have coffee and sit by the fake fire. Look outside at the people in the cold."

Dania kisses him and smiles. He can see her picturing him sitting in his coffee shop, drinking his pretentious latte—no whip cream—and watching the busy Torontonians walking on the sidewalk outside.

"There's a window off to the side," he says, "and I sit there, sometimes for a couple of hours, and just listen to the jazz on the radio or on my iPod. It's very relaxing."

"Looking at the snow," she finishes his sentence. "I bet you love the snow."

"When I'm not driving in it, sure."

"I bet it's beautiful this time of year."

"It can be. When it first starts to fall and hasn't turned to ugly, gray mush. And when the cars aren't covered in salt and dirt."

"*Miracle on 34th Street.*"

"You know that movie?"

"Of course! I wasn't raised in a convent."

He kisses the top of her forehead and smells her hair. As much as he loves being in this hotel bed and holding her as they wait for the rain to fall, he wishes he were home right now, with her. He wants to be sitting in the back of that coffee shop, watching the snow outside and listening to the music playing in the background. He could hold her hand and watch her watching the bundled up people on the streets outside.

Dania is humming again, but it's a different song this time. Steven shuts his eyes and listens to her as she runs her hand up and down the length of his body. She caresses the hair on his chest and then moves down to his belly, then back up again.

> *Silent Night, Holy Night*
> *All is calm, all is bright.*

Her voice is so deep and sultry, so sexy. He imagines that, in another life, she was a cabaret singer in an old speakeasy. That maybe she's the reincarnation of an opera singer or an entertainer from France during World War II.

> *Silent night, holy night . . .*

"I love to listen to you sing," he says, even though she's only humming.

"I'm glad someone does."

"Puh-lease. Everyone loves it. I saw the way that crowd cheered when you left the stage."

She rolls her eyes. "They're all drunk. They'd cheer karaoke if that's what they were given."

"You're being modest."

"Maybe. It's what I always wanted to do."

"Singing?"

"As long as I can remember, I wanted to make music. To perform live."

"And now you do. Mission accomplished."

She chuckles. "I guess so, yeah. But I want more than Orchard Towers."

"I would hope so."

"I want to record," she says. "Make an album."

"Yeah?" Steven runs a hand through her hair and across her cheek and down her chest and across her belly. "The next Fergie?"

"Ugh." She rolls her eyes. "Hardly. I'd rather be the next Etta James."

"Even better."

"I'd love to do an album of old jazz standards. Maybe blues. I don't care, as long as I can do it and people will listen."

"Hey, I'd buy it."

She kisses his chest. "Thanks. That's one."

He laughs and feels her mouth on his chest. It gets him a little aroused but, rather than try to start anything, he simply pulls her close to him and squeezes.

It's obvious to him now why Scotty wanted all that money. He was trying to help Dania make her dream come true. It's taken several hours and a lot of piecing the puzzle together, but—in between his intense frolicking with Dania—he's managed to figure out some of the code.

"Mick" obviously means "microphone."

"RE" means "recording," as in "recording equipment" or "recording engineer." Dania has mentioned both several times over the past several hours.

"Studio" wasn't about rent on his little apartment; it was about paying for time in a recording studio.

Steven smiles and laughs to himself. Of all the crazy jobs his brother ever had or tried to do, Steven had never thought record producer would have been one of them. Of course, with the right amount of money, it certainly wasn't impossible.

Steven kisses Dania. He almost wants to tell her that, if she wants it, he'll give her the fifteen grand that Scotty wanted. He doesn't know if she even knows that's what Scotty was doing. But Steven is willing to give the money to her if it will make her happy. If it will make her dreams come true.

If it will get her away from Nez.

"What are you going to do? About Nez?"

Dania sighs and grimaces. "Ugh. Don't remind me."

"As much fun as it was shutting him down like that, I can't imagine it helped your cause with that guy."

"I wouldn't worry about it. Nez isn't going anywhere."

"That's a shame."

"Tell me about it."

"He won't hurt you . . . will he?"

She rolls her eyes. "No, that would be bad for business. He would never be that stupid."

"Why don't you quit? You obviously hate the guy. Surely you can find another manager."

"It's not that simple. I can't leave him right now. Not yet."

"What are you, his indentured servant?" Steven gives her a serious look. He can't imagine why she'd ever even think about going back to work for Nez, especially not after what just happened.

"Feels like it sometimes."

"Whatever he's got on you, I have a feeling it can't be enough to stick with him."

She looks up at him. "He hasn't got anything on me. It's just complicated, is all."

"Apparently."

"I really don't want to talk about it." She frowns. "Trust me, if I could tell him to go to hell, I would. Right now, I can't do that."

"It just feels like something more than a contract between a singer and a manager. I've never seen someone so controlling like that. Forget about everything with my brother—that Nez guy treats you like he owns you."

"Let it go, sweetheart."

Steven leans on his elbow. "I'm serious. He treats you like he's your pimp."

"That's enough," she snaps at him. It's cold and quick. Steven holds his breath for a second and says nothing. Dania glares at him for a few seconds and then lets out a long, slow sigh. She rolls her eyes again and looks up at the ceiling.

"I said it's complicated, and you need to respect that," she says. "You're not from here, and you don't understand how it works. But it's been this way since long before you came here, and that's how it'll be when you leave. I'm a big girl; I've got it handled."

"Is this a Singapore thing I don't understand?"

"Something like that."

"Fair enough." Steven sighs and rolls back over onto his back. He thinks about that money and how he was about to give it to Scotty without even bothering to ask why he needed it. If he was so willing to give it to his brother, he thinks, why not give it to Dania instead? If it gets her to a better place, isn't that what Scotty would have wanted, too? The money's all Steven's now, anyway. What used to belong to both of them is all Steven's at this point, and he doesn't really need it. Not like Scotty did.

You are out of your mind. Scotty's empty cardboard box across the room is speaking to Steven again. There must be a few ashes littered in the bottom somewhere. *You still barely know this woman. When did you get so reckless?*

Reckless is certainly how Steven feels. He also feels insane and in love and upset and happy and full of hormones. It's all a bit overwhelming and certainly nothing he's used to. Scotty had these feelings all the time, no matter whom he was dating. He fell in love easily and enjoyed every single emotional roller coaster every single woman took him on. But Steven has never been caught up in such craziness. Not with Robin, nor any other woman in his life. He wasn't good at being a teenager in love even when he was a teenager.

"I'm sorry," he whispers in Dania's ear as he pulls her close again. She says nothing, but squeezes his hand tightly in hers.

"I never expected this," Dania says.

"What?"

"This," she says, and looks up and down their entangled bodies, both of them topless and pressed against one another. "Being here with you. It's hardly what I thought would happen."

"You and me both."

Dania smiles. "I like it, but it does feel a bit weird."

Steven smiles too. Her accent makes that entire sentence seem so proper. "*You* feel weird? I'm the one who flew across the world and wound up in bed with his brother's girlfriend."

Dania winces. "Please don't call me that again."

"I won't," he says. Looking in her eyes, Steven can tell that she wants to say something. She opens her mouth briefly, but then shuts it again and looks away. Steven kisses her on the neck, but says nothing. She rolls over onto her side, and he spoons himself against her. Several more minutes go by without either of them saying a word.

Outside, it starts to rain.

"Could you ever love me as much as you loved him?" Steven asks, and immediately bites his lip. He knows it's not a fair question, and he knows he should never have asked it, even though he's been thinking it for two days. He also knows he probably doesn't want to know the answer. He also knows he's pushing in a direction she just made it clear she doesn't want to go.

Dania is quiet for a few seconds. She sighs deeply and squeezes his hand in hers. "More," she says.

He's not sure why, but Steven instantly believes her. Perhaps it's that—if they wanted to—they could have so much more time together to find out where things could lead. Her country or his, or somewhere in between, there are places for them to go—together—and try. He has the money, if only she has the willingness and the time. Maybe, unlike Scotty, Dania is ready to stop flying by the seat of her pants.

He kisses her shoulder and pulls her body tightly against his. Three weeks ago, the last place he ever expected to be was right here doing exactly what he's doing now. Three weeks ago, he was thinking of ways to get Robin to stay. Three weeks ago everything was going as it always did, which was according to plan. Three weeks ago, he was all about his routine and liked it just the way it was.

He's never liked surprises before.

"We're very similar," Dania says. This makes Steven laugh so hard that every sexual thought that was going through his brain is now gone. His laughter booms through the room and startles Dania from her comfortable spot next to him.

"What?" she asks, turning to look back at him.

"Similar? You and me?"

"I think so."

"Please. The diva and the fuddy-duddy."

Dania makes a face. "Fuddy-duddy?"

"Yes."

"That's how you see us?"

"Pretty much."

"How do you figure?"

"The exotic sexpot singer and the pissy metrosexual," he says. "How different can you get? How on earth can you think we're similar?"

Dania shrugs and turns back onto her side. Steven curls back up next to her, still admiring how her dark skin looks next to his pasty, white complexion. "Because you hide, like I do."

"I hide?"

"Yeah, and I do, too. I've hidden from who I really am my entire life."

"What do you mean?"

"I'm nothing like my family, my parents. They were strict and serious and always about everything being perfect and in order. All the time."

"Sounds like my kind of people."

"Shush." She swats him playfully. "Not like that. Much worse than you and your picky shit."

"Hey—"

"I mean that they never really understood me." She elbows him in the ribs now. "They never really accepted me. I was never what they wanted."

"What did they want?"

"Someone I wasn't. A banker like my father or the strict housekeeper like my mother. It was never going to be my thing."

"You wanted to be a singer."

"A singer, an independent woman, and whatever else. They wanted reserved and quiet and all the things I wasn't."

"The child of 'tiger parents.'"

"Exactly."

"So, did you choose music to spite them? Or was it always your thing?"

"I never thought of it that way before. But probably a little of both."

Steven thinks about watching Dania on that little stage at Orchard Towers. He can't imagine her doing anything else. Even hosting at the restaurant seems out of place for her. He finds it odd that anyone would want her to be anything else.

"What about now?" he asks. "You're obviously doing well. You sing professionally. You're great at it. Did they ever come around?"

"Thanks, but no. They don't know what I'm doing now. Or how I'm doing now."

"Not at all? You've never even told them?"

Dania shakes her head and looks toward the window. The rain is falling hard. "I haven't spoken with my parents in years."

"Jesus, I had no idea." Steven pushes back a couple of feet and stares at her, but she doesn't turn to face him.

"They want nothing to do with me."

"Because you went into the music business?"

"Because I wasn't what they wanted me to be," she says matter-of-factly. "They never really knew me. Never understood."

The hardest part of losing their parents was that Steven and Scotty were always close with them. When Scotty had been uncertain of his future, long before the accident changed everything, their parents were patient with him. They supported his changing moods and different jobs. When Steven went from restaurant management into his sommelier courses, they were always on board.

Steven realizes that, with Scott and his parents gone, he's more like Dania than he thought. It hasn't sunk in yet just how alone in the world he is now.

He says after a few seconds, "I just want to say that none of this sounds anything like me. I repeat my objection to your implying that we're somehow similar."

Dania laughs quietly and then bites his arm. As he pulls back in mock outrage, she takes his other arm and pulls it around her belly.

"It is you," she says.

"Sounds more like Scott," he counters, and immediately regrets it. He hates bringing up Scotty. Especially when he's in his underwear.

"No, it sounds like you."

"You're out of your mind."

"Scott was always trying to find who he was," she says, still looking out the window. "Always trying to find a man he didn't know yet."

"Sounds about right," Steven says. It makes him think about Scotty at their parents' funeral. How, from that day on, he started changing his career every year. He started traveling more and randomly taking jobs in other countries. How the girlfriends he brought home were always completely different, one after another, and very eccentric and usually foreign. No one was like another.

"But you know who you are," Dania says. "You just let him hide."

"Think you're clever, huh?" He lies back and stares at the ceiling.

"It's true. Just like the story. The Minang Kabau."

"The horns."

"That's you. You always make people think you're the calf. But you're really the bull."

"I like that." He smiles. "The bull wins, right?"

She turns around and smiles and puts her mouth on his. Shifting her weight, she runs her hands back through his hair and softly kisses his neck. After a deep breath, she sits up and looks down at him, staring right into his eyes.

"My little bull," she whispers.

16

"Look at what the rain done washed up into my bar," D.Wash says as he walks into The Blue Bayou and sees Steven sitting there. "Or do my eyes deceive me?"

"Your eyes see just fine." Steven nods and raises his beer bottle in the air. Outside, the rain is pouring down now just as heavily as it has been for the past few hours. They said at the hotel that it's probably going to rain like this—off and on—for most of the day. With Dania working a few hours at her hosting job, it seemed like the perfect time to just get out and sit and have a drink by himself. It's no coffee shop and there's no fireplace, but it's a good substitute considering where he is.

He really should be booking his flight home, but he can't seem to bring himself to do it. He knows he doesn't want to stay here in Singapore. Not like Scotty did. But, at the moment, Steven can't seem to bring himself to rush home. Instead, he keeps talking himself out of leaving. Sitting at The Blue Bayou at least gets him away from his laptop back at the hotel. This way, he can't go buying plane tickets just yet.

It's cooler now, which Steven likes. The rain has slowed the city down, so now it's the only thing he hears in the background. The air is tolerable, and he's surprised at how relaxed everyone seems now for a city that is always moving so fast. The thunder and rain seems to send people into buildings to just sit and wait it out.

The Blue Bayou is busier than Steven thought it would be this time of day. D.Wash's bartender has hardly had time to slow down. People are laughing at the bar, and Steven can tell that they are Australian by listening to their conversation. One of the things he finds so fascinating about this city is that there are people from all over the world in every single place he goes. It's rarely ever locals. There are Europeans and Australians and Americans everywhere. D.Wash is hardly the only immigrant.

"Whatcha drinking?" D.Wash asks. "You ready for some more Australian red?"

"I'm good," Steven says, and holds up his bottle. "Got myself a Tiger."

"Beer?" D.Wash is surprised and pretends to be out of breath. "Mister Wine Expert over here is drinking a beer? And not even a really good beer at that."

"I like it just fine," Steven says, although he wouldn't know if it's good or bad. He hasn't drunk beer in at least five years. He doesn't even know what came over him when he ordered it. Just seemed right at the time.

"Did you get everything sorted out?" D.Wash asks. "You know, with Scott?"

"Everything is taken care of. Thanks for asking."

"Of course. I think I'm going to miss you both."

For a second, Steven thinks he's talking about him and Dania. But she's not going anywhere. Then he feels guilty about not realizing that D.Wash is referring to Scotty. Steven is still having a hard time remembering that Scotty is gone. Part of it still feels very unreal, despite Steven's having just emptied Scotty's remains all over Nez a few nights before.

Dania isn't going anywhere, Steven thinks to himself.

He still considers asking her to come to Toronto. Not for good. She doesn't have to move there permanently or anything like that. He could just ask her to come for a few weeks. Maybe see if she could get a local gig singing at a club there. Or maybe he could put up that money for a recording studio back home and see what happens.

Or maybe you'll just walk on water while you're at it, he thinks. He knows it's crazy.

At this point he wants to spend as much time with her as possible, and he wonders if flying her back to Canada is his best shot of doing just that. After all, Robin is gone. Scotty is gone. Neither he nor Dania has anything to lose. If Dania loses Nez, then all the better.

Then he realizes that the only thing he truly likes about Singapore City is her. He wonders if she'd be happy if the only thing she loved about Canada was him.

In the background, "Silver Bells" is playing on the sound system. Steven is surprised that it doesn't make him feel homesick.

"So, how much longer for you?" D.Wash asks. "You sticking around a bit?"

Steven shrugs. "Not sure. I changed my flight plans once. But I'm going to have to get home pretty soon, I think."

"Ah. Another one."

"Another what?"

"Another Canadian comes over here and won't leave."

Steven laughs and toasts his bottle in the air again. D.Wash raises his hand to the bartender and motions that he wants a beer himself and another one for Steven.

"I'm a bit taken with the scenery," Steven says, looking outside at the pouring rain.

"Such that it is," D.Wash says. It's obvious he thinks that Steven is actually talking about the view. "Did you get answers to your question?"

"Which one?"

"Your brother. The money."

"More or less. It's still a bit of a mystery, but I'm pretty sure I figured it out."

"That's good. Was I right? Was he trying to buy a car?"

"God, no. Scotty did not like cars."

"It's for the best, really. Cars cost a lot of money here. Way more than in the States."

"Or Canada."

"Or Canada," D.Wash says. His beer is delivered, and a second bottle is placed in front of Steven just as he slugs back his last sip from his first one. The two of them clink their bottles together and are quiet for a couple of minutes. They each watch the rain as it continues to pound the pavement outside.

D.Wash breaks the silence. "You doing okay? You know, with everything?"

"Thanks for asking. But I'm okay."

"Just making sure."

"Honestly, I've had a million things on my mind," Steven says. "So I haven't had to think too much about it just yet. I'll have to save some of that for when I get home."

"You gonna bury him there?"

"Already taken care of. I scattered his ashes a few nights ago."

D.Wash's eyes go wide. "Here? In the city?"

"Yeah, at Orchard Towers."

D.Wash spits his beer back into the bottle and almost chokes. "What the—why the hell would you do it there?"

"Seemed appropriate at the time."

"Where?" D.Wash asks, wiping his mouth with the back of his arm.

"All over Nez."

"I have no idea what that means."

"It's a long story."

"Well, shit," D.Wash says with a chuckle. "I guess if that's the way it had to be"—he raises his bottle in toast—"then let's drink to Scott one last time."

"Sounds like a great idea," Steven says, and returns the toast. The two of them smile and down their beers pretty quickly. D.Wash motions for another round. In the background, the Aussies are singing along with the Christmas music coming in over the speakers.

> We wish you a Merry Christmas,
> We wish you a Merry Christmas,
> We wish you a Merry Christmas,
> And a Happy New Year.

"So," D.Wash says as he tries to get one last sip of beer out of his empty glass while waiting for the next one, "you've stuck around for a week since you came to visit for a day. You've scattered your brother's ashes in the Four Floors of Whores, and now you're sitting in the rain and drinking beer."

"Right."

"This can mean only one thing. Despite my warning, you went and got involved with Dania."

Now it's Steven's turn to choke on his beer, which he does. It sprays out of his mouth and onto the table. He laughs and reaches into his pocket for the cotton handkerchief he always keeps with him. After wiping off his face, he cleans up the spray he left on the table.

"How did you know?" he asks.

D.Wash rolls his eyes. "Oh, man. Just like your brother. You think he meant to come here and stay for so long? He never planned on sticking around like he did."

"Really?"

"Really. I should have known the second I saw you today what was up."

"It's been an interesting turn of events, to say the least."

"To say the least. I think you're a good guy, Steven."

"Likewise."

"But you should probably just go on home to Canada as soon as possible."

Steven chuckles and sips his beer. Then he notices that D.Wash isn't smiling. He looks a little sad.

"What is it?"

"Dania."

"I know it's a bit weird and all. My getting involved with her."

"It's not that. That part makes perfect sense to me. I don't judge you, man. I understand. More than you know."

"Then what?"

"Look, man." D.Wash takes a sip of his beer and leans back in his chair. He looks back at the singing Aussies for a few seconds and then leans forward, close to Steven. "She's beautiful and she's exotic and she's all kinds of wild things a white boy from Toronto probably has never seen before. I get that."

"But?"

"But she's trouble."

"Funny. She said that about me. About Scott."

"Scott wasn't perfect, but he didn't come with baggage like Dania does. You dig?"

Steven cringes. If only D.Wash knew about the baggage that Scotty had been carrying around the past decade. People met him and thought that he had been a free spirit his entire life. But that side of him went into overdrive after the accident. Scotty had moved around as much as he did because staying in one place too long made him have to think about the rest of his life. He was no good at that, so he kept moving.

"Like I said, I don't judge you. I don't care about her history with your brother. There's definitely an allure to being with her. Something exciting."

"What do you mean?"

"It's cool," D.Wash says. "Just be careful, is all. I'm just looking out for you. I like Dania. Everyone does. But she's got a lot of shit she's dealing with, for obvious reasons."

"Well, yeah," Steven says, "she's got that asshole manager, for one thing."

"You've met him."

"Yeah, that's 'Nez.' That's where Scotty is."

"What?"

"Her manager. We kind of got into it the other night. I poured Scotty's remains all over him. Down his throat."

"What the hell?" D.Wash says loudly enough that the Aussies at the bar stop singing. "Why would you go and be crazy like that, boy?"

Steven laughs. "It seemed like the thing to do at the time."

"How do you figure?"

"He said the wrong thing at the wrong time."

"And so you—"

"—Shoved Scott's remains down his throat, yeah."

"And the big guy he's always got with him?"

"The bigger they are . . ."

"God DAMN," D.Wash says. "You are a crazy son of a bitch. You're lucky to be alive after pulling shit like that."

"That's what Dania said."

"She knows what she's talking about," D.Wash says. "She belongs to him."

Steven takes a sip of his beer and grimaces. "That's pretty much what she said. What the hell does that mean?"

"She didn't tell you?"

"Tell me what?"

"She's owes him a lot of money, man," D.Wash says. "He's not just her manager. He's practically her pimp."

"She doesn't like that—"

"I'm sure she doesn't. And I know she just sings. But that manager guy—"

"Nez."

"—Nez tells her what to do, and she does it. She doesn't have a choice. I get what you did and why you did it. But that shit didn't change anything, man. She still owes him. It's real loan shark shit, you dig? Guy might as well be mafia here."

Steven takes a sip of his beer and looks down at his fingernails. He could use a good manicure. "Fifteen grand? You think that's about what Dania owes him?"

D.Wash shakes his head. "Way more."

"Jesus."

"You got that right. Look, man, enjoy what you had and call it a crazy time in your life. But walk away from it. Okay?"

Steven feels that the empty cardboard box back at the hotel is laughing at him. He should have known that, sooner or later, trying to pretend he could be like Scotty was going to backfire. He should have known it was a bad idea. For the first time in his life, he acted on impulse, and all because of a woman. And, just like he feared, none of it seems to have been a good idea.

"I think Scotty was trying to be her manager," he says. "I think he was investing money in her singing."

"Maybe. But that Nez guy ain't about to take a payoff, if that's what you're thinking. He doesn't just want her money. He's obviously into her. He likes controlling her. He likes owning her."

"All because she wants to make music. That's why she's in debt."

"Nah, man. She's paying off doctor bills and medical stuff. Nez took care of that, and now she sings for him. That was the deal. That's how he likes it. That was always the arrangement. And it'll be that way for years, if he has anything to say about it."

"Doctor bills?" Steven asks. "You mean the breast implants?"

"Yeah, sure. All of it. We don't need to go into details. It's cool. Look man, she's a beautiful woman, right? But that cost money. That took a long time. She's a singer now, but she used to be just another dancer at The Crazy Horse."

Steven searches his brain and finally remembers where he's heard that name. It's the bar he went to with Dania their first night together. When he was drunk and first saw her sing. She took him to the bar with all of the gorgeous dancers. It's where the bartender recognized her.

"I've been there," Steven says. "With all the dancers and the horny men."

"If you want to call them that," D.Wash says.

"Horny men?"

"Dancers."

"Yeah. Everyone is for sale there, right?"

"You got it. And all of those dancers want to be just like Dania. They're just waiting for the right guy to come along and front the money. And it costs a shitload of money to look like she does, my friend. You'll notice none of the dancers there look as good as she does."

Steven feels uneasy all of a sudden and is now wishing he'd just stayed at the hotel. He notices that the Australians have left, and the bar now seems oddly quiet. The Christmas music continues to play, but no one is singing along.

"I have no idea what the hell you're talking about." Steven grimaces. "You telling me that Dania used to be a hooker? Like the girls at The Crazy Horse?"

"The girls at the . . ." D.Wash looks at him seriously and shakes his head. He wipes his bald head with his left hand while sipping his beer with the right. "Damn," he says. "I mean, god-damn."

"What is it?" Steven asks.

D.Wash puts his beer down and scratches his head one more time. "Part of me wants to know if you're messing with me. You really don't know?"

"I'm not messing with you," Steven says. "I have no idea what the hell is going on. Dania used to be a prostitute?"

"A man," D.Wash says, and looks Steven dead in the eyes. "Dania used to be a man."

17

Steven's hair is hanging in his face. The rain is pouring down on him, causing his bangs to slide down his forehead and into his eyes. He doesn't care. He just stands there on the sidewalk, in front of The Blue Bayou, letting it pour down on him.

A few minutes ago, he jumped up from his seat, stormed out of the bar, made his way to the street, and just . . .

Just stood there.

He realizes now that he has nowhere to go. He doesn't even know why he left the bar. It just seemed like he needed to get up and get away. Like he wasn't supposed to be there. He was supposed to be angry and outraged and offended and had to run. He had to get away from what he had just heard. Something in him felt that he had to escape.

Now he has and realizes that he probably belongs right back in that bar, sitting at that table, listening to D.Wash tell him everything. He needs to hear it.

He needs to hear the truth.

A man in an expensive suit with an enormous umbrella trudges past him on the sidewalk. He looks over at Steven and gives him a look that says "Are you crazy or drunk? Get the hell out of the rain, moron."

Steven wishes he were drunk. He thinks that might be the exact place he should start now that he's found out what he has. The shame is that he doesn't have Scotty's ashes to drink with him. He only has an empty cardboard box sitting back at the hotel.

It can't be true, he thinks, and remembers the look on D.Wash's face when he told him. But he knows that it is true. D.Wash wouldn't make up something like that, would he? That would be a cruel trick to play on a guy, especially with all that's gone on in the past few days.

It is true. Steven pushes his soaking wet hair out of his eyes and, still standing in the rain, tries to stand up straight. Tries to stand with a little dignity, even while he just lets the rain pour all over him.

It starts to all add up and make sense. How secretive Dania always was about parts of her life. How she managed to never really answer any questions. How she always seemed to just get more mysterious, even when he thought he was learning about her. She was giving him clues and hints all along, and he never saw it. She was giving him answers without his even knowing.

Her hands, he thinks to himself, and feels a lump forming in his throat. *They're so strong. I never really stopped and looked at her hands.*

He thinks back to the beginning and remembers The Crazy Horse. How the bartender gave her a knowing glance and how the dancers seemed to look her way. It was as if they knew her and envied her. He remembers the way she seemed to pity them and admire them at the same time.

"It takes a lot to look like that," she said about the dancers. "Most men couldn't handle them."

She called me naïve, he remembers. *When I said the dancers were beautiful, she called me naïve and sweet.*

They were all men. Each of those dancers, in their skimpy clothes with their sexy, long hair. Each one had perfect makeup and a toned, athletic body. They were all men—all of them beautiful—wishing they could be just like Dania. Wishing they could be women.

And Dania is a woman. She has all the right parts. Her plumbing is just what it should be. Every inch of her body that he's caressed or touched or kissed felt exactly as he expected it would, and everything about them being with each other felt right. There was nothing about it that seemed anything but perfect.

Why didn't he notice?

"You need to get back in here," a familiar voice calls from the other side of the rain. D.Wash is standing on the patio of The Blue Bayou. "Just stop standing there like that and get back in here. You hear?"

Steven says nothing. He turns and looks back at D.Wash, standing with his hands over his eyes, shielding his glasses from the rain. D.Wash shakes his head, but he's not scolding. He looks worried.

"C'mon, now," D.Wash says. "It'll be okay. Just come back inside, and we'll figure all this out, alright?"

Steven pushes his falling hair out of his face again. Like a wet mop, he feels it slap against the top of his head as some raindrops roll down his forehead. His sports jacket is soaked. He can feel the insides of his wingtips starting to get wet. He slowly straightens his back again and walks back into the bar.

Everyone is quiet, and even the Christmas music seems to have been turned down a bit. At the bar, the sexy bartender is pretending not to look at Steven as D.Wash walks over and pats him on the back and hands him a towel. People sitting at the bar stare down into their Tiger beer bottles. Steven looks at his shoes as he takes the towel and puts it over his head.

"Sit down, buddy," D.Wash says, and escorts Steven back to the table they were already sitting at. Two fresh beers await them, but, alongside them, are two shot glasses full of whiskey. Steven doesn't say a word, but quickly grabs the nearest shot glass and pours the liquid down his throat. Then he chases it with the beer, which is exactly what he needs. This doesn't seem like a red wine moment.

"Alright," D.Wash says, and downs his own whiskey. "Let's just calm down and figure this out, okay?"

"Figure what out?" Steven says, his throat burning from the booze. "An hour ago, I thought I was falling in love with a beautiful Asian singer I wanted to bring back to Canada. Now I hear that I fell for a transgendered woman who's an indentured servant to a Singaporean hustler."

"Sounds about right." D.Wash awkwardly tries to smile.

"Merry Christmas," Steven says, and tips back his beer. He finishes the bottle in one, long gulp. Then, like he's been there all his life, he tosses two fingers in the air toward the bar, just like he's seen D.Wash do before.

"It's going to be alright," D.Wash assures him. "You really shouldn't beat yourself up over this."

"Really? How do you figure?"

"Oh, man, you're not the first one to fall for her. I told you that, remember?"

"Yeah."

"I just thought you knew."

"Why didn't you tell me?" Steven asks. "Back when we met?"

"Truthfully, buddy, it wasn't any of your business then." D.Wash wipes some rain off his bald head with his palm and then wipes his hand on his pants. "You were just here to get your brother and leave. It wasn't my place to tell you Scotty's business or anything about his girl. How would I have even brought it up, right?"

"Fair enough," Steven says, and looks for his next shot of whiskey. "Did Scott know?"

"Everyone knows," D.Wash says.

"And Scott didn't care?"

D.Wash purses his lips together and sips his beer. He grimaces and looks around, as if he's not really comfortable talking about this. He leans in a little closer and looks Steven in the eye. "Scott didn't care," he says. Then, he sits back in his seat for a second before leaning in toward Steven again. "And neither should you. Not about that."

Steven just looks at D.Wash with his eyebrows furrowed and his mouth slightly open. D.Wash sighs and finishes off his beer.

"Look, man," D.Wash says, "some guys find that kind of thing exciting. You dig? Some guys love something so different like that. Being with a woman who's . . . new. You understand?"

Steven nods.

"Those guys are awful. They're users. People seeking a thrill or thinking they're being wild. It's a fetish or something. Scott wasn't one of those guys," D.Wash says matter-of-factly, and sits back in his chair. The bartender walks over with two more shots and two more beers. D.Wash finishes his before Steven gets his hands on his own. "And I don't think you are, either."

Some of this surprises Steven, mostly because he saw his brother as being somewhat superficial. Scotty never had a single woman like the last one he was with. He always sought out girls who were different, somehow exotic. He loved women with accents or something unique about them. He sought out women who barely spoke English or had some fascinating background story he could get behind. He once dated a girl with an artificial leg simply because he found it interesting that she walked with a cane. He dated a deaf woman for a few months because he loved the way she communicated without speaking. Anyone who knew Scotty all of his life would have reason to think that Dania was another unique girlfriend in a long list of unique girlfriends.

Or was she truly unique? Steven thinks.

Scotty's track record with women was long, but his time with each one tended to be brief. Not even "The Fiancées" lasted very long. Scotty got bored and moved on pretty quickly, even when it came to the women he professed to have loved with all of his heart. Dania had outlasted them, and he'd been willing to pour money into her and risk his life for her and live his life in this sauna for her. He knew everything about her, from her past to her life dealing with Nez . . . and Scotty stayed.

Yet this secret was obviously the last thing Dania wanted Steven to know.

"I just feel so stupid," he says at last. "I can't believe I didn't know."

"Didn't you notice anything different? I mean, she's a beauty, man. I admit it. But it's not the same, you know. I mean, it's different. Didn't you . . . notice?"

"I don't know," Steven says. "Maybe. I guess something seemed different. I just didn't think about it. I mean, we haven't . . ."

"Haven't what?"

"You know."

"Not at all?"

Steven shakes his head. "Not yet."

D.Wash raises his eyebrows. "Damn, you really do love this woman, huh?"

Steven doesn't say anything. He just shrugs his shoulders and takes a sip of his drink.

D.Wash nods slowly. "But you had to know something wasn't the same, right?"

Steven feels more embarrassed now than he has since he heard the news. What should he have been looking out for the entire time? Her body was flawless, toned, and tan. Her hair was so beautiful. Her voice sultry and sexy. Her breasts were fake, but he didn't stop to inspect everything else.

"I wasn't really thinking about it," he says, feeling his face getting red. "I mean, how often is that something you even think about?"

"Happens here more than you think."

"Yeah?"

"Yeah, there's a lot of that going on here, you know."

"I do now."

"That bar? The Crazy Horse? That's why some people go there. That's kinda the point."

"I never asked. She called me naïve."

D.Wash smiles softly and puts a hand on Steven's shoulder. "Not naïve, buddy. Just new here."

"Yeah."

"Her family, her parents. She said they rejected her. That she hasn't spoken with them in years. I thought it was because she was a singer."

"That, too, but she came back here because she could get by, you know? She could fit in a little better. It's not an uncommon procedure here like it is in other places."

"Like London?"

"Like London."

Steven realizes now that Dania's family didn't reject her because she wanted to sing or because her strict parents couldn't stand the thought of her being an independent woman. In reality, they just couldn't stand her being a woman at all.

"Don't beat yourself up, man," D.Wash says. "She's not a man, right? Not anymore. She's a woman. You fell for a woman, like any other woman. Just know that."

"I do know it."

"Really."

Steven takes a good minute to think before he speaks again. There are so many different emotions going through him at this moment, and he's not sure which ones are genuine and which ones are just coming at him because he has been caught off guard. Every minute he has spent with Dania is in the back of his mind now and—like watching a montage of scenes in a movie—he sees each one just as vividly as when he was experiencing them. He's been with this woman for almost twenty-four hours per day for several days, by her side most days and every night. And yet, at this moment, he can't decide what makes him angry or sad or just confused. Worst of all, he can't decide how much of a right he has to feel any—or all—of those things.

Steven takes a long pull on his beer and looks out at the street. The rain is letting up a bit. He runs the towel through his hair and attempts to dry off a little bit. Then he tosses the towel on the table next to his beer and shakes his head.

"I don't care," he says finally.

"What?" D.Wash asks.

"About her past. About any of that. I know that that's the thing a lot of guys would be upset about."

"Maybe most."

"Whatever. Any man in my place would've fallen for her, as far as I'm concerned."

"But . . . ?"

"But everything has been one lie after another. Do you understand that?"

D.Wash nods slowly. "I guess so."

"You said that everybody knew, right?" Steven points a finger at D.Wash.

"Right."

"But she made sure I didn't know. Not about her past. Not about Nez. Nothing." Steven takes a sip of his beer. "Not even about what happened to Scott."

D.Wash lets out a long, hard sigh and rubs his hands over his eyes. The look on his face seems to say "I told you so," but Steven knows he's too smart to actually say anything of the sort. Instead, D.Wash crosses his arms and leans forward on the table.

"My man," he says, "you were just some guy we knew about from Scott's stories of back home. You lost your brother, and we all lost a friend. It's been a crazy couple of weeks, and I don't know if any of us handled any of it the right way at all. And I include Scott in that, you know."

"Why didn't I see it?" Steven asks.

"Because you didn't want to," D.Wash says.

"This is why she's in so much debt."

D.Wash nods. "A lot of money, man. It takes a lot of money to look that good. That perfect."

The two of them sit in silence for a few minutes and listen to the rain as it trickles to a stop. Steven looks at his watch. Dania will be getting off work soon. He's supposed to meet her. He said he'd walk down to the Riverwalk and that they could go to dinner together before she went to her gig at The Cocktail Room. Now he thinks about just disappearing. He wonders if he can go straight to the hotel, then off to the airport. He thinks about leaving and never speaking to her again. He thinks about just getting up and leaving Singapore behind. The twenty-plus-hour flight home will give him plenty of time to wallow in this. Plenty of time to get over her.

But part of him really wants to stay. He wants to hear her tell him the truth. He wants her to tell him everything.

He wants to tell her he's in love with her. And he hates the fact that he's sure he is.

The pretty bartender walks over and puts two more beers on

the table. Before walking away, she gently runs a hand down the back of D.Wash's head. He looks up and smiles at her as she blows him a quick kiss. Steven watches her as she walks back toward the bar and can't help but wonder how many things his brother and D.Wash had in common.

"I told you not to get involved with her," D.Wash says. Steven nods at him, and the two of them sit a while longer without saying anything.

18

Steven holds the umbrella over his head, even though it's barely raining now. He's still soaking wet from just a couple hours earlier, but he stands as if the tiny amount of rain still falling will make it worse. He keeps pushing his hair back over his head with his left hand while holding the umbrella with his right. Off in the distance, he watches people walking toward him and tries to spot Dania.

He's waiting right where he said he'd be. Right in front of where people usually bungee jump and squeal as they plummet to the earth. No one is jumping today, and the entire ride looks abandoned, as if it has been years since it was last open. The outdoor cafés along the Riverwalk are empty, and all of the restaurants and bars have pulled their sandwich boards inside. A few random people are walking in the rain, but the area mostly looks abandoned.

Behind him, cars zip past, splashing water up onto the sidewalks. It's surprisingly quiet here, despite the fact that there are still tons of people hiding inside, waiting for the rain to completely stop.

After what feels like an hour of standing there—but is only about ten minutes or so—Steven notices a familiar figure walking up from the distance. He sees Dania in her tight black skirt and form-fitting white blouse. She's holding a tiny umbrella over her head and adjusting the small purse around her shoulder.

She looks beautiful.

As she gets closer, she looks up and notices Steven standing there. She stops for a second and tilts her head to one side, as if she's making certain that it's really him she sees. When she's certain that it's actually him, she smiles and waves her right hand in the air. He can see every one of her teeth and her bright red lips as she gives him the same sultry smile she's given him several times before.

He doesn't smile back.

Steven stands there, motionless, holding the umbrella over his head. The blank look on his face can be seen from across the city. He makes eye contact with Dania, and she keeps her waving hand in the air. She continues to smile but, when he doesn't return it, she slowly lowers her hand to her side and tilts her head to her left. Her long hair falls over one shoulder and behind her back. It's still perfect, despite getting a little wet from the light rain that is still falling.

She can tell that he knows.

Her smile fades quickly and, even from this distance, Steven can see the creases form on her forehead. From a good twenty feet away, Steven can already see her mood completely changing. She raises her hand and covers her mouth and then looks over her shoulder to see if anyone is watching. Then she bobs her head slightly and covers her face. Steven stands there for a moment and watches her.

After what feels like more than the thirty seconds it probably is, he slowly walks over to where she is standing. She has her head down, and he can see her shoulders shaking a bit as his umbrella touches hers. This close to her, he can almost hear her breathing as she looks down at his feet. When she finally looks up at him, Steven is surprised at how pretty she still looks, despite the fact that she looks as if she may cry.

"I'm sorry," she says to him. Steven realizes she's apologizing for being upset and not for lying to him. He reaches over and touches her cheek. It surprises them both how gentle he is when he does it. He has been thinking for a while now what he would say, but, seeing her like this, he realizes nothing he prepared is going to come out. Instead, he just touches her cheek and lets their umbrellas bump into each other a few times.

"Why didn't you tell me?" he asks quietly, feeling his throat close up as he speaks.

"Do you really have to ask that?" she says. She seems almost angry. As if he has just slapped her across the face.

Steven stands there for a few seconds without saying anything. He looks around as if there are people watching them, even though they are the only two people standing out in the rain, next to the river. Two people loitering next to the bungee jump.

"The boy in the photo," he says finally. "It's you."

Dania doesn't nod, but her look tells Steven that he's right.

"You took it from my hotel room," he says, realizing he left an extra key card on the nightstand.

She nods. "It doesn't belong to you. It's mine."

"Did you give it to Scott?"

"No."

"How did he get it? From Nez? Did Nez give it to him?"

"Are you crazy?" She seems offended. "Nez doesn't want people to know."

"People do know."

"But it's not like anyone announces it. Jesus, you think that would help me? That it would help Nez?"

"No, I guess not."

"How did you find out?"

"Doesn't matter. How did Scotty get the photo?"

"He found my parents. He knew that we don't talk anymore. He wanted to visit them."

"In London?" Steven asks.

"Yes. He didn't tell me he was going to do it. I had no idea."

That's what the money was for, Steven thinks. *Music and a trip to London for two. Something to help the two of them start a new life together.*

"He wanted to take you to see them?" he asks. "To meet them?"

"He wanted to marry me. He wanted to tell them and get

their blessing. It was just some crazy idea he had. He thought he was helping."

"What did they say?"

Dania sighs and adjusts her umbrella. A single tear falls from her left eye as she looks up and, for the first time, into Steven's eyes. "They sent him the photo," she says. "They said they didn't have a daughter. They only had a son. And that he was dead."

Steven feels a sting in his own eyes and realizes he hasn't felt like this since he looked at Scotty's dead body at the morgue. Something about this doesn't feel like he expected it to when he thought about it an hour ago. He thought he would be angry with Dania and that he would scream at her. Now, seeing her crying, listening to her and realizing what it all means, he only feels pity.

And she really does look beautiful.

"Is that when you told him?" he asks.

"I don't tell anyone. It's not their business."

"But he knew."

"He knew almost from the start."

"You didn't think you should tell me?"

She looks up at him angrily. "Did you tell me everything about your past?"

"That's not fair."

"Only because you're ashamed of yourself for being with me now."

"No, I'm not."

"Would you still be saying that if we'd had sex?"

"Is that why you didn't?"

"I wouldn't sleep with anyone without telling him everything first."

"Is that why you told Scotty?"

"You know, you can be a real jerk sometimes," she scoffs harshly, and gives him a look that might as well be icicles shooting out of her eyes. Steven notices her hand clench around the umbrella. He wonders for a second if this is a conversation she's had before with other men.

"I might not have had sex with you," she says through

clenched teeth, "but don't pretend for one second that I haven't loved you."

"It's different," he says.

"No. You just think *I'm* different. If I had never told you, you never would have known or cared about my past. You would have just gone home to Canada and never spoken to me again, and we'd both just have the memory of this time together as being wonderful."

"It's not like that."

"It's just like that," she says. "This has been amazing, Steven. But where was it really going? Surely you've thought the exact same thing, that this was a beautiful thing but only temporary?"

"I don't know."

"Don't you?"

He stands there and looks over her shoulder. None of this is going as he planned, and he can't seem to get the words to come out right. He's not sure how it happened, but he feels as if he's on trial and can't quite figure out what crime he committed. The smell of her perfume is in his nostrils and part of him wants to bury his head in her hair right there in the middle of this sidewalk.

"I haven't figured it all out yet," he says quietly, "but I was hoping there was something, yeah. Some kind of future."

"You really are sweet," she says. "But you really are naïve."

"And had I never asked, you would have just kept me in the dark?"

"Maybe," she says, and looks down at her feet, "but everyone who does know only winds up being miserable."

"Including Scotty?"

"Stop."

"You should have told me," he says.

"Why?" She looks up at him. "Then this would have only happened sooner. At least I got time with you. This brief and wonderful and terrible, mixed-up thing we have may be twisted and unusual, but at least it's something. If I'd told you everything, you'd already be back home in Canada."

Steven looks at her for a full minute before he speaks again. "That's not true," he says. "I don't care about your past."

"Please—"

"I care about the fact you lied to me."

"It wasn't a lie."

"Not about that. About everything else. About Nez and Scotty and all of it."

She looks over her shoulder and away from him, anything to keep from looking into his eyes. There are no tears there, but she's obviously holding back a million thoughts and emotions as hard as she can. Steven wonders if, like him, she's one second away from running away and one second away from embracing him at the same time.

"I never thought any of this would happen," she says.

"That I would find out about all of it? Everything?"

"That you would even be here."

"You thought I'd leave."

She shakes her head. "I never thought I'd fall in love with you."

Steven knows this is where he would normally tell her he loves her, too. This is where he would tell her that all is forgiven and they'd throw their arms around each other and live happily ever after. The sun would come out and they'd bungee jump together and—holding hands the entire way down—plummet happily to earth. Instead, he says nothing at all.

"And now you're ashamed," she says. "What do you think? That you fell in love with a man? Does that scare you, Steven?"

"Stop saying that. I don't care about that."

"Of course you do."

Dania looks at him and tears well up in her eyes again. Steven isn't sure if he wants to hold her or push her away. Part of him wants to touch her face and feel her warm tears on his fingers as he tells her everything is okay. Then he can tell her he can forgive her and that she's still the same woman he fell for, and then he can prove to her that her past doesn't matter to him.

And then he walks away.

"Where are you going?" Dania says to him as he turns and

walks away from the river, toward the busy street up ahead. Steven says nothing, but simply keeps walking.

"Steven!" she calls to him, but he pretends he's not listening. If he does listen, if he stops even for a second and lets anything she's said seep in, he may find himself admitting that she's been right all along. Her voice gets louder, deeper, which almost makes him cringe. He doesn't look back. He just keeps walking away. He realizes again he's not good at being a teenager in love, especially in his thirties.

"Steven, wait!" she calls out again, and he can hear her starting to cry. It's harder this time, and Steven can hear her doubling over as she does it. He hears her umbrella hit the ground as she lurches over or walks forward. He can't tell which one.

"STEVEN!" she screams this time. To Steven it sounds like she has just been shot. It sends a cold snap like an ice pick into his spine, and he wheels around to see if she is okay. It's the most terrified she has ever sounded, and the scream almost scares him out of his wet shoes.

It was a warning.

Steven turns around just in time to see Nez pull back a fist and send it squarely into his face. Where the little bastard came from, Steven can't say, but the fist to the jaw sends him back a few steps and causes him to drop his umbrella. Raindrops pelt his face at the same time the stinging pain of Nez's punch kicks in. Steven shakes his head and pushes his hair out of his eyes just in time to look up. It's at that moment that another punch connects with his left cheek.

In the background, Dania is screaming, but Steven doesn't really hear her. He is too busy trying to catch his balance and stop the ringing that suddenly fills his ears. He thinks he sees his open umbrella on the ground next to him and, for a split second, thinks about grabbing it to use as a shield. Before he can do anything, he feels his arms being pulled tightly backward, behind his back. They feel as if they are about to be broken.

Nez's bodyguard is behind Steven, yanking his arms back as tightly as possible. Steven can barely keep his balance as he realizes that he's being propped up for another round of punches.

They come quickly and harder than expected. Nez isn't a big man, but he knows how to throw a punch when the target is standing still. Through blurred vision, Steven can see the brass knuckles wrapped around Nez's fist. Each time they connect with his face, Steven feels as if he is being hit by lightning.

"Now you get it," Nez says, grabbing Steven by the jaw and spitting in his face. "Not so funny now."

The next blow sends blood pouring out of Steven's nose, and tears begin welling up in his eyes. Steven sees a bright flash of white before he shakes off the pain and catches a glimpse of Nez pulling back his fist for another go-round. This time, Nez gives him a good one square in the chest. The sound of the impact tells Steven it hurt them both. He gasps for air as Nez massages his fist and moves the brass knuckles to the other hand. The bodyguard is laughing and still holding Steven back. Steven feels his legs growing weaker even as he hears Dania yelling at Nez to stop.

There is another punch. Then another. First comes one to the stomach and then another to the kidneys. Each one feels harder than the last.

Steven uses what is left of his strength to try and pull free from Nez's bodyguard. But he can barely stand and feels as if his arms are about to snap. Another punch from Nez almost knocks him out, but he manages to shake it off long enough to see Nez smiling at him. His grin looks evil. Nez is laughing loudly, and the bodyguard laughs with him. Nez pulls back his fist for one more blow. Steven is clear-headed enough to know that this one will finish him off.

Nez looks shocked, and his eyes go wide. With his hand cocked back, ready to give Steven one last blow to the jaw, something comes down hard upon the top of his head. It hits Nez so hard, he almost falls to the ground. He spins around to see Dania hitting him over the head with the handle of her umbrella. When Nez turns to look at her, she takes the opportunity and swings the umbrella like a baseball bat, making direct contact with his face. He stumbles back a few feet from the blow.

Steven almost smiles, but feels his broken lip bleeding into his mouth. The bodyguard loosens his grip a little bit, but not enough for Steven to escape. They're both caught up in watching Dania deliver a nice ass-kicking to Nez.

Dania yells something in Mandarin to Nez, who yells something in Mandarin right back at her. The two of them point and yell at each other for a few seconds before Nez pulls back and full-on punches Dania in the face. Her head snaps back from the blow, and her beautiful hair whips around, now soaking wet and sticking to her face. She opens her mouth to scream, but nothing comes out. She looks at Nez, who pulls back to hit her again.

"You sonofabitch," Steven slurs through his swollen jaw. He feels the bodyguard loosen his grip even more and then finally drop him to the sidewalk. Steven feels his legs give out underneath him as the cold, wet concrete meets his body. Out of the corner of his eye, he sees Dania wheel around and push Nez back at least three feet.

Steven tries to get to his feet, but is pushed back down by the bodyguard, who is watching Dania and Nez hit each other and doesn't know what to do. The bodyguard doesn't move, but holds Steven back. Steven reaches up with his hands, trying to make contact, but the bodyguard holds him off and keeps him at arms' length.

"You do what I say!" Nez screams at Dania in English for the first time. Dania is massaging her face where she was hit while obviously trying to catch her breath at the same time. Steven thinks that, for the first time, she really looks angry. More than he's seen her look before, even moments ago when he thought she couldn't look meaner. He feels his head spinning and thinks he's going to pass out. He tries to stand up, but can't make it.

Then, Nez rushes toward Dania. He laughs at her when she steps back from him, obviously afraid of getting hit again. He dances around her and laughs and points. On cue, the bodyguard starts laughing, too. Steven feels his head getting heavier.

"You not so tough," Nez says to Dania. "You make a good little girl."

Nez laughs and moves to kick Dania. He brings his expensive

right loafer into the air and aims for her midsection. Dania moves back a couple of feet, and Nez lifts his foot higher. So high, in fact, that he topples backward. The pavement is slick from the rain, causing him to fall right on his ass. Dania uses the opportunity to try and get away. Seeing this, Nez's bodyguard jumps into action.

It's just the distraction Steven needs.

Feeling as if he may pass out at any moment, Steven uses every ounce of strength he has to get to his feet. As he does, the adrenaline kicks in, and his head suddenly clears enough for him to see Dania is backing away from the bodyguard, swinging her umbrella each time he tries to lunge at her. He pulls a fist back, about to clock her any second. But it's not the bodyguard who is in charge, and Steven knows it.

Before Nez can get all the way up off the pavement, Steven's hands are wrapped around his neck and squeezing the life out of him. The look in Nez's eyes shows that he didn't see this coming at all and that he knows Steven isn't going to let go this time. He claws at Steven's arms, his own hands flailing desperately, trying to break free.

"Steven!" Dania screams again, and Steven wheels around before Nez's bodyguard can make contact. As hard as he can, Steven throws Nez away from him and right into his own henchman. The bodyguard tries to help Nez regain his composure but—gasping for air—Nez pushes him off. He lunges at Steven, who cocks his fist back and lets it connect in the middle of Nez's forehead.

Nez falls backward, his feet slick from the rain that has soaked the sidewalk. Steven watches him, almost in slow motion, as he hangs in the air for a second, one foot higher than the other. He almost looks like one of the tourists on the bungee jump. When Nez hits the ground, his head is the first part of his body that makes contact.

The sound is sickening. Nez's body lands after his head and falls limply against the cold, wet concrete with an awful and heavy-sounding thud. His body twitches for only a second and then just lies there. The bodyguard stands silent and stares at his boss lying on the ground.

Steven shakes his head and feels his knees starting to tremble. Out the corner of his eye, he sees Dania standing motionless, her mouth wide open. He hears the bodyguard speaking, but doesn't know what language he's using. Steven shakes his head again and tries to put his weight on the noodles he calls legs.

Even in this state, he can tell that Nez is already dead.

The bodyguard bends down and touches Nez's body. There is blood on the sidewalk, swirling around in the rain that is already getting heavier. The bodyguard touches Nez on the face and tries to get him to wake up. Then he shakes Nez by the lapels of his expensive suit. Looking back at Steven, the bodyguard turns completely white, and his mouth drops open. He looks back at Dania, back at Nez, and then stands straight up. Looking around to see if anyone is watching, he slowly walks away. After the bodyguard is halfway down the Riverwalk, he starts running.

Steven collapses and feels the same wet pavement that just ended Nez. Blood fills his mouth, and he tries to spit it out as his face connects with the ground. The front of his pants feels cold as the wet sidewalk soaks into them. The last thing he hears before everything goes black is the sound of Dania's voice.

"Steven," she cries. "Steven, do you hear me? Steven?"

He looks up and she is standing over him, a look of complete shock on her face. That's the last thing he sees as everything goes quiet and dark.

19

Steven feels like he is floating. Falling. There's a soft feeling that embraces him and makes him feel warm. A tingling runs up the length of his right arm and, even though there is a slight pain, he barely notices it. He mostly feels numb. He simply continues floating and falling.

There is darkness and talking, a voice in the distance. It's too muffled to understand. Then it's louder and clearer. A second later a very bright light appears out of nowhere, shining right into his eyes. It hurts. He squints and feels his eyes rolling back. There is a deep pain in his eye sockets—pain from the light and all around his eye. The light stings when he looks toward it, but his eye hurts more when he tries to look away.

And then there's the voice again. It's speaking to him now. Clearly now, it says, "There we are. Looks like you're in there after all."

The light goes away. Then it returns. There is a clicking sound, and then the light and the pain, followed by the voice.

"Here we go," the voice says. "Don't worry, it's a bright light. But it's not *the* bright light. You don't have to be afraid of walking toward it."

The voice laughs, and the light goes away. The pain is okay, and suddenly the light is dimmer. Everything is clearer. His eyes are opening now. Everything is coming into focus. His eyes hurt, but he is no longer squinting.

Steven sees a tall, Singaporean man in a white doctor's coat looking at him. Putting away the penlight he was just shining into Steven's eyes, the man smiles warmly. He's balding, probably in his late fifties, and he is holding a medical chart in one hand. He clasps his hands together, holding the chart in front of him. He smiles again as he cocks his head slightly to the side.

"There you are," the doctor says. "You're back with us now."

"I—" Steven feels a pounding in his head, but most of his body just feels warm and numb.

"Don't try to sit up." The doctor holds out a cautious hand. "Just stay right where you are, okay?"

Steven would nod if he could move his head. Instead, he hopes his painful eyes convey that he understands. The doctor is standing over him in a very small, but very clean hospital room. The warm numbness that covers Steven's body no doubt comes from the IV that Steven sees attached to his right arm. Still, even with whatever is in that IV, Steven knows that parts of him are aching very badly right about now, even if he can't quite feel those parts.

"Where—"

"You're in the hospital, son," the doctor says. His English is perfect. He sounds vaguely British, like Dania. "You've taken quite the beating. But here you are, still with us."

"Singapore," Steven says.

"Yes," the doctor says. "Good. You know where you are. Now can you tell me *who* you are?"

"S—Steven. Kelly. Steven Kelly."

"Very good," the doctor says, and pulls out the penlight again. He looks at Steven's eyes again and then returns the pen to his jacket pocket. "You have a slight concussion, so you will have a sore head for a while, I'm afraid. But at least all the wheels are turning, it seems."

"What happened?"

"You tell me. You've been beaten quite badly, son."

"How badly?"

"Three cracked ribs. Your eye socket was nearly broken. Many, many bruises. Two bones in your right hand were broken. So was a finger on your left. Your left wrist is cracked. And your nose. We had to reset it. Probably good you don't remember that part."

"Jesus."

"Yes, but you're okay now. Nothing permanent. Nothing that won't heal. Lucky. Very lucky."

"Shit." Steven wants to shake his head but can't. "Lucky."

"You don't think so now, but yes. Your lady friend brought you in. And that's good. Because you would have been much worse off if she hadn't."

"Lady friend?"

Dania.

"Don't worry," the doctor says. "She's fine. She's waiting outside to see you."

"How long?"

"How long have you been here or how long has she been waiting?"

"Both."

"Many hours."

"Christ," Steven says. "My face hurts."

"I would imagine so. Your face is what took most of the beating."

Steven doesn't want to know what he looks like right about now. He looks down at his body and tries to count the fingers and toes. He notices the bandages taped to his body and is sure the pain in his ribs will be insufferable. His right hand is in a tight bandage and completely covered. Even with the painkillers he can feel the bruises on his face. He doesn't want to think about what it will feel like when the drugs wear off.

"I was attacked." He remembers how strict Singapore is and how severe their laws are. He starts to concoct a story. He knows he's slurring and wonders if it's from the bruises or the medication or both.

"Yes, you were." The doctor holds up his hands to stop Steven from saying more. "But you're okay now. That's all that matters. We'll worry about all the rest another time. Okay?"

Steven thinks he nods. He's not sure.

"Lady friend?" Steven asks.

"She's outside," the doctor says. "I'll come back and check on you again soon. Okay? You rest for now."

"How long am I here?"

"You can leave soon enough. We'll keep you and watch you until then. You rest now and let me do what I do. Then you can leave, okay?"

Before Steven can answer, the doctor smiles again and steps out of the room, tapping his chart on the end of the bed as he walks out. Steven looks around the tiny room and realizes that he's alone. It's quite small and bare. Not at all as he would think a hospital room would look. It's not at all like the room where he visited Scotty after the accident.

Steven remembers a fight. He remembers getting hit. Did he bungee jump? He remembers Dania getting hit and punched in the face. He remembers a fall. A crack. Then everything went black. The bodyguard punched him. Nez's bodyguard.

Nez, he thinks to himself. *What happened to Nez?*

The door opens again, and Steven looks over to see Dania walk slowly into the room. She has been crying, and her makeup is almost all gone, cried away or rubbed away. On her lower left jaw there is a small, dark bruise. Her eyes are puffy and red. Her hair is wet from rain or sweat or both. She looks exhausted.

"Hey," she says quietly. Steven doesn't like the word "hey." He wants to speak, but his throat is dry and his face hurts. He makes a face that might be a smile. He can't tell. Dania walks up to the bed and looks as if she's going to cry again. Tears are in her eyes. She leans in and kisses him on the forehead. Her lips feel warm on his skin. A single tear rolls down her cheek, and Steven feels it land on the bruises on his face.

"How do you feel?" she asks.

"Hurt."

"You're okay. I mean, you're going to be alright."

"How did I get here?"

"I threw you in a taxi. I brought you here while you were out."

"You brought me to the hospital in a cab? Not an ambulance?"

"I had to be discreet. You understand?"

Steven now remembers what happened. He remembers all the punches and his arms being pulled back. He remembers the awful cracking sound.

"Nez?" he asks.

Dania looks out the window in the door to the hallway outside. She looks over her shoulder to see if the tiny room is, indeed, empty. Then she leans in to Steven's ear and whispers:

"I didn't see who attacked us, and neither did you. I don't know anyone named Nez. And neither do you."

She steps back and looks into his eyes. Does he understand? She nods slowly at him, and he tries to nod back. His head really hurts. But he understands.

She pulls up a chair and they sit in silence for a few moments, and Steven suddenly realizes that Dania is holding his hand. The left one, not the one with the IV sticking out of it, wrapped in the tight bandage. Every so often, a tear runs down her face and she pushes it away with the back of her free hand. Steven can hear the air-conditioning in the background. He hears it louder than she does.

"Money," Steven says after a few minutes.

"What?" Dania asks.

"You don't need it anymore. Nez. The money."

"Don't think about that. It doesn't matter."

"You don't need the money."

"I never needed any money," Dania says. "Okay? I can't tell you that enough. I didn't want money. Not from Scott. Not from you. I never even knew about the money."

"But now you're free."

"Whatever. Free to do what?"

"Leave."

"And go where? I don't know anything else. I don't know anywhere else."

Steven pulls his hand away from hers. "Leave. Leave me."

"What?"

"I want you to leave," he says.

The look on her face is crushing. The tears start to form in her eyes, and she stands up and takes a few steps back. Steven can smell her perfume. It's that same flowery scent that always comes from her hair. She stands there and looks at him questioningly for a moment.

"Is that what you really want?" She clears her throat.

"What I want," Steven says, slurring his words, "is to leave this place. To heal and pack and get the hell out of this godforsaken city. I can't leave fast enough. As soon as they let me, I'm gone."

"Just like that?"

"Just like that. And then I'll try to forget I ever came here at all."

Dania leans forward again. She tries to touch his hair, but he pulls his head back. His head hurts so much when he moves it, he feels as if he'll pass out again.

"Please don't say that," she almost whispers.

Steven scoffs and feels his throat, dry and hoarse. "Look me in the eyes and tell me why not," he says. "Better yet, look at my face and tell me. Look what happened to my face. And then tell me why I should stay one more minute here."

"I'm sorry."

"You win," Steven says. "You're free now. So just go and be free from all the shit you were in."

"I don't want to be free. I want you."

He shakes his head. "No, you wanted him. You got me because he's dead."

Dania looks shocked. She looks out the doorway again to see if anyone is watching. She clasps her strong hands together and tightly squeezes them. Steven notices again that she really does have strong hands.

"You don't mean that," Dania says.

"I mean every word of it. Ask yourself if I'd even be here if Scotty were still alive."

"That's not fair."

"Isn't it? If he hadn't died, you'd probably be planning your wedding right about now and I'd just be the brother-in-law you hadn't met yet."

"I didn't want to marry Scott," she says. "That's what he wanted."

"Christ, this was crazy." Steven rolls his eyes and can feel how the socket of one of them was beaten to a pulp. It's a very unusual, very unique pain.

"So that's it, then?" Dania sniffs loudly and glares at him. She looks angry.

"After you lied to me? Lied to my brother? Essentially destroyed our family? Everything I had, gone. Yes, that's just about it. I think that's enough."

She wants to scream at him; he can tell. She wants to curse at him and scratch at him. If he were standing in front of her right now, she would slap him. Slap his bruised and beaten face. Instead, she just bites her bottom lip. He can see how hard she is biting it.

"Don't blame me for this," she says through her teeth. "Scott never would have blamed me."

"You'd be surprised how little you knew about Scott."

"And you'd be surprised to find out how much he knew about *me*. He wasn't ashamed of me. He knew everything and stayed with me."

"Because Scotty liked being different. He liked being unusual. He liked to shock people. It turned him on."

"It wasn't like that," Dania says. "You don't even know."

"I knew my own twin brother. I knew him better than you ever did."

"He loved me."

"I'm sure he did."

"He didn't care about my past."

Steven rolls his eyes. He can feel the bruise on the left one and imagines that's the eye socket that was pummeled. "I'm sure he loved it. He just wanted to do anything he thought made him different or special or eccentric."

"It wasn't like that."

"Don't you get it?" Steven asks.

"What?"

"All this talk about what Scotty was or wasn't ashamed of. All this talk about how he knew about your past and wanted to know more." Steven tries his best to lean in closer to her. "Of the two of us, I'm the only one who really fell in love with the real you."

He looks away from her. He sees people walking by the room, down the long hallway outside. He can hear nurses or doctors or whomever walking on the hard tiled floor. He hears random beeps and machines. He can still hear the air-conditioning. All of it makes his head hurt. He wants to make all of the sounds go away. He so desperately wants silence.

"If I had told you everything from the beginning," she says softly. "If I had told you about Nez and my parents and all the surgeries and all the therapy. About being the wrong person for most of my life. About feeling hated by my own parents and still feeling like I was born completely wrong and no one listened or understood when I begged them. If I had told you everything from the start, would you have stayed?"

"If you had, would I be lying in this hospital bed right now?"

"You think this is my fault?"

"You don't have a clue what I'm feeling or thinking."

"I think you're scared."

"Oh, screw you."

"It's true," she says, stepping closer. "I think all of this scares you, and that's why you're so angry with me. That's why you're lashing out at me. You don't even see that everything I've done since you got here was for you. To try and keep you happy and keep you safe. To keep you from learning the things you were better off not knowing."

"Thanks for nothing."

"That's the biggest difference between you and him, you know. He wasn't scared."

"You really never knew him at all, did you?" Steven asks as he tries his best to sit up in the bed. He feels the IV tug at his skin when he moves his arm to steady himself. "Scotty was the most terrified little boy I've ever known."

"That's not true," she says.

"Are you kidding? He killed our parents."

Dania makes an audible gasp and covers her mouth. Her beautiful hair falls down into her face, and she pushes it away with a sniffle.

"Didn't know that, did you? Well, that's what he did. All because he was careless. And then he never could even own up to that. Instead of getting his life together, he just got worse. He just ran away. The rest of his life, he was just running. Just a scared little kid always running away." Steven holds his left hand up to his face and is surprised that it's not in pain like other parts of his body.

Dania turns and looks away from him. She stares off into the corner, putting her back to Steven.

"Why do you think he never drove anywhere? Why do you think he could have gotten a car and never did?"

"He had headaches," Dania says quietly.

"Oh, yeah," Steven says, "the headaches. Because he wouldn't wear his glasses. Please. He got the headaches from his head hitting the windshield. Underneath that long hair was a nasty little scar you never got to see."

Dania says nothing and does not turn back around. Steven sees her shoulders moving and can tell that she's crying. He's said enough and knows he should let it go. He should stop talking now and just let her weep. But he wants to keep pushing. He wants someone to finally know the truth about Scott. He wants to stop pretending his brother was something he never was. Everyone thought Scotty was always the life of the party, when Steven knew that Scotty wasn't even that nice a guy.

"He ran away from everything," Steven says. "He was scared of driving and scared of dying and scared that one day he'd realize that he had done nothing but constantly run away. Anything to keep from having to simply grow the hell up and just forgive himself."

"He was a good man," Dania says.

Let her believe that. Steven can hear Scotty talking in his ear. But he tells Scotty to go to hell.

"He was a liar, and everything about him was a lie."

"You don't mean that."

"I mean all of it," Steven says, "but maybe you're right, too. Maybe you're not the one I should be angry with. Maybe this isn't your fault."

"Don't—"

"Maybe this was all about him all along. In the end, Scott did this to both of us. He screwed us both over. And all because he was too much of a coward to do anything else."

Dania turns to look at him, but she is not angry. She is not going to yell at him or throw a tantrum, and she isn't going to hit him. Her hands are open, and she holds them out in front of her, as if pleading with him to stop. He's hurting her now, and he knows it. She just wants him to stop. She opens her mouth, but nothing comes out. She then looks off to the side, as if trying to pretend he's not even in the room with her. Pushing the hair out of her face, she starts to speak but, instead, turns around and walks out of the room.

Steven looks the other way. He doesn't want to see her walking down the hallway. He doesn't want to see if she looks back toward the room. He doesn't want to hear her footsteps on the hard tile floor in the hallway. He hates that he can hear her footsteps and wishes he couldn't hear them. He just wants silence.

After a few minutes, he feels the stinging in his face, but this time it's in his eyes. Everything gets blurry as the pain radiates to the back of his head. After a minute he realizes that the pain he's feeling is caused by his own tears.

There is a light, but not in his eyes this time. It's not a flashlight, just the fluorescent lights overhead being turned on. Steven sees red through his eyelids. He can't quite open his eyes all the way. He has to adjust to the brightness. He sees a slender figure approach and lean over the bed.

"Dania?" he asks.

"Who?" a man's voice responds. Steven tries to shake his head and wake up faster. He still feels the IV attached to his arm. His face hurts more now than it did before. The drugs must be wearing off. There are fewer painkillers pumping through him now that he's been here for a while.

His eyes adjust and lock in on a tall, thin, white man standing over him. The man snaps his fingers several times in Steven's face.

"You in there, chief?" the man asks.

"What's going on?"

"Steven Kelly?" he asks. Steven nods. The man stands up straight and closes the door behind him, then steps back over to the bed. "You know where you are?"

"I already did this with the other doctor," Steven says.

"I'm not a doctor, chief."

"Then who are you?"

"My name is Bobby Clayton. I'm with the consulate."

"Which one?"

"Funny. The Canadian one, of course. The High Commission of Canada, if you want to be precise."

"Am I in some sort of trouble?"

"Should you be?"

Steven shakes his head. "No," he says, although it comes out as a question.

"I'm just kidding with you, mate," Bobby says. He has very short hair and a thick jawline. Definitely a military guy. "Just checking up on you to make sure you're okay and alive."

"I'm alive," Steven says. "The jury is still out on the rest."

"Sure. That's what I heard."

"So, that's why you're here? Is that typical?"

"No, to be honest. But you know what's also not typical? Violent crime in Singapore."

"Could have fooled me," Steven says.

"Yeah, I guess so. But I wanted to see if you were okay with my own eyes. You don't remember me, but we've met before."

"We have?"

"Yep. Two years ago, my sister got married in Toronto. We had a huge dinner at your restaurant. You talked about wine with me for a good hour."

Steven realizes that if he tells Bobby he remembers the conversation that he'd only be lying. And he's pretty sure that Bobby would know he's lying. Instead, he tries to smile and nod.

"Anyway," Bobby says. "When we got the report that you were here and pretty banged up, I did some looking around. I'm sorry to hear about your brother."

"Thanks."

"Rough week, huh?"

"Yeah."

"All of that and then you took a bit of a beating a couple of days ago," Bobby says. It's only then that Steven realizes how long he's been out.

"Pretty bad," Steven says flatly.

Bobby leans in and gives Steven a sly grin. It's surprisingly warm. As if—if Steven were in better shape—Bobby would give him a playful slug to the shoulder. "Didn't get a look at who beat you up, eh?" Bobby asks.

Steven shakes his head. "No, not really."

Bobby hums. "Well, it was dark and rainy. It gets dangerous around here when it rains. Lots of accidents. That sort of thing. Not a lot of crime but—boy—there can be some accidents when it rains."

"Oh, yeah?" Steven looks warily at Bobby.

"Yep," Bobby says, looking out the window to the hallway. "Hell, just on the other side of the city, over by the Riverwalk, some guy slipped in the rain and died."

"Jesus."

"Bashed his head against the curb."

"That's terrible," Steven lies.

"Not really." Bobby turns and looks at him, right into his eyes. "Spoke with the locals about him. The cops. He was a real scumbag. Just a total piece of shit, this guy."

"You don't say."

"A hustler. Pimp. Just an all-around lowlife, if you ask me. Everyone who knew him is pretty much glad he's dead. *Everyone*."

"Wow, just like that, huh?"

"Just like that. He's gone, and no one will miss him." Bobby leans in again. "Not one bit."

Steven nods and tries to gesture in a way that thanks Bobby at the same time. Bobby gives him a wink and stands up straight again.

"So," Bobby says, "they say you get to leave in a couple of days. The hospital, I mean."

"That's what they say."

"Well, if you need anything at all, we're here for you. We'll support you all the way."

"That's great news. But I think I'm ready to put it behind me now."

"Sounds like the right idea," he says. "Singapore City is an amazing place. But I bet you probably want to get going home, eh?"

Steven nods and realizes Bobby isn't asking a question. "More than you know," he slurs.

Bobby smiles. "That's good. Probably the sooner the better, right?"

"Right."

"You leaving anything important behind in Singapore?"

Steven shakes his head. "Nothing I will miss."

20

He feels his entire body jump and realizes that the plane has touched down. Pulling out his earplugs, Steven is surprised to find he must have slept through the past seven hours. The painkillers he was prescribed at the hospital did the trick and, with a couple of glasses of awful airplane wine, he managed to close his eyes a bit and suddenly wake up in Toronto. He wonders if he can get these same pills for the next time he travels.

Behind him, he hears people rustling and getting ready to leave the plane. The sound of what must be a bag of chips being folded up and shoved into a carry-on bag tells him that it's a good thing he remembered earplugs this time around. He's not sure if he could have put up with all of that noise while dealing with the pain in his face at the same time. As luck would have it, he wasn't awake for most of it anyway.

His neck hurts from being pushed up against the window, but it's nothing compared to the pain he still has in his face and jaw and ribs. Still, this was one of the easiest flights he's ever had to endure. Modern medicine is a wonderful thing. He can easily tell why people become addicted to these pills.

Just to be sure, he pulls the bottle out of the inner pocket of his sports jacket and pops a few more of the little capsules into his mouth. He likes the way it makes everything bother him a little bit less.

There is a lecture on the plane about where to find his bag, where to follow the arrows, who to talk to, and everything else they tell people arriving from overseas. All he cares about is getting off the plane, getting home, and being there as long as humanly possible. He has a suitcase to pick up at the baggage claim but—besides that—feels oddly like he's bringing more with him than just luggage.

He hates that feeling. He wants to be home where he can lie down, sleep another day, and just put the past few weeks behind him. A new year is coming. He wants to start all over and can't wait until he starts to do so.

He aches all over, and walks through the airport as if he's an eighty-year-old man. People practically sprint past him, tugging at their wheeled suitcases as they hurry to be the first person through the doors and down the escalator. Steven hobbles slowly, content to be the last person in every line.

It's a long line to be last in, and Steven winces as he steps into the large customs room at the Toronto airport. A dozen border guards, each sitting in his or her own cubicle, wave people forward one at a time, examining travel documents and stamping passports. The line wraps around the room several times, like everyone is waiting to board a ride at an amusement park or make a deposit at the world's busiest bank.

The wait seems even longer when he realizes that everyone can't stop staring at his face. People are looking at him, checking out his bruises. They probably imagine all kinds of exciting stories. They wonder if he's some kind of thug or deadbeat, sneaking his way into Canada. Or maybe they think he's a mixed martial artist, coming back from a prize fight overseas. He waits for someone around him in line to ask him what happened.

I'm a cage fighter, he'll tell them. *You should see the other guy.*

A young couple, barely in their twenties, is standing in front of him in line. They were on a school trip or something. They smell like cigarettes and excitedly talk about how they can't wait for New Year's. The young man looks over at him and catches his eye for a brief second. He nods as if the way Steven looks is completely normal.

Slept with a transgender lounge singer, Steven thinks. *Her pimp beat me up.*

It's at that moment that he realizes the truth is far more exciting than any story he could make up.

No one speaks to him. Some people politely smile and try to pretend they don't notice him. He wonders if any of these people have ever ordered wine from him in his restaurant or if they ever will. How will they look at him when he's wearing Armani and pouring a two hundred dollar bottle of Pinot Noir into their glasses? Will they remember the man with the beaten face?

Probably not, he thinks. *No one ever remembers me anyway. I'm just the guy who brings the wine.*

He loves the fact that the pills make the pain go away, but he hates that they make him so groggy, so cranky, perhaps even more than usual. They make him snooty in a different way. He preferred it when he was just a wine snob. But he also knows he likes the buzz from the pills. He's just as cranky as ever, but at least he doesn't care as much.

"Next, please," the customs agent says. Canadians are so polite.

Steven steps up to the booth and hands over his passport. It had so few stamps in it until now. There were Italy and France and the States. Now Singapore becomes fourth. Steven has Scotty's passport in his luggage. There are many stamps on that one. The customs agent looks at Steven's passport, then looks at his face. He furrows his brow.

"Purpose of your trip?" the agent asks. Steven slides the extra piece of paper across the counter to the guard, who unfolds it and reads it carefully. That piece of paper might as well be a golden ticket or a Get Out Of Jail Free card. It explains the bruises and comes with a nice, official stamp from nice, official people. The agent reads it again. "And this . . . Robert Clayton is with the consulate in Singapore?" he asks.

"Yes, sir," Steven says.

The agent reads the paper a third time, looks at the passport again, and looks up at Steven. "Are you bringing any alcohol, tobacco, or firearms back from Singapore, Mr. Kelly?"

"No, sir," Steven says.

"Are you okay?" the agent asks. His concern is genuine.

Steven shrugs.

You screw with the bull, you get the horns, he thinks.

"Welcome home," the agent says, and stamps Steven's passport. Steven collects it and the letter from Bobby Clayton and puts them both into his jacket pocket. He walks to the baggage claim and thinks about just leaving his luggage there. At this point he'll do anything to get home faster. As soon as his luggage comes around on the belt, he grabs it and wheels it outside.

The cold air hits him immediately and feels amazing. All around him, other people coming out of the airport pull their coats on and adjust their collars. They bundle up and go searching through purses and briefcases for scarves and gloves. Steven stands and closes his eyes.

If his face didn't still hurt so much, the look on his face would resemble a smile.

The town car feels nice. Much nicer than the taxis he had gotten used to taking in Singapore. The leather of the seat is cold, but there is hot air coming from the front of the car. Steven looks out the window as the lights go from small to bigger and the buildings come closer out of the distance. The traffic is busy, but moving fast. The cars are reckless. The drivers are terrible.

It's Toronto.

In the distance, he notices the CN Tower. Normally lit just like the surrounding landscape of tall, brightly lit buildings, it now shines red and green. Its usual blue and white lights have been switched to match the season. Towering above the city, the tower is clad in a trademark set of the two most festive colors.

It's Christmastime.

Steven almost forgot that December isn't over yet. It's only a week until Christmas, and he's back in Toronto. There's slush on the roads from a snowfall a couple days earlier. The cab driver is wearing a heavy coat. People everywhere are bundled up, battling the wind and the chill that pushes through the city.

There are Christmas lights everywhere, and the tall buildings are made up to look festive. There are billboards with Santa

Claus advertising products that supposedly he's all about endorsing. Ads for Christmas movies and holiday cell phone plans and all kinds of gifts you owe it to loved ones to buy them this year. Yonge Street has neon snowflakes hanging off of street lamps. Everything he normally loves about Christmastime is right here waiting for him, as if the city knew he was coming back. This is the real deal, not that imitation he was surrounded by in the Far East.

The cab driver has the radio playing, and Steven recognizes the song immediately: "Merry Christmas, Darling" by the Carpenters.

He looks out the window at the passing lights. The people dressed in Canada Goose down jackets. The cold December weather in the cold city that he loves. Tim Hortons' red storefront sign telling him the perfect place to go for a double-double. A billboard telling him to be sure to listen to Skip and Spence in the morning on The Wolf FM, the station that rocks. For a moment, he catches his reflection in the taxi window. He still looks awful.

Karen Carpenter is telling him about how much she misses him this Christmas Eve. This has always been one of Steven's favorite Christmas songs.

"Can you turn the radio off, please?" he asks the driver.

The concierge at his building nods from behind his desk, but doesn't say a thing. He never does. The same man has been working behind that desk for over two years, and Steven can't for the life of him remember the guy's name. He thinks he should ask him tomorrow. He remembered Lee at the hotel in Singapore. He should at least know the name of the doorman at his own condo.

Steven puts his key in his door and, for a second, wonders if Robin will be there. If she had a change of heart and, because of all the Christmas lights in the city and all the festivities, can't be without him any longer. She missed him and is glad he's home. She was worried about him and just wants him to come in and sit on the sofa and let her take care of him.

But then he realizes that she's been here all along, in this city.

The holiday isn't special to her. She's glad to be somewhere else. He opens the front door and looks around. The entire apartment is empty.

She took everything.

There's nothing left for him to come home to. Not Robin and nothing that could possibly remind him of her. All of the furniture is gone. There are no paintings on the walls. The enormous sofa is gone, as is the uncomfortable chair she used to read in. The floor is bare and missing the area rug that covered the entire living room. Even the things that he had long before she came along are gone. She took all of it, even the things she didn't like, the things that weren't hers.

Steven puts his keys on the kitchen counter and steps into the big empty space. Sitting in the middle of the floor is the smaller of the two television sets they had. It's the one she owned before she met him.

Steven walks across the room, wheeling his suitcase behind him. He hears the hard plastic wheels scraping across the bare hardwood floors. Somewhere halfway across the living room, he drops the handle and leaves his luggage right there in the middle of the apartment. He walks over to the large window and looks out at the city. He's always loved this view. It's the main reason he bought the place. Way off in the distance, he can see downtown Toronto, the CN Tower, and other tall buildings.

Home.

He suddenly realizes that the apartment feels very cold, and he goes to adjust the thermostat. It's set at normal room temperature, but he guesses that the apartment's being empty makes it feel chillier than it should. He walks into the bedroom, which is almost as empty as the rest of the condo. His bed is gone, and so are both of the nightstands. She left the chest of drawers with his clothes in it. He looks in the closet and finds that an extra set of blankets and sheets are still there—the black ones that she always hated. The ones he had on the bed when he met her. He takes the large comforter and carries it back into the living room. Once there, he drops it on the floor and looks in the kitchen at his wine chiller.

Empty.

Did you have to take all the booze? he thinks to himself. *You didn't even like it.*

He is relieved to see there is still plenty of food left behind. Above the fridge, in the small cabinet where he mostly keeps empty boxes, he finds what he really wants. There, in the back, is the old bottle of Johnnie Walker Black. The scotch she would never touch. The stuff she hated.

He opens the bottle and resists the urge to take a pull standing right there. Instead, he tries to pretend he has an ounce of class left in him and finds a rocks glass she left behind. He pours himself a good four fingers and takes off his sports jacket, which has seen better days. Out of habit, he checks the pockets, even though he never keeps anything in them.

There, in the left breast pocket of his jacket, he feels a little lump. He digs his hand in and scoops out the contents onto his kitchen counter. It's gritty and coarse, like a handful of dirt.

It's Scotty's remains.

Some must have spilled out of the bag he used to carry Scotty around Singapore. They most likely poured out a little bit when Steven pulled out the bag to assault Nez with the ashes. It's not much, probably enough to fill a shot glass, but that's definitely what it is and definitely all that's left of Scotty.

Steven stares at the remains scattered across his kitchen counter and suddenly feels the stinging coming back into his eyes. His vision is getting blurry again, and he feels his breathing getting quicker. He takes a long gulp from his glass of scotch as he closes his eyes.

What a sad sack this guy is, Scotty's ashes tsk-tsk from the kitchen counter. *You'd think you were the one who was dead, not me.*

"Shut up," Steven says as he walks over to the cupboard and fetches a small bowl. With one careful sweep of his hand, he scoops the rest of Scotty's remains into the bowl and places it on the corner of the counter.

I'm serious here, Scotty says. *What the hell are you moping about? This is everything you wanted. You're home and you're free.*

"Free?" Steven asks.

Absolutely. Free of everything. No more Robin. No more Dania. You're home in time for Christmas, and the rest of your life is ahead of you. It's just what you wanted.

Steven catches a glimpse of his reflection in the window. "I didn't want this," he says.

Bah, humbug. Bruises heal.

"She took everything."

She left your pride. You can get new stuff.

"Start all over, eh?"

What choice do you have? You don't want her back.

"Which one are you referring to?"

Does it matter?

Steven chuckles to himself and finishes off the scotch in his glass. He was in such a hurry to get home, he never stopped to realize there was so little he cared about coming back to see. For all the prestige his job offers, he's barely thought about it in days. Robin might as well be a total stranger at this point. And the most enjoyable thing he's seen this holiday season is the doorman at a hotel in Singapore.

"This is all your fault, you know."

And I'm sure you'll never let me forget it. Said some pretty harsh stuff about me back East, you know?

"If you weren't dead, I'd kill you."

You seduced my girlfriend instead. That's the best revenge.

Steven walks around the counter and back into the living room a few feet away. There, with his luggage behind him, he sits down on the cold, hardwood floor and wraps up in his comforter. He doesn't even know what time it is.

The doctor told him to take a couple of the painkillers every six hours or so. It's been about an hour since he took two of them, so he pulls the bottle out of his pocket and tosses down another four. He washes them down with the scotch and looks outside at the lights just off in the distance. After a few minutes and a few large gulps of the scotch, he feels a warm tingle start to spread all over his body. He lies down on the floor and wraps himself into a cocoon inside the old comforter.

Silent night, holy night.
All is calm, all is bright.

"Wish you were here, bro," he slurs to the bowl in the kitchen. Scotty always called him "bro." He always hated it.

Merry Christmas, darling, Scotty says from the kitchen, sounding a lot like Karen Carpenter.

The sound of his cell phone ringing startles him awake. He hasn't heard it ring in what feels like months. He can't even remember the last phone call he got. He reaches for it just before the call goes to voice mail and answers without bothering to see who is calling.

"Yeah?" he says.

"Oh." A familiar voice on the other end sounds startled. Robin clears her throat and speaks quietly. "You're there."

"Yeah," he says as he rolls over and untangles himself from the comforter. His head and eyes hurt, but not just from the bruises. Too much scotch and too many painkillers, and the blinds being left open have the sun slapping him right in the face. He has no idea what time it is, but the sun is higher than his apartment, which tells him it's easily midafternoon.

"I thought I would get your voice mail," Robin says. "But you're back, I guess, huh?"

"Got in last night," he says, and brushes his hair out of his eyes. He looks around for his glasses, which he apparently managed to toss across the room before he passed out. "What's up?"

"So, everything is okay? You got in alright and got home?"

"Such as it is," he says.

"Yeah," she says. "Well, I told you I was leaving."

"Leaving me with nothing, yeah. I gotcha."

"Hey, I took what was mine. It's only fair."

"Whatever you say," he says. He could argue with her, but, as usual, feels no need. It's not like she's going to move the furniture back if he puts up a stink. "Why are you calling?"

"I'm fine, thanks," Robin says. Steven wants to throw his phone out the window. "How are you?"

"I'm home," Steven says. "So, what's up?"

"I was just checking on you," she says.

"And?"

"And what?"

Steven sighs. "Look, you moved everything out and you got your own place," he says. "You barely spoke to me when I was in Asia, so I can't imagine that you suddenly care about how I'm doing."

"That's not—"

"So, what can I do for you? What do you want?"

That's it, big guy, Scotty says. *Give it to her good.*

"Fine," Robin says. "I just wanted to see if you were there because I've got to come by."

He looks around the empty apartment. "Here?"

"Yes, there," she says. "I still have some things to get, and I figured it'd be awkward if I did it while you were there. I knew you were supposed to be coming back and all, so I called to check first."

Steven hears his voice echoing off the empty walls. "What on earth could you possibly have left here?"

She scoffs. He can see her rolling her eyes when she speaks. "Lots of things," she says. "My TV, for one."

Steven looks at the old television, unplugged, sitting on the floor. He looks at the empty wine chiller just off to the side of the kitchen. He looks at his empty living room, which looks much like it did the day he moved in, long before he even met her. It looks like it did before he even bought the place.

"Now I will say it," he says.

"Say what?" Robin asks.

"Go to hell," he says, and hangs up the phone.

It's dark outside now, although it's only early afternoon. It gets dark so much faster in Toronto than in Singapore. It feels like it has been months since he has been home, like it will take him weeks to adjust to the time and even to the cold in the air. Snow is falling outside, and he thought that the sight of it would make him happy.

He's still just lying on the floor.

The bottle of scotch is almost empty. There are take-out food cartons on the floor. He had some poutine delivered just so he could try and feel at home. Steven barely ever eats poutine, but Scott insisted. Steven scarfed it down with more scotch and pills. Then he slept. Then he ate some more and slept some more. The pills make it easy to sleep.

On the floor, next to his laptop, he has marked pages in an IKEA catalogue. The TV is still unplugged, but he keeps checking his e-mail and doing nothing online. He pretends he's looking for furniture. Ordering a new place to live without leaving the place where he lives.

He goes online and checks the time and weather in Singapore. It's boiling hot there, despite the fact that it's the middle of the night. He checks his e-mail, wondering if he'll hear anything . . . from anyone.

The phone rings and startles him again. It takes him a moment to find it because his hands are a bit numb from the pills and scotch. He knows he's going to have to get more booze and pills soon if he wants to keep lying here like this. He'll have to stop altogether in another day or two when he goes back to work.

"Hello?" he asks when he sees that the phone number isn't Robin's. He doesn't recognize it at all, but sees by the area code that it's someone in Toronto.

"Mr. Kelly?" asks a woman's voice on the other end.

"Yes?"

"I'm sorry, is this Scott or Steven Kelly?"

There is no Scott Kelly, he thinks. He's going to have to get used to saying that, much to the chagrin of the bowl sitting on the kitchen counter.

"This is Steven," he says instead.

"Oh, hi, Mr. Kelly. This is Grace McDonald. From Scotia-bank."

"Yes?"

"I'm sorry if I caught you at a bad time, sir."

"That's okay. What can I do for you?"

"Well, I have been trying to reach you for a few days now," she says. "Have you gotten my messages? I wasn't sure."

He keeps checking his e-mail, but hasn't once checked his phone. He wonders how many messages are waiting on his voice mail. Some from Robin, he's sure, and maybe someone from work checking up on him, even though he's not due back until next week. Maybe even a friend here or there offering condolences.

Did Dania call?

"No, I'm sorry," he says. "I've been out of the country. I just got back and haven't checked my messages yet."

"Oh. Well, I just needed to confirm your wire transfer. The one you requested several weeks ago."

Steven sits up on the floor and looks around the apartment. He keeps wondering if he's going to blink and suddenly all of his belongings will magically return. They never do.

"Wire transfer?" he asks.

"Yes, sir," Grace says. "You requested money from your trust account into your checking. That was you, correct?"

"Yes," Steven says. "I did."

"Well, I just wanted to speak with you before we went through with it."

"Is there a problem?" Steven asks.

"No problem. Just covering my bases, if you know what I mean. It is a good-sized amount."

"Yes," he says. "I guess so."

"So, should I go ahead with it?"

He looks around at the empty apartment and realizes that it's going to cost a good bit of money to refurnish it. At the very least, he needs to buy a bed and some living room furniture. Something—anything—to fill up the space.

"Yes, please. Go ahead with it," he tells her.

"Alright. And you still want this to be accessed by Scott? His name is on the receiving end."

"No, Scott won't be needing it. You can just have it put into my account."

"Just yours?"

There is no Scott Kelly, he thinks.

"Yes, please. Scott isn't . . . that is . . . he won't be needing it. It's for me."

There is a pause on the line and the sound of a woman's hands typing on a keyboard.

"Alright, then, you're the one authorized on the account. I'll just go ahead and make the transfer."

"Thank you very much," he says, and starts to hang up the phone. At that moment, he looks down at his laptop. There's nothing new there, other than some random nothing messages and a few offers to get cheap drugs online or increase the size of his penis.

But one e-mail catches his eye:

Steven,
Hope you made it home okay. Let me know. Good on you.
—D.Wash
PS: No regrets.

"Are you still there?" Grace asks from the other end of the line. Steven looks at his cell phone as if she's actually standing in front of him. He feels almost embarrassed. As if Grace caught him doing something sneaky.

"Yes," he says, "I'm here. Sorry, I was just . . . I was just in the middle of something. Go ahead with the transfer, please."

"Yes, sir. Have a happy holiday, sir."

"The happiest," he lies and hangs up the phone.

Is that my money? Scotty says from his bowl on the counter. *Are we going to live happily ever after now?*

Steven looks at the bowl and feels a dull pain creep across his chest. He knows it has nothing to do with his injuries, so he doesn't reach for the painkillers this time.

There is no Scott Kelly, he thinks, and looks out the window. The snow is falling again. It's going to be a white Christmas. He suddenly remembers that poster hanging on the wall in the morgue, the one with the symbol that meant *peace.*

21

"How was your Christmas?" The woman behind the counter at Second Cup smiles politely at Steven as she hands him his large coffee. She's served him dozens of times before and knew instantly what he was going to order before he even asked for it. He can tell that she's dying to ask him about the bruises on his face. If only she knew what they looked like two weeks ago.

"It was nice," he lies. "Yours?"

"The usual."

"Happy New Year, I guess."

"You, too." She smiles and goes back to cleaning the cappuccino machine.

Steven turns to make his way to his usual seat at his usual table, when he stops himself and turns back around. He's been coming here for years, ordering the same coffee from the same handful of employees. There are always some new faces here and there, but it's been pretty much the same staff for the better part of the past year. He steps back up to the counter and catches the barista's eye.

"Hey." He extends his hand. "I'm Steven."

"Marie." She smiles, and her teeth almost outshine the Christmas lights still hanging in the window.

Steven gives her a nod, then turns around and leaves her to her work, slowly limping his way to the back of the café. His ribs still ache with every step, and he can barely grip his coffee cup because of the brace on his wrist. But somehow he still manages. At least his face is starting to look a little normal again. He's gotten pretty tired of being stared at everywhere he goes. He probably should still be taking the painkillers he was prescribed, but he figures that all the wine he's been drinking is pretty much having the same effect. At least he's not mixing the two anymore.

As luck would have it, his favorite table is empty, and he slowly lowers himself into his usual chair. This time of day, middle of the week, there are only a couple of other customers, and they chose to sit in the comfortable leather chairs near the middle of the shop. Just the way Steven likes it, he's practically alone, right next to the electric fireplace that is pretending to crackle in the corner. Outside, the cold January wind is pushing pedestrians up and down the street. It snowed last week, but it's been raining all morning. The city looks like one big ball of dirt and slush but, somehow, Steven thinks it's still quite pretty.

He gently puts his messenger bag on the chair next to him and leans over his coffee while staring outside. It feels as if it's been months since he was here last, although it's probably only been about six weeks. On the plane coming home from Singapore, he imagined this was the next place he'd go after getting back to his condo. Instead he stayed away for almost three weeks. As if this little coffee shop were a wife he cheated on overseas and was too ashamed to confront. Sitting here now, he feels as if he never left. That is, of course, until he moves and every aching muscle and bruise brings it all screaming back to him.

After a minute of staring at the electric fireplace beside him, he reaches into his messenger bag and pulls out the contents. There's paper, envelopes, and an old fountain pen that once belonged to his father. He's kept it in a shoebox in his closet for over ten years. As he puts the messenger bag back on the chair and places the fancy stationery in front of himself, he bumps his broken finger on the side of the table. The pain causes his entire arm to jerk back, and he winces hard from the shock it sends up his arm. The pain is gone almost as quickly as it comes, but he drops the fountain pen and it goes rolling out of his hand, onto the table, and then onto the floor. It doesn't stop there, but instead rolls a few feet away. Steven slumps in his seat, staring at it for a minute, cursing under his breath.

Sonofa . . . he thinks, looking at his wrist brace, which might as well be shackles at this point. Somewhere in the background, he hears Dean Martin singing. The café probably stopped playing Christmas music on New Year's Day.

Taking a deep breath, Steven starts to stand up, but is stopped by his injured ribs, which feel as if they are shooting through his skin and into the back of the chair. He sits down again and tries leaning forward instead of attempting to stand all the way up. This hurts more, and he leans back again, trying to breathe calmly while staring at the elusive pen lying a mere five feet away.

"How was your Christmas?" a pretty voice asks as a pair of women's winter boots steps directly behind the fountain pen.

Steven looks up and is surprised to see her standing there. She looks exactly like she did the last time he saw her, and he swears she's wearing the exact same perfume. Her hair is mostly bundled under a knit cap, her bangs sprouting out from beneath the front. She blows on her coffee and gives him what could almost be called a smirk.

"Hello, Robin." Steven smirks back.

"Oh, my God." Robin's expression changes when she gets a good look at Steven's face. "What the hell happened to you?"

"You should see the other guy."

"Jesus."

"No, really. You should see the other guy. I really do look better."

"What the hell happened? Did you get mugged?"

Steven shrugs. "Killed a pimp."

"Are you okay?"

"Just dandy, thanks. You wanna hand me that pen?"

She picks up the fountain pen and places it gently on the table, as if setting it down harder would somehow bruise Steven more than he already is. Steven inspects the pen as if it were made of glass and the fall to the floor nearly shattered it. Satisfied that there has been no permanent damage from its being treated like a pen, he puts it down on the table again and looks back at Robin.

"What are you doing here?" he asks.

"I knew you'd be here," she says, and motions to the chair directly across the table.

"By all means." Steven sighs. As Robin sits, he looks around the café at the other customers, at Marie, and at any possible escape route he can plan. Then he thinks about jamming the fountain pen into his own neck.

"How are you holding up?" Robin asks, taking a sip of what is probably a soy chai latte. "All things considered, I mean."

"One more time"—Steven raises his eyebrows—"what are you doing here?"

"Just seeing if you're alright. I haven't heard anything from you, so I was just hoping you're okay."

"I'm fine, thanks. How's my stuff?"

"My stuff," she says, and pushes one of her bangs out of her eyes and under her hat. She's wearing a turtleneck sweater that Steven knows is one of her favorites. "It was our stuff, but now it's my stuff. It's only fair."

"Fair? How do you figure?"

"It's all I have left."

"Well, that makes one of us," Steven scoffs. "You cleaned me out. Most of that stuff was there when I met you."

"We bought a lot of it together—"

"I bought it."

"Because I couldn't afford it." She starts to raise her voice, but catches herself. Taking a breath, she bites her bottom lip for a second before she starts again, this time with a calmer tone. "Look, I don't want to argue with you, Steven. I really don't."

"Fine," Steven says. "Keep the furniture. I'm going to replace it anyway."

"And that's what you don't get." She pats the table with her left hand while sipping her latte with the right.

"What?"

"You can easily get new furniture. You always could. You

can afford it with no problem. You could have anything you
wanted and you always did, unlike some of us."

"What's that got to do with anything?"

"You don't remember, but the entire reason we have all that
furniture is because you made me get rid of mine."

"I did not—"

"You said it was awful and, no matter how great a decorator
I might be, you'd never have any of that in your house. Everything I tried to bring with me when we moved in together, it was
gone."

Steven scrunches up his face and takes a big gulp of his coffee. What started as a perfectly nice winter's day—the kind he
dreams about all year long—has suddenly turned more bitter than
the wind outside. Ten minutes ago Robin was the ex he barely ever
thought about. He even thought his anger toward her was pretty
much behind him. Sitting here looking at her now, he realizes
that's not remotely true.

Then he realizes that she's right.

He hated almost everything she owned. She sold it online or
gave it away because he promised to buy anything they needed.
After all, he had money and she never did. She came into the relationship with almost nothing, but only because he made it be
that way. He's not sure if he completely forgot or just never gave
it much thought in the first place. He takes another gulp of his
coffee and suddenly doesn't feel as smug anymore. Now he
wishes there was booze in his cup.

"You're right," he says, and it stings almost as much as the
bruises on his face. "All that stuff should be yours."

"Thank you." She seems sincere and gives him a tiny smile.

"But what about all the wine?" he asks, still trying to win an
argument he lost the day she moved out.

"I didn't take it. I moved it. It's in the storage locker in the
basement."

"What? Why?"

"It's expensive, and I didn't want the movers to break anything when I was leaving. I know it's important to you."

Steven is ashamed of himself and starts to chuckle. "Why didn't you tell me that before now?" he asks.

"To be an asshole," she says. This almost makes Steven laugh out loud. Instead, he just smiles and raises his cup to her.

"Happy New Year," he says, and thinks about ordering another coffee. He wonders if he can talk Robin into getting it for him so he won't have to stand up.

"Are you okay?" she asks again. "I mean, about your brother and Singapore and everything?"

Steven looks out the window and tries to think about the wonderful, awful, bitter wind and snow and freezing temperature that is blanketing the city. He thinks about his topcoat and scarf and thick sweater. He thinks about his winter boots and people trying to start their cars. He tries his best not to think about the intense humidity and heat in Singapore City. He tries not to think about the spicy food and the Four Floors of Whores and about the Minang headdress.

The bull wins, he thinks.

"I'm fine," he says. "I mean, I'll be okay."

"I went by the apartment, before I came here. To see if you were there. Have you been sleeping on the floor?"

"Haven't picked out new stuff yet. Was waiting for after Christmas."

"Anyway, I just want you to be okay."

"I will be."

She starts to get up, but stops herself. Steven can tell there's more she wants to say, but that she's holding back. He's actually surprised that the conversation went as well as it did, and wonders if it'd be best for both of them if they never said another word again. At least then they could actually say it ended well and they both moved on with relatively little drama.

"I almost didn't recognize you. You're not wearing a tie or a blazer."

"I'm trying a new thing. Casual Wednesday."

"What's with the fancy pen and paper?" she asks, although Steven knows it's not what she was thinking. She's using it as an excuse to stay a few minutes longer and then will maybe decide whether or not she wants to spill her guts out a little bit.

"Writing a letter." He flicks the cap off the pen and holds it out as if he's just invented it.

"Really? Is your laptop broken?"

"Nope."

"Then why?"

"No one writes letters anymore."

She starts to ask him another question, but stops and stares at him for a minute, her mouth slightly open. That one strand of hair has fallen out of her hat and is now hanging over her right eye again. She doesn't seem to mind, nor does she make any effort to push it away. In the background, Paul Anka is playing on the radio. After a few seconds, Robin sits back in her chair and drums her fingers on the table. Steven is surprised that it doesn't bother him in the slightest.

"Who is she?" Robin asks, grinning slyly.

"Who is who?"

"The woman you met over there in Asia?"

Steven's eyes go wide, and he nearly drops his precious fountain pen on the floor again. Fumbling with it, he puts the cap back on and places it in the middle of the table. He shifts in his seat, feeling his ribs stab against him as he does.

"There is no woman in Asia."

"Of course there is. I know it."

"And how's that?"

"Because I remember what you were like when that woman was me."

Steven starts to speak, but is left with nothing to say. He takes the last sip of his coffee and then looks at the fake fire pretending to crackle in the corner. He looks back at Robin and thinks he should smile or something, but instead he just shrugs his shoulders and says nothing.

Robin says, "It all makes sense. You miss her."

"Maybe," Steven says softly. "But it's nothing."

"Doesn't seem like nothing."

"It is. It's over."

"That's too bad."

"Really? That seems weird coming from you."

"Believe it or not," she says, and starts to button her over-coat, "I want to see you happy. Just because it won't be with me doesn't mean I don't want it to happen."

"You were the one who was unhappy."

"That's not true."

"No?"

"Well, I wasn't happy," she agrees. "But you hadn't been for a long time, either. You just don't like change. Or changing your routine. Or confrontations. It was easier for you to stay than to leave and have to start over again or change anything you were doing. Or just tell me to get the hell out. Any other man would have kicked me out a year ago."

She's right, and Steven knows it. He deliberately sabotaged the relationship while thinking it was her. He grew complacent and simply went through the motions, doing nothing. Rather than fight for her or even with her, he just pretended the problems weren't there at all. It's why she broke bottles of wine and picked fights. She was trying to get him to realize what she had accepted months ago.

"So." Robin stands up and takes one last, long gulp of her latte. "If this woman in Asia or wherever has somehow got you pulling out of this never-ending rut you seem to have been in for God knows how long, I say write whatever letter makes that happen."

"You don't even know who she is."

"But I can tell she obviously matters to you, so that's all that really matters. What's left besides that?"

Steven sighs. "I'll probably never even send it."

"You should. She's definitely special."

"How could you possibly know that?"

"Because I've been cracking my chewing gum the entire time I've been here and you didn't even notice it. Not once."

This hits Steven in the face like a hammer, and he is left with nothing to say. She blows a bubble that pops loudly, then leans over and kisses him on the cheek that isn't bruised. Steven looks up at her and, for the first time in what is probably months, gives her a genuine smile. She pushes her hair back up into her hat again and returns the smile as she starts to walk away.

"Hey"—she turns around—"did you start smoking?"

"What?" He looks at her as if she's just grown a tail.

"When I was at the apartment, there was a dish on the counter. Looked like it had some ashes or dirt or something in it. I figured you were using it as an ashtray."

Scotty, he thinks.

"It's nothing," he says.

"Well, I rinsed it out and tossed it in the dishwasher for you."

"I appreciate that," he says as he watches her walk out the door and back into the cold.

22

Dania drops her keys on the little table right next to the door. Like every other winter she's ever lived in Singapore, it's still quite hot outside and, even with the air-conditioning on high, she's still sweating a bit when she walks in. There is a tiny mirror on the wall right there and, every time she walks into the little studio apartment, she catches a glimpse of herself. The bruises are gone, but she can still feel the ache in her chin. She looks to make sure there is nothing visible, but she still feels as if the marks are there.

She can't believe it's almost February. She wonders where the past several weeks have gone. It's a brand new year with a brand new job. Nez is gone and, with him, so is the gig at Orchard Towers. She isn't upset, and she doesn't miss it. She never liked the job that much anyway. She works more shifts at The Shark Fin. She does more looking for new gigs and new managers. But she can deal with it. She likes this better.

She sings at The British Club a few nights a week. It's not the same as the last gig, with the full band and the weird men in the audience; just her and a guy on piano, doing quiet songs and jazz standards. It's just the way she likes it. There's less money, but she's okay with that. She gets to keep all of it for herself this time. There's no one she owes anything to anymore. No one knows anything about her, and she likes it that way.

She likes singing for the British ex-pats and workers. It's

mostly bankers and finance guys and their wives. The people who go to the club every night to pretend they are still back home or—at the very least—anywhere but in Singapore. They sit at the bar and listen to her sing Rosemary Clooney and Etta James and Lena Horne. They pretend they are still in England and, for a while every night, she pretends she's there with them.

There are no more floors with whores for her now. There are no more of the sleazy drunks leering at her across the room. No one trying to buy her for the night. No more of the dancers at The Crazy Horse looking at her like they know her, or like they want to be her.

And yet, when she looks at herself in the mirror, she doesn't smile.

Tossing her purse aside, she goes through the mail that was slipped under the door. There's never anything worth keeping, just the occasional bill and the occasional junk. It's just enough to make her feel like she's still alive. At the bottom of the stack, she finds the one envelope that feels out of place and holds it up to the light. The international postage envelope catches her eye, and she immediately feels her heart stop.

Canada.

She rips into the envelope, already feeling the tears welling up in her eyes. Even before she knows what it could be. Before she knows if it's good news or bad news, or something she doesn't even want to read. She kept wondering if this would happen and, if it did, how she would react. Without even bothering to sit down or make her way into the apartment, she tears into the envelope as if she has just won the lottery.

She has been trying not to think of Steven. Trying instead to hate him. She gets angry at herself for it, but she instead only wound up hating Scott. She still doesn't even know why. She unfolds the letter and is surprised at how little he wrote. She feels herself cry out—just a little gasping sound—when she sees he's written the letter by hand. It makes her smile, even before she reads it.

D,

I've only just now realized that I ran away from you.

I spent years being angry at Scotty for always running away. Then I went and did exactly the same thing.

It's not the same without you.

There is no snow. Rain is falling outside the coffee house. The jazz is playing, and it makes me miss you.

I wish you were here to see and hear all of it.

I would love for you to consider forgiving me.

Can you?

You have already lived two lives.

Would you be able to live a third?

I hope you will.

You know where I will be sitting.

I love you,

S

Dania raises her hand to her mouth and chokes a bit. She's both inhaling and laughing at the same time. Tears roll down her cheeks, but she's not sad anymore. She holds the letter to her face and smells it, just to see if it smells like him. It doesn't; it just smells like paper.

But it's enough. It's enough to know that he held this paper and wrote on it and then sealed it in the envelope that he addressed to her. Even though it doesn't have the smell of his cologne or his hair that she can easily recognize, it's somehow enough. She feels as if he just wrote it a moment ago and handed it right to her. The tears roll out of her eyes and onto the paper, causing the ink to splotch. She looks inside the envelope, and there's more: a sticker of a Canadian flag, and something else.

A photograph.

She sits down on the tiny loveseat in her apartment and all of her emotions come gushing out. She holds the letter in both hands and cries, her tears hitting the paper, her bare legs, and the floor below her.

But she can't stop smiling.

The photograph is recent and was obviously printed out on a computer and then cut to size. In the photo, Steven is sitting on the floor of a large, empty room. There's a city skyline behind him and a tiny smile on his face. He almost looks as if he's unsure of himself. On his head he's wearing an unusual hat. Dania squints and looks closer and can see it's not a hat at all, but some kind of headband or costume. When she realizes what she's looking at, she laughs hard and loud.

Horns. He's wearing a tiny set of horns.

The bull wins, she thinks, and laughs even louder. She's crying and laughing at the same time, and feels she probably should get a drink of water. But she doesn't get up from the loveseat. Instead, she reads the letter again, and then a third time.

You know where I will be sitting.

His handwriting isn't so bad, she thinks. It's actually quite pretty. She wonders if he wrote several versions before he finally chose this one, the one that looks the nicest.

Of course he did.

Dania looks at the photo again and feels her lungs filling with air. She holds her breath for a minute and then folds the letter and the photo together and puts them back into the envelope.

Not yet, she thinks. *Not here. It's a test. Don't fail it.*

She looks around her tiny apartment at all that's left. There isn't much. She wonders if she should leave and—if she does—if there is anything here she'll miss. Scott would always just jump up and go wherever he wanted. He would pick up and leave and go wherever he felt his life was supposed to take him.

Scotty would have liked that. She hears Steven's voice in her head.

But there is no Scott.

Before she even realizes that she's standing, Dania pulls her suitcase out and begins to throw clothes in it. It's an old suitcase, being shoved full of even older clothes. But that doesn't matter. She doesn't have much, but she'll take what she can. She'll fly away as soon as she can.

Fly away to him.

Dania smiles as she looks around at the tiny room. She feels she should start her new life with nothing. For once, she doesn't feel like she's running away from anything. The rest of her life is waiting, and she's ready to live it. She's ready to make it happen, so she should start with nothing. Just like that.

They will both start their new life together. She knows it can work. All of this will be behind them both, and she'll learn to live her new life with him, in the cold. In that freezing, awful cold country she's never even seen. Just like all the terrible winters in London. But she's ready to have those winters, as long as she can have her new life with him in it.

It can work, she thinks. *Can't it?*

She stops for a second and sits down again. There's no reason to rush this. She can take her time and pack and let everyone know where she's going. She can take a day to collect her things and cancel her rent and quit her jobs. She needs to calm down and just let it all sink in. Prepare everything and calmly get ready for the trip. There is much to do. She has time.

She takes out the sticker of the Canadian flag and takes a long look at it. Her tears are gone now, but her face is still wet. She wipes it with the backs of her hands and looks at the silly sticker he decided to include in the letter. Then, without thinking about it, she puts it on her old suitcase and smiles.

No one writes letters anymore, she thinks again.

Outside, it's sunny and bright. She wants to call him, but knows that's not what he really wants. It's the middle of the night where he is. Will he even be awake? She decides instead not to call. She will wait and speak to him later.

When she sees him.

It's so hot outside today, but she knows it'll be very cold where she's going. She'll pack her warmest clothes. She'll travel light and pack warmly and that way she won't be so shocked when she first gets there. Then she'll be ready when she goes to find him.

Second Cup. Isn't that what he called it? Just like Starbucks. Didn't he say it was near Yonge Street? It's where he always goes. She will find it and, waiting in the back of the room, she will find him. He will be sitting alone, drinking some silly coffee drink. She will see him sitting there next to his fireplace, looking outside at the cold. He will not be looking, but he'll know she's there. He'll smell her perfume. He always loves the way she smells. He'll know she's there when she leans close to him and he smells her hair.

She will touch his shoulder and whisper in his ear, "Hello, my little bull."

Acknowledgments

To Jonathan Atherton, Brendhan Lovegrove, and Shazia Mirza.

Also to Ralph and Rhonda; Rob and Renita, Doug and Vickie; Michael, David, and Chloe; Pearl Green and Lil Gruneir; David Grunier.

To Eric Alper; Ian Atlas; Ilene Benator; Julita Borko; Andrew Bradley; Kathy Buckworth; Andy Burns; Rick and Angie Campanelli; Jodi Cohen; Candace Covington; Michael Dahlie; Kate Drummond; Matt Dusk; Terry Fallis; Joanne Feldman; Jeremy Freed; Aoife Gold; Meli Grant; Denis Grignon; Tina Gruver; Dustin Hertel; Denise Hofmann; Humble and Fred; Charles Kaminski; Andrea Lakin; Katherine Lam; John Lewis; Irem and Markus Lutz; Victoria Makhnin; Shaun Marvell; Kristin Matthews; Andrew McMichael; Jessica Megly; Terry Mercury; Richard Mills; Ben Miner; Marc and Tanya Morgenstern; Larry Nichols; Tom Nowell; Paul Ogata; Aron Papernick; Greg Pappas; Shaun Proulx; Nathan Quinn; Tracy Rideout; Dan Riley; Luis Ramirez; Meghan Robertson; Nicholas Rosaci; Rob and Debbie Rosen; Davin Rosenblatt; Heazry Salim; B. Mark Seabrooks; Matt and Gabi Syberg-Olsen; Ralph Tetta; Joe Thistel; Jeremy Thompson; Rob and Gillian Tudhope; Christopher Turner; Cal Verduchi; Barbara Wheeland; Celine Williams; Mike Wixson; Peter Zakarow; Peter Senftleben, Vida Engstrand, and everyone at Kensington Books; everyone at SiriusXM, especially Allison Dore.

And—most of all—to Laura and Marlowe.

A Conversation with Ward Anderson

Your first novel (*I'll Be Here All Week*) dealt with stand-up comedy. This book is quite a departure from that subject matter. What inspired such a move?

I had been developing the idea of a twin dealing with the death of his brother for quite some time, with nothing more than that basic premise in the back of my mind. Then, in 2011, I got to visit Singapore as part of an international comedy tour. The places I visited there and the people I met inspired the events that eventually became *All That's Left*. I was there in December, so all of the references to the Christmas celebration and decorations are as I remember them from my visit. The hotel bellman really wore that Santa Claus costume every day in that intense heat and humidity. I knew I had to write about that.

Steven suffers from misophonia. Where did that come from?

I have it! It's an intolerance to certain sounds. For me, it's background noise that really sets me off. The sounds of people eating, especially. But it can also be little things people normally ignore or don't hear, like whistling or humming. Even the sounds of hands typing on a keyboard or music bleeding through a person's headphones. The opening chapter—with Steven on the plane listening to the man behind him eating chips—is straight out of my life. My parents gave me a pair of noise-cancelling headphones a few years ago as a gift. I never travel without them now. Like Steven, I spent years just thinking I was a fussy snot. But I've lightened up over the years and learned to deal with it better than I used to.

Steven isn't a very likable guy when we first meet him. People have said the same thing about Spence, the main character from *I'll Be Here All Week*. What is it with you and unlikable protagonists?

Well, neither Steven nor Spence are terrible people. At their worst, they are each a bit selfish and perhaps narcissistic. But I've always liked the idea of a character who is essentially good trying to find his way out of a bad shell. Steven knows he's a snob and wishes he weren't that way. It takes a free spirit like Dania to open his eyes a bit and help him find the good man who longs to break out. Spence—in the previous novel—is the same way. In both books we have a decent guy who has lost his way, and it takes the love of a good woman to help set him straight. I've always liked the idea of redemption.

There's a good bit of that in *All That's Left*.

Yeah, Steven finds redemption. So does Robin, a woman we think the worst of throughout the story, until we find out who she really is near the end. Steven has been an unreliable narrator in many ways, painting her as a worse partner than she actually was. In the end, she gets redeemed a bit. Even Scotty (or, rather, his ashes) gets a shot at forgiveness.

Although Steven finds happiness with Dania, there's always the death of his brother hanging over his head.

And Steven never really gets over it. Not until the very end. He talks to Scotty's ashes as if his brother is still there. He continues doing this when he's back in Toronto, even. It takes Robin throwing out those remains for Steven to finally move on. He accepts a lot of truth throughout the story, but I think it takes Robin stepping in and accidentally throwing out Scotty's ashes for Steven to finally accept that his brother is gone.

This book deals with a controversial topic: Dania is a trans-sexual woman.

When I was in Singapore City, I found it so fascinating to hear about men from other parts of the world traveling to Singapore and falling in love with women they met at Orchard Towers, which is a real place. Sometimes the men wind up moving to Singapore. Sometimes they marry and take the women back home with them to wherever they're from. And, yes, there are transgendered dancers and bartenders at some of the clubs there. To me, it was a love story that no one was telling.

Steven falls in love with Dania before he finds out about her past.

Steven falls in love with Dania for who she truly is. It's not a fetish. He meets and falls in love with a beautiful, talented woman who makes him feel alive. It was important for me to show that the two of them fall in love with each other for who they both truly are, not because of Dania's past. They don't even have sex. Their relationship is purely romantic and from the heart. It is, after all, a love story.

But Steven doesn't deal very well with finding out about Dania's past at first.

Steven doesn't like the fact that he's been lied to and that she kept secrets about Scotty from him. But he doesn't question the fact that he fell in love with a woman. He's smarter than that.

You describe the weather in Singapore as being intensely hot. Why set the story during the winter then?

It's brutally hot and humid, pretty much all the time. Especially for a Canadian guy visiting in the middle of December. I liked the idea of having the story set at Christmastime, because so many people can't imagine that holiday in a place that is so hot on the other side of the world. And I liked going instantly back to Toronto, where Steven suddenly finds comfort again in the bitter cold. Most Canadians (and Americans) can't wait to get away from the cold winter weather, but Steven longs for it . . . except when he's with Dania.

It all comes back to falling in love?

Of course! Doesn't that bring out the free spirit in all of us? Because of Dania, Steven finds joy in the very things he would normally despise, from the crowded bars to eating with his bare hands. She opens his eyes to things that aren't normally like him at all. He doesn't hate it; he loves it because he's with her. At the same time, Dania finds that she loves the stuffy gentleman who is nothing like what she's used to being with. At the end, she's excited to fly into a snow-covered country just to be with him. We've all discovered new ideas and experiences because of a person we loved. Falling in love makes people take chances they normally would never take. Sometimes it all works out.

Where are Dania and Steven now?

They're probably living in Toronto. Dania is singing. They're happy. It's a love story.

Don't miss Ward Anderson's debut novel,

I'll Be Here All Week,

available now!

Turn the page for an excerpt. . . .

1

Spence turns the volume up on his laptop because the girl in the bathroom is being so loud. She's talking about comedians she thinks are funny, but he's watching clips of himself on YouTube and wondering when she's finally going to take the hint and leave. On the screen he's watching a set he did once on *The Late Late Show with Craig Kilborn*. At the time it seemed like a really big deal. Now it just depresses him. He still can't help but watch it from time to time, even though it never makes him feel very good.

"Do you like Dane Cook?" Brandy or Mandy or whatever her name is says while fixing her hair in the mirror. He chuckles at the thought of her putting in so much effort just to make the walk of shame out of his hotel room in a few minutes. All the primping in the world isn't going to erase the "just sexed" look she has.

"Sure," he says back, even though he didn't even hear the question.

"What about Daniel Tosh? You like Daniel Tosh?"

"Yeah." He nods. He pauses the clip and realizes for the first time that he still owns the shirt he wore on the TV show. It was eight years ago. It might be time to change things up a bit. He wonders if there's an outlet mall or something nearby that he can stop at when he heads out of town. His wardrobe has consisted of the same five shirts and pairs of jeans for so long, he doesn't remember the last time he tried something new.

"I think Dane Cook is hilarious." She emerges from the bathroom, still wearing nothing but her panties. In this light, he can see how poorly done the tattoo of the kitten just below her navel really is. Last night he thought it was Pac-Man.

"Don't you think he's funny?" she asks. "Dane Cook?"

"Sure." He goes back to watching the video of himself.

She sits down on the corner of the bed just behind where he is sitting at the tiny hotel desk. She's pushing thirty and talks like she's fifteen. Everything she says sounds like a question, even when it isn't one. She twirls her hair around her index finger while she talks and bobs her foot up and down to whatever song is in her head. He looks down at her toes and thinks it's kind of cute that her feet sort of look like hands.

"That you?" she says and points at the laptop screen.

"Yeah."

"From TV?"

"Yeah."

"What show was it? *The Tonight Show?*"

I wish, he thinks.

"*The Late Late Show,*" he says.

"Oh, yeah. With that guy that was on, like, that Drew Carey show."

"Craig Ferguson."

"Yeah. That guy. He's funny, too."

"This was when it was hosted by Craig Kilborn."

"Who's that?"

"Some other guy."

"Is he like the guest host or something?" she asks.

"No, he was the guy who used to host it before the guy doing it now," he says.

"Oh," she says, "when was that?"

"Eight years ago."

"Oh," she says. "Wow."

"Yeah."

"So," she says and then sits in silence for thirty seconds.

"Dane Cook is probably my favorite comedian of all time. Daniel Tosh, too, but Dane Cook is better. He's, like, the funniest comedian I've ever seen."

He pauses the video and looks at her over his shoulder.

"What?" she asks and looks confused.

"Really?" he asks.

"Oh," she says, "you're funny, too. I mean, I just think, like, Dane Cook is awesome, you know? He's like my all-time fave. But I still think you're funny, too."

"I slept with a chick in Florida once who was absolutely gorgeous. She had the most amazing body I've ever seen. I've never been with a woman as gorgeous as she was. She was amazing. But you're pretty good, too." He raises his eyebrows. She has stopped playing with her hair and has her lips stuck out like she's pouting.

"What the hell is wrong with you?" she asks.

"Nothing," he says.

"That wasn't very nice."

"Tell it to Dane Cook."

She rolls her eyes and then stretches out across the bed. He's kind of surprised she didn't just get up and leave, but he guesses she's smarter than he gave her credit for at first. Maybe she got the point. Either way, she doesn't seem too upset by it and isn't leaving. He goes back to watching the video.

He killed that night, eight years ago, in front of the studio audience and in front of everyone watching it at home. It was an incredible set and, for a while, he used the TV recording as a demo tape. For the first couple of years after it aired, he got a good bit of work. He killed last night, too, right there in Enid, Oklahoma. Eight years ago he was on TV and hoping to be headlining Vegas within the year. Now it's 2010 and he's at the Electric Pony bar in Enid. There's even a mechanical bull next to the stage.

Welcome to Hollywood, baby, he thinks. *Could be worse.*

At least the audience was good to him and at least he got laid last night. He's been treated worse in better cities and had worse looking women than Mandy or Brandy or whatever her name is shoot him down. He reassures himself that there are worse places to be. They like him here, so he should consider himself lucky.

They treated him like a TV star. From the moment he set foot onstage, they treated him as if he were Steve Martin making his triumphant return to stand-up comedy. For a brief moment, he forgot that he was unknown and broke and actually felt like a celebrity. The bright lights shining in his face hid the fact that he was performing in a shitty bar and not an A-list comedy club. Those same lights also hid the fact that the place was half empty. They loved him so much, they sent drinks to the stage and bought him shots of liquor after his set that made Enid *feel* like Vegas. Or at least like Reno.

He looks around the hotel room and sighs. It isn't dirty as much as it's small and musty. The bedspread is frayed and a bit worn out, even though it smells like it's pretty clean. He hates places that only give you a single bar of soap and no other toiletries. He's got at least six little bottles of shampoo in his suitcase, but that's not the point. He just likes to have them available even if he has no intention of using them. He also likes hotel rooms that have two double beds. That way he can have sex in one and sleep in the other when What's-Her-Name finally leaves. Feeling like a celebrity wears off very quickly when the sun comes up.

"Do you like Carlos Mencia?" She picks up the TV remote and starts flipping through the channels. He remembers an interview with Charlie Sheen in the nineties. He was asked why someone as rich and successful as he was felt the need to pay prostitutes for sex. Sheen told the reporter, "I don't pay them to have sex with me, I pay them to leave." It makes perfect sense now.

His cell phone rings on the corner table, and the caller ID reads that it's Rodney. He's tempted to let it go to voice mail because Rodney knows damned well that he's normally still asleep at this hour. The problem is that Rodney never calls this early unless there's something wrong, so he answers.

"You having fun out there, dumbass?" Rodney says. Rodney has never so much as had one drag off a cigarette, yet he sounds as if he's been smoking since he was three. His sinus medicine apparently sucks because it never seems to work.

"What do you mean?" Spence asks.

"I mean did you get laid last night?"

He looks at his laptop to see if the webcam is on. "Why do you ask?"

"Because I hear you had some broad hanging all over you, you filthy man-whore."

"I had fun. It was a good show," he says.

"Oh, I see," Rodney says. Rodney is easily fifty, but the way he talks makes it apparent no one ever told him that. "She's still there, isn't she?"

"Did you call for any other reason than to live vicariously through me?" Spence asks.

"Hey, screw you," Rodney says. "I've got better clients than you I could vicariously live through, you know. You think you're the only client I have that ever gets laid?"

"I'm the only one you're calling at nine a.m."

"You should be flattered."

"What's the problem?"

"How do you know there's a problem?" Rodney asks. "How do you know I'm not just calling to check up on you and see how you're doing?"

Spence sighs. "Because I know you, Rodney. What's the problem?"

"There was a complaint," Rodney says as he switches gears. It has become routine. Rodney always starts by building people up before he tears them down. It comes from something he read called *The One Minute Manager.* Ever since then, Rodney tosses out a few compliments before delivering really bad news. It would actually be pretty nice if it weren't so predictable.

"Where?" Spence asks.

"At the Pony."

"Jesus." Spence closes his laptop and gets up from the tiny hotel desk. "Already?"

"Yeah," Rodney says and pauses for no reason other than the fact that he's trying to do too many things at once. He's probably checking his e-mail, clipping his fingernails, and reading *Variety* all while doling out the bad news from the night before. "Somebody said you weren't that great or you said something offensive or pissed someone off or something."

"That's a little vague, don't you think?"

"I guess," Rodney says. "I'm just telling you that someone bitched about you so they called me."

"Who was it?"

"Who was what?"

"Who'd I piss off?"

"I dunno," Rodney says. "Some guy. Or some broad. They didn't tell me. Just said someone complained."

Spence looks in the mirror and frowns. It's not going to be a good day. He looks like shit. Like he hasn't slept in a couple of days or is hungover. The fact that he managed to get laid looking like this is somewhat of a miracle. "This is about one complaint?" he asks Rodney. "They had one complaint, and you're calling me at nine a.m. to gripe at me about it?"

"I'm just telling you what they told me," Rodney says. Spence pictures him sitting at his cluttered desk with his feet propped up, wearing the same ratty baseball cap he's been wearing for years. He thinks that the way Rodney dresses is lazy. The irony is not lost on him, since he hasn't worn a suit or even a tie on-stage in years. Still, he thinks that an agent should dress the part more often. Rodney looks more like a drunken golf caddy.

"There were almost a hundred people there last night," Spence says. He remembers it well because he killed. That's what all that laughter was about. That's what the free drinks were all about. That's why Brandy or Mandy is now lying half naked on his bed and watching *Full House*.

"Yeah, but they're pretty big on not getting complaints," Rodney says.

"One freaking complaint? Jesus, Rodney. That's a bit much, don't you think? You'd think that a hundred people laughing would outweigh one jackass, right?"

"Hey, I'm just telling you what they told me."

"Oh, for Chrissakes."

Rodney pauses for a minute to finish whatever else he's doing and says, "Look, just go back there tonight and have a great show, and they'll forget whatever it was that pissed them off. I just wanted you to be aware of it."

"And you don't see how telling me this is going to make me paranoid now?" Spence asks. He's pacing around the front of the room now and starting to realize why he looks like hell. Too many early phone calls from Rodney that stress him out for the rest of the day.

"Not paranoid, just aware," Rodney says.

"I'm supposed to just walk in there and be all carefree and jolly or something?"

"Hey, today is a new day," Rodney says. "Just don't do whatever you did last night. I dunno."

"Don't do—" Spence bites his top lip and makes a fist. He wants to throw the phone against the wall, but it would only freak out the girl on the bed and he'd have to go out and buy a new phone later in the day. "I was doing my act. A hundred people loved it. How the hell should I know what pissed off one person?"

"It was probably more than one person," Rodney says.

"If it was less than a hundred, they lose," Spence says. "It's a goddamned comedy show, Rodney. Majority rules."

"And I'm on your side," Rodney says. "I'm just telling you what they told me. If you wanna get booked back, you need to take it easy on them tonight."

Sure, you're on my side, Spence thinks. *Fuck you, Rodney.*

"Do something different. Mix it up a bit," Rodney says.

"Oh, okay, I'll just write a whole new act today. A full hour of squeaky clean jokes for the one table of people who complained last night and won't be back tonight anyway."

"Did it ever occur to you that you'd work more if you could work clean?"

"Did it ever occur to you that I know more about being a stand-up comedian than you do?"

"Just trying to help you," Rodney says without skipping a beat. "You can't get on TV saying 'fuck.' "

"This isn't *Letterman,* Rodney," Spence says, "it's a cowboy bar. It's not even a real comedy club, for Chrissakes."

"Really?" Rodney says. "Because I could have sworn that you were working there last night and that you're a comedian."

"You know what I mean."

"You can call it whatever you want. They pay you the same as any other place," Rodney argues.

"Right, but I can't perform clean in front of a roomful of drunk rednecks, Rodney," Spence says. Rodney never understands this argument, and they've had it a dozen times already this year. "The drunk cowboys want the dirty jokes, whether the idiot running the place understands that or not."

"You could be clean if you wanted to be," Rodney says.

"No way. They would eat me alive."

"Please," Rodney says, "save the drama for your mama."

"Save the—" Spence rolls his eyes. "What are you, calling me from 1998?"

"Don't kill the messenger here. I'm just giving you the news. That's my job."

"Are you reading from a book of clichés?"

"Are you listening to me, you ass?" Rodney says. "I'm trying to help you."

Spence looks back in the mirror. He really looks awful. Two years ago he was thirty-five and looked twenty-nine. Now he looks fortysomething. When did that happen? He wonders if maybe he should go back to highlighting his hair.

"Just once," he says, "I'd like for you to call me with good news. I had a great show last night, Rodney. Do you understand what it feels like to have you shit all over it like this the next day? Any idea how awful that is?"

"Look, it sucks and I know it," Rodney says. "But that's business, my man. This is show *business*. And it may suck sometimes, but it's better than sitting in an office. Last I checked, you haven't had a day job for, what, ten years?"

"Nine."

"Nine. Whatever. If I were you, I would stop feeling sorry for myself, check my ego at the door, and just do what they ask. Plenty of clubs love you. This one will, too. Just lay low tonight."

Spence sighs. "Alright, fine."

"I'm serious," Rodney says. "Check your ego at the door."

"Fine."

"And be careful where you stick your tallywacker, will you? I think the broad you're with is the bartender's ex or something. That may be what started this whole thing."

"So that's what the complaint might be about? Not about the show but . . . you know," Spence looks over at What's-Her-Name. She's still watching *Full House* and doesn't seem to even notice that he's been about three seconds away from an aneurysm this entire time.

"Yeah, maybe," Rodney says.

Unbelievable, Spence thinks.

"Fine. Anything else?" he asks.

"Yeah, scratch Rockford, Illinois, off your schedule. The club went out of business."

"Aw, hell," Spence says. It was just a one-nighter in a bar, but he needed it. The gig paid four hundred bucks for one night and led right into a weekend of other gigs along the way. He booked it because the routing was perfect and gave him a hotel to stay in on his way east from a string of western gigs.

"Yeah, I know it sucks," Rodney says. "I'll try to fill it in with something else. Maybe Baltimore or Cleveland. I dunno."

"Lemme know, okay?"

"And send me more headshots. I'm all out of them."

"Already?"

"Yeah, send me at least a hundred."

"Alright."

"Now go tell that girl you're with you just gave her the clap."

Rodney hangs up before he's even finished with his zinger. It doesn't matter because it's essentially the same joke every time he calls. If it's not the clap, it's syphilis or herpes or genital warts.

Damn it, Spence thinks and stares at his phone.

Another call from Rodney to ruin a perfectly good day. It has become so predictable that it's almost a routine. A show will go great only to be followed eight hours later by a call from Rodney telling him that the club is pissed for some stupid reason. They hated the shirt he wore or didn't like his joke about epilepsy or thought that his act was too dirty. Or maybe someone just hated the fact that he got laid and the bartender didn't. It's always something, and it usually has nothing to do with stand-up comedy, which is supposed to be the job description.

He tosses his cell phone on the bed and looks at Mandy or Brandy as she's watching TV. He's tired and he's hungry, but he's also a bit horny and thinks he could probably have sex with her again. She just fixed her hair, though, so she might not be up for it.

"What's up?" she asks, and he realizes he's been staring at the wall behind her head. She's attractive, but she could stand to do a little less tanning. If she keeps it up, her face will be leathery by the time she hits thirty-five.

He clears his throat. "Nothing."

"You okay?" she asks.

"Yeah," he says. "I've just gotta get out of here."

"But you have another show tonight."

"I mean I have to get going. Out of the hotel. I have to do an interview for the radio."

"Which station?" she asks as she gets up from the bed and puts her jeans on. They're bedazzled and have writing on them, and he suddenly wonders if she realizes that she's not a teenager anymore.

"I don't know," he says. "The rock station."

"106.7 or 92.9?" She pulls her T-shirt over her head, and her bracelets get caught in her sleeve. She stumbles around for a second, stuck in the middle of her shirt. He almost laughs at the way she wrestles her way into her clothes, her head buried somewhere inside and her arms just two awkward stubs trying to poke their way through. He thinks she looks like a low-budget *Star Trek* alien.

"106.7, I think."

"Oh, I like that one. I'll have to tune in and listen to you."

"Yeah. I'll be on with the morning crew, I think," he says. "Or maybe they'll tape it and play it later."

"*The Cubby in the Morning Show?*"

"I guess so," he says. All of the radio shows are the same. Some "Morning Zoo Crew" sitting around pretending to laugh at each other while playing ZZ Top. He probably knows three DJs named "Cubby" at this point and has met at least six guys named after animals.

"That's pretty cool. You get to, like, hang out on the radio all day and then, like, do shows at night."

"Something like that, yeah."

"Better than having a job," she says. He cracks a smile and tosses her a pair of tiny pink socks he found on the floor. He has had this same conversation so many times, it's almost as routine as the one he just had with Rodney.

Spence puts on his jeans and a sweater and checks out his hair in the mirror. He keeps wondering if maybe he should go back to highlighting it. He grabs his sunglasses off the small hotel desk because he's certain he won't be able to stand the sun when it hits him in the face. The one good thing this fleabag hotel has going for it is the blackout curtains. He opens the door, and the cold hits him at the same time as the bright sunlight. Neither feels very good, and he instantly wishes he was back in bed.

What's-Her-Name drives a Jeep. She followed him to the

hotel and parked it right beside him. She must've been drunker than he remembers because her parking job sucks, and she has taken up two spaces next to his old Toyota Camry. She throws her purse into the passenger seat and then leans up against the door with her thumbs in the belt loops of her jeans. She must be at least twenty-nine but, just like Rodney, she's having a hard time accepting her age.

"I had a great time." She bites her lower lip and looks up at him. The eyes she's making remind him of why he brought her back here in the first place, and part of him is tempted to just take her back inside and have sex with her again. But then she'd probably never leave and wind up sticking around the rest of the day.

"Drop me an e-mail or something," he says and unlocks his car. As he opens the door, she leans in and puts her lips on his. He puts one hand around her waist and lets her tongue slip into his mouth for only a second. Before she can really connect with the kiss, he pulls away.

"I had fun," he says and slips into his car. He rolls down the window and leans out.

"Me too." She gets into her Jeep and sits there with the door open. "You're gonna, like, be famous one day. You know that? I bet you will. I believe it. You're really funny."

"From your mouth to God's ears," he says as he starts the car.

"One day, I'll tell people I knew you when."

It's more likely you'll tell them that you slept with me when, he thinks.

"I hope so," he says.

She shuts her car door and starts the Jeep at the same time. He doesn't say anything, but he smiles at her and gives her a wink. She's probably a pretty cool girl, and he realizes he'd probably like her if he wasn't in such a foul mood.

Thanks for nothing, Rodney.

"See you later," she says. She waves at him as she pulls out and drives away. He sits in his car for a minute, screwing around with the rearview mirror. Maybe later today he'll get some highlights. Then he won't look quite as old. Maybe there's a hair salon and an outlet mall nearby. He can kill two birds with one stone.

When she has pulled out of the parking lot, he shuts off his engine. He sits there for a minute, then goes back inside his hotel room and goes back to bed.